To my mother, Dorothy

THE PRUSSIAN CAPTAIN

ANN BROUGH

*E*ighty four years old! There's a number for you! Eighty four years! Born in 1921, my mum, Dorothy, lived through a war for six years, from eighteen to twenty-four, when life should have been at its best. She was wrinkled and old, her skin turning a dull yellow, to match the whites of her eyes. Me, her daughter, not knowing the reason for the yellowing was to be pancreatic cancer two years later. Her hair was a beautiful silver colour and still thick, with a slight natural wave in it. Feisty as ever! She'd pick an argument with a cat if she thought she'd win. Well, come to think of it, when didn't she win an argument? Every single person in this family backed off as soon as she got that glint in her eye and sharpness to her tongue.

Why does eighty-four strike such a chord? I worked it out and realized that my mother's grandmother, Emma, was eighty-four when she died. I was nineteen. I didn't think it was anything special to still have a great grandmother alive at nineteen, but I guess it was. She was very tall and thin, though my mother told me she had been very fat until old age had shrunk her. She had the same yellowing wrinkled skin as my mum, but her hair was thin and white and I couldn't help staring at it because I could see her pink scalp through the hair so clearly—it almost looked like the hair was just a halo of light, though she was no angel. She was very unhappy and lived in a horrible new flat up the Meir, where all the slum-dwellers of Longton had been relocated.

This part of Staffordshire was called The Potteries, where all the fine china was produced for the rich and famous. Royal Doulton, Wedgwood, Minton and hundreds more factories, employed an under-paid labour force to create the world's most beautiful and sought-after decorated china.

People were poverty stricken and worked either on "The Pots" or in "The Pit". They were either potters or coal miners. Riding a bus at the end of the work day, I'd see half the people very "white" covered in clay powder and half the people very "black" covered in pit dust.

Dorothy's family all worked in "The Pots," from mould-running to decorating. The china was fired in coal fired ovens then; the china stacked into saggers and piled high inside the bottle neck ovens to be fired. China could spoil in the firing process, destroying days of work, so it was experienced men who had this task of stacking and building the coal fires. As a result of the bottle neck kilns the entire Potteries was covered in an aura of black, sooty smoke all the time. Every building was black, even the beautiful town hall in Longton built from sand stone.

Great Grandmother Emma never left her flat. My great aunt did the food shopping for her—such as it was, and picked up bottles of thick black stout—one for Emma's night cap and the rest for Tom's several hours of stout drinking each day.

My great grandfather, Tom, died just a year before his spouse. They didn't speak to each other. They hated each other. I had to visit them every Sunday afternoon after Chapel, dragging my little sister with me on the bus. When I think of it now, it was like a comedy sketch.

"Ask 'im if 'e wants a cup o' tay," my great grandma, Emma, would say to me.

"Do you want a cup of tea, Grandad?" I'd yell at him. He was almost deaf.

"I want bloody nothin' from 'er." He'd reply and glare at the gas fire, fitted into the wall, which burnt winter and summer alike. Then he'd get up, grab his walking stick and hobble into the kitchen to make his own tea. I don't know how they kept it up, or for how many years they had been "not speaking."

Great Grandma would look at her husband with an evil look in her eyes and say, "I'll dance on 'is bloody grave one dee."

And he would say, glaring into the fire, "Not if she bloody dies fost."

Tom did die first, but it didn't make the old woman happy. She died a year later after a brief illness. My mother told me Emma warned the people caring for her, my great aunt Madge mostly, "I'll tak a couple o' ya with me." Wicked old woman! I'm sure she would have been happy if her care-givers had indeed died before her, as she wished.

She would say some odd things to me from time to time would my old great grandmother Emma.

"Where were yow last night then?" she'd ask on those Sunday afternoons.

"Just at the youthclub at Chapel. There was a dance."

"With lads?" she'd glare at me.

"Yes, a few boys were there."

"Yow'll fall on your arse yow will, lark ya grandmother."

I didn't know anything about my grandmother. Who was she? I just had a great grandmother—no grandmother. Why did she say I'd "Fall on my arse"? What did that mean?

"Who was my grandmother?" I asked the old lady once.

"Never yow mind," she snapped, looking at me with one eye closed, like an old witch. "We don't talk about 'er".

That was the end of that. I didn't dare ask my mother about it.

Another funny thing. My mother told me once that she was born in Blackpool. Blackpool? By the seaside? Why was she born there? Everybody else was born in Longton, including me—in the slums of Neck End. No explanation was ever given.

When I was a very little girl a very tall distinguished man, who talked posh, like the Queen, came to visit us. My dad was a tall man— over six feet, but this man towered over my dad. He seemed to fill our tiny living room. He wore a black great coat and a black trilby hat. I'd never seen a trilby before. He was very kind to me. I sat on his knee. He spoke quietly and gently. I didn't know what to call him, so I didn't call him anything. He kissed my mum on both her cheeks and when he left my mum cried—I'd never seen her cry!

My mum and dad never said who he was until later that year when my mum had to go away overnight to somewhere near

London, which was far, far away from where we lived. One hundred and fifty miles, my dad told me. She had to go on the train. She went because her dad had died. He was the man in the trilby. He was eighty four years old!

PART I
BORN INTO PRIVILEGE

TURNING SEVEN

*T*he picture my mother held in her withered hands showed the family in a straight line on the left, and the servants in a straight line on the right, standing at the front entrance of the Elizabethan red brick house with white stone pillars and stairs at the front entrance. Somewhere near Birmingham, she thought her father had told her. It was the only picture she had of her father's family and it was dated 1893 when her father, Edward, was twenty-four years of age.

∾

Edward Wrightson was born into a privileged life—a rich life. There were servants, a cook and a livery man, a butler, a valet, a lady's maid and a nanny for him and the other children. Edward was a middle child, one of eight children. They wanted for nothing.

It was the year 1876. The nursery was cramped! Robert, Edward's youngest brother, was just a few months old. He'd been born in Wilsbaden, Germany earlier in the year and now they were all back at Nine Elms in Kings Norton, near Birmingham. Life seemed to revolve around the newest member of the family. In addition to Robert, Lucy, Harold and Edward all shared the nursery space, even though they were not babies. Lucy was four years old, so she quite liked to help Nanny with the baby, but Harold and Edward couldn't wait to get away from the day-to-day chores of nappies, bottles, rocking and burping that went on in the nursery.

Edward envied his four older siblings, who had long since moved into their own rooms in the east wing of the house. He waited patiently for his seventh birthday, when he too would be moved into his own room. He counted the days down on the monthly calendar on the wall in the nursery.

"Do you think Mother would let me move into my own room when you move, Ed?" Harold asked. "I do not want to stay in the nursery with Lucy and the baby without you."

"No Harold, you cannot move until you are seven. It would be unfair. I have had to wait forever, and you will have to wait too," Edward replied, while he piled his toy soldiers into their metal box, ready for the big move.

Edward and Harold were best friends. There was a strong bond between the two brothers, who were inseparable. Their father, Dr. Francis Wrightson, encouraged independence from a young age and gave the boys freedom to break free of the nursery and explore their small world in the vast grounds of the house. Mornings were filled with writing out letters, numbers and shapes over and over again until they were perfect. Edward quickly moved on to putting letters together to form words, learning to read effortlessly, which opened up a new world for him. He read stories to Harold and Lucy at the end of each morning, which made him feel very important.

Lunch was served in the nursery. Edward would have eaten the same thing every day—cook's wonderful flakey pastry shells, filled with vanilla custard. Nanny had different ideas and the lunch menu was usually an array of cold meats, cheese and fruit.

Baby Robert and Lucy both napped after lunch, which was the boys' cue to escape to the big outdoors. Every day was an adventure as they looked for the perfect spot for their games of knights and dragons, or cowboys and Indians, or African explorers.

They built a bridge of sorts across the stream running through the bottom of the property, using wooden planks from the old garden shed, which had recently been replaced. Dragging each plank down to the water was a mammoth task for the two small boys, but inventing ways of moving them became part of the fun. An old wheelbarrow, discarded at the back of the kitchen garden, was swept into action. The handles had fallen off long ago, but the boys found that by laying a wooden plank on what was left of the bucket part, they could push it along quite easily.

"Do you think the planks will reach across the stream, Ed?" panted Harold as they pushed the fifth plank of old wood down to the water.

"Of course they will," assured Edward. "But we should try one just to be sure."

They struggled to stand a plank on end at the very edge of the stream. Then, with a *one, two, three*, they let it drop with a splash, soaking the two of them from head to toe.

"Hurray, it reaches!" they both yelled at once.

They worked at placing the next four planks beside the first one, getting wetter and wetter with each splash as the planks hit the water.

"I think one more will do it," said Edward, and off they set with their transporter to bring the final plank down to the stream.

Once in place, their bridge was almost finished. They ran across it to the other side, wobbling on the unsecured old wood.

"I think we need to stabilize it a bit," Edward suggested.

"What does that mean?" his brother asked.

"To stop it wobbling so much. Also, if there's any amount of rain and the stream swells, our bridge will likely float away."

The boys decided to ask John Briggs, the groundskeeper, for help. John thought the two young masters from the big house were "grand" boys. Always outside and up to something. Not like most posh youngsters who spent their days indoors, dressed in their stiff clothing. John was happy to help Master Edward and Master Harold finish their bridge, providing them with twelve sturdy timbers, screws, angle brackets and a ball of twine. They loaded their wheelbarrow bucket with the wood and carried the twine and screws that would have fallen through the many holes in the bucket of the barrow.

John Briggs followed them down to the water and helped sink the timbers into the bank of the stream with a sledge-hammer, then he showed the boys how to secure the planks to the timbers with angle brackets and screws, letting the youngsters use the screwdriver to do most of the work them-selves. Lastly, the brothers took off their boots and socks, pushed up their knickerbockers as far as they could, and waded into the stream to wrap the twine around the planks to make them extra secure. Harold stood upstream and let the ball of twine float under the bridge, where Edward caught it and threw it back to Harold.

What a great bridge!

The boys thanked John Briggs for his help and returned the old wheelbarrow to the kitchen garden. They raced into the house, having completely lost track of time, to find they had missed tea. As they ran through the back door into the small hall at the top of the kitchen stairs, two of their older sisters came out of the drawing room and stared in horror at the boys.

"What have you two been up to?" squealed Louisa. "Look at the mess you are in. Where have you been?"

"Horrible boys," said Margaret, wrinkling her nose. "You are in so much trouble for missing tea. Wait until Nanny sees you. You are really quite disgusting."

The sisters turned and hurried back into the drawing room, obviously to tell whomever was there what a mess their brothers were in.

Edward and Harold burst out laughing. The girls, dressed so finely, had no influence on them whatsoever. Who cared what they thought?

However, they did care what Nanny thought. Edward looked down at his boots in dismay. The boys took off their boots, but as they did so mud and water poured out of each boot onto the immaculate hall floor.

"Cripes!" said Edward. "We are in a bit of a mess, old man.

Maybe we should take off our socks and knickerbockers too, so as not to splodge all the mud and stuff up the stairs."

They stripped down to their drawers and, holding their sodden clothing and boots, headed for the back stairs up to the nursery.

"Edward, Harold," Father's voice behind them stopped them in their tracks. "What are you doing, half naked, creeping up the stairs?"

Dr. Wrightson had a very hard time keeping the smile off his face as he looked up the stairs at his two sons, covered in mud and wearing only their drawers.

"We were building a bridge, Father," explained Edward. "Very hard work indeed—and quite messy. It's a marvellous bridge though."

"Is it indeed? Then you had better get bathed and changed quickly so that you can take me to see what has made you miss tea, and arrive in such a condition."

"Yes Sir," said the boys in unison as they sped up the stairs.

Francis gave way to his amusement, and the boys could hear him laughing as they headed for the nursery. *Of all my children*, Francis thought, *these two boys are something special. Wonderful boys!*

The bridge was pronounced a great success by Father. He was very impressed by the work and ingenuity it had taken to build. Such a sturdy, well-constructed bridge would be the source of many adventures for the boys for the short time they would have to enjoy it.

Annie Wrightson read to her eight children every day before dinner, gathering them around her and making each one of them feel she loved them most. She always kissed each of them tenderly as they entered her sitting room for story time and asked how they had liked their day. Edward adored his mother.

On his seventh birthday Edward was escorted by his mother, with great ceremony, to his very own room. His sheets were the finest linen, his pillows and bedcovers were filled with goose down. He had a mahogany desk with matching chair, a dresser filled with handmade clothes and leather boots in the boot cupboard He had pyjamas, slippers and a warm new dressing gown. Every morning William arrived with a tall jug of warm water to fill his basin and help him wash and dress for the day.

Edward spent his days in the study now he was old enough. The governess, Miss Carter, taught him and his siblings the classic languages, history and geography each morning. Miss Carter was tall and severe, with greying hair and an unsmiling demeanour. She was, however, an excellent tutor and the children learned quickly. After lunch Father would tutor them in mathematics and science, when he wasn't lecturing or away on business in Germany. After tea, Miss Carter instructed the girls in the art of needlework and made sure they practised piano—Mrs. Meadows came to the house every Thursday, after tea, to conduct a group piano lesson with Louisa, Margaret and Alberta.

Harold hated being left behind in the nursery. He became so distressed with his situation and missed Edward's company so much, that Mother decided to allow him to work in the study with the older children, although he was really too young. Afternoons, after tea, still belonged to Edward and Harold. The two brothers would make for the bridge to fight a battle, or rescue a maiden, or save a comrade from certain death. Even their brother, Arthur, at the advanced age of thirteen, occasionally made the trip to the bridge to join in the fun.

A year later, when Harold turned seven, he moved into the room next to Edward. Overjoyed to be on their own and "grown up," the two brothers relished their independence away from Nanny. How great life would be now they were both sleeping in the east wing. What fun to be next door, visiting back and forth between rooms, sharing toys and having adventures. Life couldn't have been better!

FATHER'S SURPRISE

"$\mathcal{M}$ove to America!" Annie Wrightson dropped her fork onto her breakfast plate with a clang. "Have you lost your mind?"

"It is a once in a lifetime opportunity, my dear," encouraged her husband. "The offer is too good to miss and just think of the benefits for the children."

"What benefits?" Annie blurted out, rising from the table. "It is a wild country, full of wild people. They carry guns. People are killed every day. Shot down. I have read it all in the Times. There are no refined people there, Francis. Our children will become cowboys and saloon girls."

"Now, now, dear. You have been reading all the silly stories the Times writes just to sell its paper. They are not true. There are great cities being built. It is a new country and they are looking for people like us to help build it. That is the reason I have had this offer to go out there and be part of this. It is so exciting I could burst! We have been asked to go to a place called California. I have invested in a piece of land there. They need a soil specialist and I am the best. It is on the west side of America on the Pacific Ocean. It is warm all the time and lush with vegetation. Correspondence with my old friend, Conrad Peters, tells me that it is a paradise just waiting to be developed. I just cannot turn this down, Annie."

Annie looked at the man she loved with her big brown eyes and knew that it was fruitless to argue. Francis was determined to have his way in this matter. She needed time away from him to think this through. She walked to the door, but Francis stopped her, placing a gentle hand on her arm.

"I promise you, my love," he whispered into her ear as he drew her close, "I will keep the house going here the entire time we are in America, so that we can return, when or if we need to. I cannot do this without you beside me. Let us have an adventure, Dearest. Let us go to America!"

He could always inspire her with his enthusiasm for life. He just seemed to make all the problems disappear, until just the "adventure" was left. This was how life had always been, married to Francis, and was going to continue to be. How could she dampen his dreams? She knew, as she raised her mouth to his, that she would always be by his side.

∾

Edward's Father, Dr. Francis Wrightson, Ph.D, eminent Chemist and Professor of Chemistry at Birmingham University, was middle aged when he met and married Annie Prosser in 1858. She was a mere girl of twenty. He purchased Nine Elms, a large house in Kings Norton. The house was vast and in no way a comfortable "home" when they moved in, but Annie was determined to turn the large, empty mansion into a welcoming, homely place to nurture her

family. Little by little she sought out furnishings and beautiful draperies and carpets; rooms were tackled one by one until the living areas of the first floor were splendid in appearance and comfortable as a nest.

Only the bedrooms remained empty and cold, except for the one bedroom which housed the marriage bed with its four posts, thick mattresses and Italian linens. It always smelled of rose petals, and fresh flowers were placed daily on the round table in the bay window. Francis arranged for the very latest water closet to be installed in an adjoining dressing room. Water closets were unheard of in England at the time, although Germany was years ahead with their plumbing arrangements! A beautiful bathtub with clawed feet stood in the centre of the room with two wash stands on either side, below oval mirrors. Thick white towels hung over wooden racks beside each wash stand as well as an extra pile on each of two low stools flanking the bathtub. Hot running water came right out of the tap—a miracle of invention. Annie was thrilled!

Mrs. Brookes was hired as cook-housekeeper and John Briggs as groundskeeper. Mary Bail, a young girl from the nearby village, was hired as general helper to Mrs. Brooks.

As the years passed, Nine Elms was filled with children, arriving one after another, until there were eight. Louisa the eldest, now sixteen years old, down to baby Robert.

The family thought they would be living at Nine Elms forever.

Now the incomprehensible was happening. They were going to America and eight-year-old Edward was overjoyed. So were Harold and Arthur.

"Ed, we will see cowboys and Indians for real," said Harold,

his face red with excitement. "I'm going to ask Father for a gun, so I can protect the family."

"I know, I cannot wait," Edward joined in. "Although I am sorry to leave our bridge."

"When we get to America we could build a fort," said Harold. "I bet there are a ton of trees there. We will need an axe to chop down the trees."

Arthur laughed at the two of them, but secretly envied their youthful enthusiasm. He rather liked the idea of building a fort too. He would offer to help when the time came.

Edward and Harold burst through the door of the study and pulled out their slates and began drawing out designs for their fort, and a list of materials they would need. Miss Carter had been instructed by Dr. Wrightson to begin a short, in-depth study of the new world. So maps, books and magazines lay strewn across the big table in the middle of the study room. Edward traced his finger from New York, where they would arrive, across the vast expanse of land to California. Their journey would take them from the Atlantic Ocean to the Pacific Ocean. What an adventure!

The three eldest girls sat in the bay window seat with sour faces, watching their younger brothers draw out their plans and talk excitedly about America. They were not at all enthusiastic about the prospect. They were under the impression that there were only men and boys in America. They had only read stories, like Mama, about gun-packing cowboys shooting everything that moved. Other stories were told of lumberjacks, railroad men, Indians and forts. There was no mention of any women or girls in these stories. Louisa, Alberta and Margaret thought they would be the only girls in America. Father laughed when they told him their fears, and

assured them that there were many girls there, and that they would not be deprived of female company.

"I have read stories of families disappearing in the wilderness," said Louisa, "never to be seen or heard of again."

"I have looked through all the magazines and the only civilized place seems to be New York," nodded Alberta. "Why can we not stay in New York, if Father is so determined to go to America?"

Margaret listened to the two older girls, nodding in agreement. "How will we manage? Mother said only Nanny will go with us. She will be taking care of Robert and Lucy, so who will help us with dressing and keeping our clothes in good order?"

The more they talked, the more fearful they became. What about the long journey on the ship? What about the even longer journey to California on the train? The boys would not care about washing every day, or having clean clothing. They would not care about eating strange food or seeing strange people. America was a world for men and boys, they agreed—not for ladies and girls.

SS EGYPT

*T*hey were to leave in August of 1877. The preparations were great indeed, and the whole staff at Nine Elms were busy for weeks packing for the journey. Father was away most of the time supervising the packing and dispatching of the chemistry equipment he would need. He arrived home on August twelfth to collect his family.

Edward's clothes had been carefully packed by Nanny along with a choice of three of his favourite toys. He chose his box of Prussian infantry soldiers, dressed so splendidly in their blue uniforms, his wooden Noah's Ark, complete with two of every animal, and his bag of marbles—he had the best shooter in the whole world!

Early in the morning of the fourteenth they set out from the house, with many tears from the servants. They travelled to Liverpool and stayed overnight in Durham's Inn, where they had a fine time eating thick slices of ham and roasted potatoes—the boys sucking up the foam from Father's beer. After a night of restless non-sleep for the big family, they were away to board the ship that would take them to America.

Nanny fussed and fussed. Small trunks packed separately for the journey had each child's name written on the top. Edward wondered to himself if it really mattered if the girls had their correct brush or ribbons, or if his deck shoes were in Harold's trunk. No, Nanny made sure there were no mistakes. Each trunk was checked numerous times, it seemed, before she gave the all clear for them to be taken down to the carriage and away to the dockyard.

The ship, called the SS Egypt, was beyond anything Edward could imagine, towering over them as they walked along the dock behind Father. The gangplank sloped steeply onto the ship's deck, making the going slow, especially being behind the girls, who took tiny steps. Francis led the way, Annie held Lucy's hand and Nanny, carrying Robert, brought up the rear. Porters greeted them to take them to their cabins, where Nanny fussed again, making sure each trunk was delivered to the right cabin. Edward shared a cabin with his brothers. Arthur, being the eldest, took the best spot, a comfortable single berth nestled into the wall of the cabin, with its own oil lantern and nooks everywhere to put books, candles, or precious belongings. Edward and Harold had bunk beds. Each of them dived for the top bunk and fell in a pile on the floor. They decided the issue with a toss of a coin, borrowed from Arthur, and, winning the toss, Edward climbed onto the top bunk. Harold was left with the bottom.

Their parents' cabin was more luxurious and contained a bed almost as large as the one at Nine Elms. Mirrors, lanterns and shelves lined the walls, and a carved wooden desk stood under the porthole window. The girls were happily housed in two adjoining cabins, sharing one room with Nanny, who could fuss all she wanted over the four "silly" girls, as Edward called them. Their hair dressing notions alone seemed to take up most of the shelves in the cabins. Then there were the dresses to be hung, with petticoats galore, silken under-garments, perfumed soap, shoes and slippers. Baby Robert's cradle was tucked in beside Nanny's berth, so that she could attend to him easily during the night. Edward was thankful that boys travelled light and had very little to unpack.

Francis had arranged for two servants to be at the family's disposal during the voyage. One to help Nanny with the children and the other to assist himself and Annie with dressing and keeping their clothing in order.

Edward, Arthur and Harold explored every nook and corner of the ship during their ten-day crossing. How exciting that this was a steam ship and the Atlantic crossing, so dreaded by travellers before them, was not the six-week long voyage on a sailing ship which left the passengers sick and fatigued. It was calm and beautiful and nobody was sick. The girls stayed close to Mother, but the boys were never to be found and only appeared, ravenously hungry, at meal times.

Francis laid down some basic rules of conduct for his sons, but felt their formal education could take a back seat to the life education they would experience exploring the ship and its inhabitants.

Life experience was certainly what they found in volumes! With hundreds of people, from every different walk of life, crammed into such a small space, the boys learned life lessons they would never forget. The boys were soon bored with walking the decks with the elite, dressed in their finery, stopping to exchange polite conversations with their peers.

Finding the stairs that took them to the lower decks, they joined the families in steerage, who were far more interesting.

Down in the belly of the ship, with only oil lamps giving a dull yellow glow to their quarters, the people of steerage shared their food and drink with each other, which seemed precious little to the boys from the upper deck. They made it their daily mission to bring fat loaves of crusty bread from their deck to steerage, watching with delight as the hungry filled their bellies. Then came jam and cheese and even a half bottle of wine—re-corked and left over from dinner—it would have been thrown away or drunk by the waiters!

"This is a king's life, don't ya know," laughed Mr. Caraway, who had four little Caraways to feed, along with his pretty, dimpled wife, Betty. "You boys 'ave dun us proud, right Betty?" His eyes twinkled as he shared the wine, from the bottle with his sweetheart.

The Caraway children, laughing as they ate their bread and jam, tried to kiss the Wrightson boys with their sticky, jammy faces. The boys had so much fun watching the food disappearing into those hungry mouths.

On their excursions around the ship, Edward, Harold and Arthur saw the very rich walking around the deck and taking the sea air, resting on white wicker chairs, and being served with iced lemonade or hot tea by barely noticed waiters. The great dressing up for dinner happened each night and the gowns the ladies wore were astonishingly beautiful, even to three boys of fourteen, eight and seven. The white bosoms overflowing the satin and silk were riveting, and only once did Father catch the stares and flick Arthur across the head with his table napkin. They were expected to behave their best at dinner and had many compliments from the other first class passengers, including unwelcome wet kisses bestowed on their foreheads by grey-haired ladies.

After dinner, they were supposed to go to bed. The girls were always so eager to please and followed Nanny without a murmur. Mother was lenient about bedtime, as long as they were in their quarters before ten. As the boys left the dining room promptly at nine-o-clock, Alfred winked at the younger boys and they knew where they were heading.

Scaling the rigging which held one of the life boats on deck eight, hiding under the tarpaulin, they could peek over the edge of the boat and right into a cabin occupied by the most beautiful young lady they had ever seen. They were all used to having girls around, having four sisters of their own, but this was different.

A maid assisted her out of her outer garments and brushed her hair until it gleamed. Her maid poured warm water from a huge jug into a silver basin and put white cloths in the water and white towels beside the water. Every night was the same ritual, and the boys had discovered this treasure just three days into their trip. As they watched from their vantage point, the maid would unfasten undergarments that seemed to have laces all over the place, and the garment would finally be lifted away and the boys would draw in their breath so sharply they feared being discovered.

As the object of their adoration walked toward the basin to begin to bathe, they would have to go. Running along the decks to make sure they were in their quarters by ten, Edward wondered, if only they could stay longer, what else would they see? The thought of discovering what was below the pantaloons sent his body into a warm flush. He would glance at Arthur, the main instigator of their nightly returns to the life boat, and see the beads of sweat above his upper lip. Edward liked that the three of them shared a secret; he liked that the secret was something they could never tell. He liked that Arthur would wink at him and Harold when they were back in the cabin and heading off to their bunks.

CASTLE GARDEN PIER

The Wrightson family lined the railings of the upper deck to watch as the Egypt made her way through the narrows, flanked by Staten Island and Brooklyn, to New York Harbour. On the south shore of Staten Island the ship ground to a halt and the anchor was dropped.

"What is happening, Father?" asked Harold.

"We are anchoring here because we are in quarantine," explained Francis. "There may be sick people on board and the American authorities do not want them bringing disease into the country."

"We must wait here quietly," said Mother. "I am sure we will be on our way very soon."

Edward looked over the railings to see the decks below filled with people. Their friends from steerage were herded onto one of the lower decks, packed in like sardines in a can. There were children crying, men yelling and women trying to keep their families together.

As the officials boarded the ship, they made their way to the upper deck first. They barely scanned the wealthy passengers waiting quietly in family groups. The head of each family was given a stamped document and told the importance of keeping that document in a safe place. The upper-deck passengers were then ushered into a comfortable lounge area and served food and drinks. Father read the paper and Mother read stories to the younger children. The three boys itched to stay outside and watch what was happening, but were told to stay with the family. Edward caught a glimpse of "the beautiful bathing lady" on the other side of the room, sitting demurely with her family around her. He flushed just thinking about the water trickling down her body in tiny rivulets. He looked up at Arthur, who gave him the knowing wink.

It seemed like half a day had gone by before they felt the boat lurch into action as the anchor was raised and they were on the move again. Not a long journey this time—just to Castle Garden in the bay. Now began the disembarkation; going ashore! Dr. Wrightson's name was called and the family proceeded to the doorway two decks below, led by their porter. A small launch carried them to Castle Garden Pier.

Father's stern voice and solemn face came close to the children as he crouched down and faced them. "You are to stay close to your mother and myself as we leave this vessel. You are to hold hands with each other and remain close to us. Do I make myself clear?"

His steel grey eyes looked into each pair of wide eyes individually as if he was imprinting his words into each child. They all nodded sombrely, hearts racing at the thought of the dangers ahead in this huge, bustling city.

Castle Garden was a writhing sea of people, as they left their tender and climbed onto the dock with porters dragging their belongings behind them. Dr. Wrightson, wearing his top hat, was head and shoulders above the crowd, which seemed to separate before him as he walked, followed by his entourage of children and porters. It did indeed matter, in this new country of equality for all, that the family who cut through the crowd with ease and confidence was so obviously wealthy and influential.

They were looked at briefly by a doctor, who did no more than look into their mouths and feel each forehead. Then off they went to another part of the huge fort-like building to register.

The paperwork was dealt with and names and details were entered into the thick ledger by a small, quietly spoken man. Edward noted he had a drip at the end of his nose and wondered why he didn't use his pocket handkerchief. The drip was on an eye level with Edward and he stared at it, fascinated, as it seemed to disappear into a nostril as he drew a breath and descend again as he exhaled, each time threatening to drop onto the ledger, but never doing so.

Edward was hot and he hated holding hands, particularly with his brother. Their hands seemed glued together with moisture, but Father's words echoed still and they dared not disobey, at least while they were standing next to him. They were soon on the move; Mother fussing with the smaller children and Father striding ahead, so easy to follow because of his stature, his black top hat a beacon for the whole family.

The passengers were gathering in an enormous rotunda. They were buying railroad tickets, being met by friends and family, or arranging with boarding house keepers for their stay in New York. Edward had never seen so many people at one time and was terrified he would lose sight of his parents and be lost forever in the bedlam of that rotunda. He kept his eyes glued on Father's hat.

Francis went to seek out a money changer, exchanging his British Pounds for American Dollars. Edward was about to follow the hat, but Mother's urgent voice called him to her side. "Stay with me, Edward. Father will be only a few minutes." Still Edward could see the hat, over many heads, waiting in line like a common man, something the Wright-sons had rarely had to do.

As Francis turned away from the kiosk where he had been doing business, and made his way through the human tide of people, two rough-looking men took each of his arms and began to move him in another direction. His hat, Edward's focal point, was knocked to the ground. Hands moved deftly in and out of Father's pockets, searching for the hidden stash of cash. They hadn't reckoned a dapper-looking gentleman would put up much of a fight. How wrong they were! Francis was no stranger to violence; he had seen and taken part in his share of brawling and could take good care of himself. He was strong and tall and not past his prime; he easily escaped their grasp and ducked the right fist before it collided with his chin. Instead, the fist smashed into the nose of the accomplice, sending blood spraying over the people closest. Uproar ensued, as the people scattered away from the fracas. Exposed on all sides, the villains charged through the crowd towards the departure door and Francis came towards his family, grin on his face, hand above his head carrying his hat.

Edward ran towards him and was lifted up high by his father. "Did they rob you, Father?" he panted. His father gave him a wink and tapped his secret pocket inside his waistcoat. "Not on your life Edward! The money is quite safe, and so am I."

A GENEROUS HOST

*A*rrangements had been made for the family, and Dr. Wrightson led them outside, where two very large black carriages took up most of the space for private transportation. They were tired, hot, and more than a little irritable by the time they reached their lodgings in New York.

Dr. Ravensburg was their generous host. He had been a close friend of the family in Germany before going to America. He was curator of the New York Museum of Natural History and, although it was such a new country, no expense had been spared to begin an arts community including museums, galleries and an opera house. He had acquired the second floor of an elegant house facing Central Park for the Wright-sons, with beautiful large rooms, high ceilings and enormous windows.

They were greeted by Klaus and Hilda Peters, who lived on the ground floor in a small apartment, and were to take care of the family during their stay. While Klaus attended to the bags, under Nanny's watchful eye, Hilda led the way up the wide wooden staircase and into the living room, where they sank into the soft seats.

"Welcome!" Hilda said in a soft voice, lilting with a slight German accent. "I'll show you to your rooms in a few minutes. There are ample bathing facilities, which I'm sure you want to take advantage of. The water is hot and piles of fresh towels have been laid out for you. There's a hot meal waiting, once you have settled in. How would one hour be before I serve? Before anything though, you'll all need a drink I'm sure. There's pink lemonade for the children. Dr. Wrightson, please help yourself to anything from the drinks cabinet; it is well stocked. The kettle is boiling in the kitchen, if you would like tea."

She paused for breath at last. All the suggestions had been greeted with nods of approval and smiles of thanks.

"I will take you up on the tea, please," said Annie. "And would you be kind enough to include an extra cup for Nanny? I am sure she is going to need it after sorting the bags."

"Me too," added Francis. "Although I think I do need something a little stronger before I drink the tea." He made his way over to the well-stocked cabinet and poured himself an aged whiskey with a little water. A few sips would make him begin to feel human again.

After drinks, baths, clean clothes and much running around the house exploring all the rooms and visiting back and forth between bedrooms, the family sat down to the best meal they ever remembered eating. Maybe because they were all so hungry and tired. Maybe because it had been cooked by Hilda, whom they all now perceived as an angel in disguise. They piled their plates with delicious braised beef in a succulent gravy, tiny potato wedges, dumplings filled with soft cheese, vegetables even the children ate, bread sauce and afterwards lemon cake with sugar icing and strawberries with cream.

Stuffed to bursting, the younger Wrightsons headed to bed. Nanny helped the girls with their nightgowns and brushed their hair. They were so tired they could barely climb into their cosy beds, piled high with goose down pillows covered in silk pillow slips. They lay bathed in mellow light from the gas lights over their beds. The pink walls and white furniture looked so much like their room in England, that they were instantly at home. When Mama came to kiss them and sing lullabies, their eyes were already closed; they managed a faint smile as they heard the familiar singing and felt the sweet kiss.

Edward, Arthur and Harold had an amazing room. Three beds on three different walls with curtains around each bed. Each had a desk, each had a dresser and wardrobe, each had a wash stand. The window covered one wall and looked out over the park. The boys didn't think they could sleep, but when Mother came into their room with her soft-spoken way to encourage them to get ready for bed, they did as she asked, knowing that she would give them a few minutes before returning to tuck them in and kiss their heads. Although they scoffed about it with each other, they secretly loved having that kiss at the end of the day. They had outgrown the lullabies, but not the kisses.

THE PRUSSIAN CAPTAIN

They were to be in New York for a week, while Dr. Wrightson arranged their trip west and completed all the necessary paper work for their journey. He spent the first few days busy with meetings and arrangements, but then the carriage he had hired was at the family's disposal for sight-seeing trips around New York.

What a city it was! To Edward's eyes he had never seen such a place.

Madison Square Theatre had been newly renovated and completely remodelled. They attended a play called Hazel Kirke, staring Effie Ellsler in the title role. It was a small theatre, seating only 500, but with wonderful atmosphere. There was an elevator stage and "ice air" brought in every day and filtered through the same system as used for heating during the winter. The children sat still as stones, enraptured and silent.

The family loved Central Park. The smallest children joined

the outing to run and play in the middle of the bustling city, Robert's chubby little legs trying his first steps in an effort to follow his siblings.

Macy's Dry Goods Store seemed like wonderland to Edward. It took up a whole city block and was eight stories high. It had a whole department devoted to children's needs: clothing, boots, books, and the most impressive collection of games and toys on earth. Father had to set some rules to keep the children from scattering in a dozen different directions. His hat was always the beacon for them, sitting tall and black above the heads of the regular height grown-ups. He expected they would find him easily after the designated thirty minutes to explore in small groups.

Edward didn't like the fact that he and Harold had to be with Margaret during their adventure into toy land, but Father insisted they stay in their groups. Arthur was worse off, because he was to watch Alberta and Lucy. Louisa had gone to the lady's department with Mother, as she considered herself too mature to look at toys and games. Robert was with Nanny at the apartment taking a nap.

Edward loved the hustle and bustle of New York City. People everywhere! He didn't mind being jostled and bumped, or dodging the constant tide of carriages, carts and hand barrows on the overcrowded streets. New Yorkers were friendly and loud, and never passed by without a nod, or a "hello." Even Edward, at eight, who would have been ignored by all adults in England, had his hair tousled, or his head patted, as the sea of strangers passed him by.

I wish we were staying here forever, Edward thought as he roamed around Macy's, looking at the sets of soldiers. *I wish we didn't have to go to California, wherever that is, at the end of the week.*

Then he spotted it; a captain on horseback from the very same regiment of Prussian soldiers as his set packed in the big "Edward" trunk. He looked around for Father's hat. There it was, over in the book department.

Edward raced over to the hat.

"Father, Father, you will be amazed when I tell you what I have just found," he gasped.

"I am sure I will," Francis said, looking down on his small son. "Show me."

They set off, with Edward in the lead and Father following behind.

"Here," declared Edward, holding up the captain of the Prussian army. "It's my captain. He is from the same Prussian regiment as my soldiers, Father. My regiment really needs a captain."

"Well, well. Then we had better take him with us. What is a group of soldiers without a captain?" smiled Francis.

"Thank you, Father. Thank you so very much. I will never forget this day as long as I live."

Francis smiled and said nothing, thinking it would probably be only a few short months before his son forgot about the captain. But he would be proved wrong.

They were to begin their journey west the next day and Nanny had spent the afternoon preparing in advance for their departure. They were to travel by train, but nobody realized the length of the journey, nor the conditions they would find. Train travel in 1877 was not for the faint of heart. It would take many days to reach their destination, changing engines and taking on supplies at Philadelphia and

Chicago. This would be nothing like the crossing to America as first class passengers on the luxurious SS Egypt.

Edward wanted to stay in New York, the bustling city he loved.

PULLMAN CAR

"*E*dward, wake up." Nanny was shaking him gently. "Harold, you too." Nanny continued her shaking.

"Arthur is already up and dressed, and you two are behind your time. You must be up and dressed in the next ten minutes, so I can put your things in your trunks."

She bustled out of the room, threatening to come back in a few minutes to find out how they were "getting along."

Edward stretched, yawned and ran to the water closet before Harold could make a move.

Ten minutes later they were dressed, trunks packed, and had joined the rest of the family in the dining room. Hilda had prepared a simple breakfast with scones, fruit, cheese and warm cereal for Robert and Lucy. She had also packed a large basket of homemade baked goods for the journey.

Father counted the trunks as the porters took them down to the carriages waiting in the street. All being in order, he led his family out of the apartment where they had been so comfortable for a week, and into the carriages which would take them to the railway station.

Grand Central Station was the destination. The whole family gazed, open-mouthed at the railway station on 42nd Street, which looked like an enormous palace.

Scurrying everywhere were travellers, porters, carriages. Edward and the other children stayed close to their parents as they left the carriages and made their way through the vast arches to the platforms and the trains. It was difficult for Edward to keep focused on staying alongside his family, as there were so many distractions surrounding him on every side. Francis led the way, parading his family through the crowds, onto the platform where the train stood. Porters followed with the trunks piled onto their carts.

Annie was very worried about this train journey with so many children. *What kind of train goes so far across such an immense country? Would there be facilities on the train to accommodate the smaller children? Would there be food? How long would it take to get to San Francisco? What am I doing, following my husband on such a journey as this?* She wasn't feeling particularly well herself and suspected another pregnancy was well under way, although she had not shared that information with Francis.

Francis' eyes glowed with anticipation of the adventure ahead. None of his wife's anxieties concerned him. If she had shared them with him, he would have brushed them aside with a kiss on her cheek and told her not to fret. *The children are strong and healthy and will find the journey full of interest; what an education to travel from one side of America to the other in just ten days, as promised in the Harper's Monthly Magazine article. California is the place to be, and we are going to be part of this new land.*

The vast interior of the station didn't disappoint! There wasn't time to stop and take it all in as Father marched in front of the line at a great rate, with the children scurrying to keep up, and Mother and Nanny a good way back taking care of Robert and Lucy.

Francis had purchased passage on a Pulman Hotel Car for the ten-day journey to the west coast. At the time, it was the most luxurious way to travel by train. To this day there is no more elegant rail car in existence. Francis knew, with eight children in a confined space for a week, they would need room to move, play, sleep and eat.

The hotel car came with its own kitchen, two drawing rooms lavishly furnished with arm chairs, a dining table and chairs, and two writing desks. The sleeping arrangements consisted of a state room containing two double berths, and six open sections of two double berths each. If every bed were to be occupied, the hotel car could sleep twenty-two people in all. A small dressing room and water closet was accessed from the open section by the berths. Stewards had been hired to cook and take care of the family and, as always, the small trunks were put into use, packed with all the necessities.

Edward was in a state of pure excitement as they boarded the car. All thoughts of staying in New York now vanished with the prospect of spending ten days on the train heading west. The first thing he did was find the captain of the Prussian army and stand him on guard on the shelf at the head of the berth.

He and Harold were to share a top berth; how great was that? Arthur was in the berth beneath them - a double to himself!

Louisa and Alberta shared a top berth with Margaret and little Lucy beneath. Baby Robert had his own wooden cot beside Nanny's berth. Father and Mother had one of the beds in the state room to themselves.

The two boys were up and down the steps to the top berth dozens of times before the train was even under way. They raced around the entire car in circles, until Nanny's frown stopped them in their tracks. Edward was convinced he would never sleep.

Once the trunks were installed beside each berth and their other belongings were safely aboard the baggage car at the back of the train, Francis called a meeting.

"We are going on a great adventure!" Father began. "I expect us all to live together well during this journey. We will be confined in this railway car together for ten whole days." He paused to look at each child, letting the magnitude of this length of time sink in.

"I expect subdued behaviour. We cannot have you running around Edward and Harold! It will be difficult for you two in particular, I think. But I have foreseen this and have decided that we, as a family, will have regular exercises three times every day."

The girls sighed and rolled their eyes, looking at Mother for reprieve.

"No one is exempt," said Father. "The girls will exercise too."

"Also, I deem this journey as an incredible opportunity for learning. Every morning we will meet at breakfast and go over the itinerary for the day. There will be many amazing discoveries along the way. We will see parts of America very few people in the world have ever seen. We are part of a privileged few. We will remember this journey for the rest of our lives."

Francis choked as he said the last words. Then he beamed at them all.

"Now, on with the adventure!"

TEN DAYS ON A TRAIN

*T*he next ten days were burned into Edward's memory forever, as his father had predicted. Ten days of wonder. From leaving New York to arriving in Philadelphia, then Pittsburgh, then Chicago, the days were spent with noses pressed against the windows, watching the life outside unfold before them. As planned, Father held a morning meeting to tell them about the city they would see that day and some of its history. They did jumping-jacks and push-ups and running on the spot three times a day. Father even invented a game of netball by tying two of Mother's extra long stoles across the width of the car, from window to window, and having the children, in teams, hitting a soft ball over the "net." It was their favourite game and kept them moving and happy for many hours.

In Chicago they got a new engine, but they didn't have to move into another car, as the Pulman Hotel Car remained on the line while the new engine was hooked up. Francis told them about the stockyards of Chicago. And indeed all they saw, on entering and leaving the city, were miles of holding pens housing sheep, cattle and pigs.

Where are the people? Edward thought.

"Now our journey to the west really begins," Father said at the morning meeting.

"Will we see Indians, Father?" asked Harold.

"Yes we will," was the answer. "But do not believe all you read Harold. The native people have lived here for thousands of years and are a proud and brave culture. We must respect them, as we respect all human beings, no matter where they are from, or where they live. Whatever you hear to the contrary, you must always think for yourselves whether you are hearing the truth of the matter, or just somebody's version of the truth. This is a new country for the Europeans who are settling here, as it is for us, but we must never forget who was here first."

Edward sat quietly during this speech. He had read stories in the newspapers in New York which told a very different tale. Stories of battles with the Indians, of scalps being taken, of families being killed. Stories of the "Wild West," where men carried guns; where there were outlaws and sheriffs constantly shooting each other. Stories of wild animals, unheard of in England, like grizzly bears and mountain lions. He hoped he would see these exciting things on their journey, but only from the safety of the railway car.

Ten days in the Pulman car proved to be a test on everybody's nerves. Even for parents as even tempered and caring as Annie and Francis Wrightson there was a limit, and about five days into the trip they had reached it. The constant energy of their big family stifled by the confined quarters erupted into arguments and fights, especially between the boys and girls, who had very different ideas of what was fun. Edward longed to get out and run beside the train. Arthur lay on his berth, sulky and silent, reading book after book. Harold didn't want to play any more games of marbles because they kept rolling in the wrong direction as the train moved. The girls whined and the baby fussed.

The meals the two cooks worked hard to prepare were plain and tasteless. The only exception was the dining car. Each evening Mother and Father dined in style, sampling several courses of delectable food. Mother listed the names of the six older children. Several times during the journey west, two at a time, the children were invited to join their parents in the dining car. During the journey, Edward and Harold were invited twice. Edward stuffed himself with wonderful food and counted the days until he would be invited again.

Their saving grace was the frequent stops for water and coal, when the children could leave the carriage and spend time running and jumping. Annie was always nervous that one of the small ones would be missing when it was time to climb on board. She counted their heads as they came bursting back into the carriage. There were always seven plus Nanny, holding Robert, bringing up the rear.

Only once was there trouble; Harold was missing for the count! Edward had been rolling down the embankment with him, when Harold had taken off into the long grass for a call of nature.

"Back in a jiffy, Ed," he called over his shoulder as he ran, already unbuttoning the front of his knickerbockers. He disappeared into the long grass just as Father called for them all to get on board.

"Where is Harold?" Mother asked. Edward explained where

he was and all eyes watched the long grass. He did not reappear. The guard's whistle blew twice, indicating that all should now be on board. The family all stayed outside the Pulman still watching the grass.

"Get on board, please," yelled the guard from the brake car at the back of the train, looking irritated and waving his yellow flag around frantically. "On board right away!"

"Where the devil is he?" muttered Father under his breath. "How long does it take to urinate?" Father began to stride towards the long grass. "Get everyone on board, Annie," he instructed. "I will find Harold."

By this time, passengers were hanging out of their windows to find out what the holdup was and the guard was hurrying towards their Pulman Car.

"Sir, sir," yelled the guard. "Get on board. Where are you going? The train needs to get underway immediately."

Francis didn't answer, but continued to hurry towards the long grass where Harold had last been seen. It took a few minutes to find him, but they all finally saw Father bend down and pick up Harold and begin to carry him back to the train. Harold was crying and sobbing into Father's shoulder. He had twisted his ankle badly when he ran into the long grass. He had heard the whistle and the guard yelling and thought the train would leave without him.

"Get on the train immediately." The guard was now waiting at the Pulman, face red with anger. Francis quietly lifted Harold onto the train, into Nanny's hands and turned to the guard.

"There has been an accident. My young son has badly injured his leg, so stop shouting. It is not helping the situation. You may now go back to your carriage and wave the train into action."

The guard gaped open-mouthed at Father. He turned and hurried to the end of the train and within a few minutes they were on their way.

This was always Francis' way of dealing with situations; quietly and gently. Seeds were sown in each of the children as they watched and listened to their father. More was achieved by his gentlemanly manner than loud, gruff, confrontational behaviour. Edward admired his father in every respect and wanted to be just like him.

Harold's ankle was iced and bandaged. He was excused exercises until it was healed. Edward thought he was making more of it than he should. He enjoyed the attention! Even the girls offered to bring him drinks and treats and placed a cushion under his leg when he was sitting. Edward's job was to help him to the water closet - hopping on his good leg, then wait for him to finish and hop him back to his chair.

Days passed when they saw nothing but flat prairie spread in every direction. Where was the edge of this vast country? The children were the first to see the mountains. Bumps on the horizon at first, then grand and majestic as they neared them. The flat prairie was behind them and the Rocky Mountains provided hours of breathtaking scenery. The children ran from one side of the train to the other, not wanting to miss a single mountain, cascading waterfall or rushing river. The sun made patterns on the faces of the rocks, changing them into different colours, making them look like great giant dancers against the blue sky.

"Mother, look at this mountain," called Edward. "It is surely the biggest one we have seen. See the snow covering the tip? See where the trees stop growing? Look, Mother, look."

"Yes Edward, I see it," laughed Annie. "It is indeed a marvelous mountain."

The mountains brought fresh air into the train. The mountains brought hope that the journey was almost over. The mountains brought out sketch pads and pencils, as the Wrightson children sketched and wrote down their first impressions. The arguments stopped and the time seemed to speed up as they headed at last towards San Francisco.

SAN FRANSISCO

*E*verything was more difficult when there were eight children involved. Moving everybody from the train to the hotel in San Francisco, involving a ferry ride across the bay, needed planning and precision. Francis, as usual, had everything under control: carriages to meet them, porters to transport the trunks, and his optimistic spirit supervising all with good nature and encouragement. He helped Annie from the train with a kiss on her cheek. She leaned against his shoulder for support as she rested on the last step.

"Francis, what was I thinking to agree to this?" she whispered.

"You were thinking it would be wonderful to be doing something that practically nobody else has done," he answered with a gleam in his eye and another kiss on the other cheek.

"Come, children," Father called. "Into the carriages and away to the hotel."

It felt like they were still on the train, their legs wobbling and their heads swimming. The ground felt like it was made of mercury or soft sand as they walked out of the station. It would take a few days of being on firm land before the strange feeling went away.

They were only to stay in the hotel for a week or so before moving out to the valley, where Francis had bought land seventeen years earlier.

~

When the land was purchased and Francis had the deeds in his hands, he had begun to dream what he would do with the land.

He remembered travelling through France as a young man of eighteen. He was with his father, who had been lecturing in Germany, and they travelled through the French wine regions to Calais, where they were to board a ship for England. He remembered the beautiful Chateau in Bordeaux. He had been so inspired by the building that he had returned several years later to tour the region and particularly to take a closer look at the chateau. He had toured the lovely residence, built on the banks of a tranquil lake, drinking in the beauty and remembering every detail. He had filled his notebook with sketches, jotting down details of floors, ceilings, windows, everything that was unique to the building.

His dream had been to replicate the chateau one day.

It became an obsession over the years, and once the land in California was his, he spent a great deal of his life travelling to Germany to meet with the architect who worked on the plans Francis outlined. Would he be able to build such a place in the new country far away?

It took years to develop his dream, years of pouring over drawings with the German architect, years of sourcing the stone they would use, years to discover a way of transporting stone to the new world, and then from the docks of San Francisco to the inner heights of Wild Horse Valley. Even when the stone arrived, it still took years to find the craftsmen skilled enough to build the chateau.

The stone was transported from Italy, travelling around Cape Horn for many months to reach its destination. More shipments followed, with doors and window frames, floor tiles and furnishings, and even a grand piano. The "castle" project had taken an unbelievable sixteen years from beginning to end. Pride of place was the fused window facing west, catching the sun's rays and reflecting the spectacular sunset colours across Napa Valley. Francis had not seen it, but the reports from his friend, Conrad Peters, and Mr. Poole, who had supervised the project, were impressive.

During all these years of building, Francis had kept the house a secret from his family. At first it was a dream that he dared not let himself admit possible. Then children were born one after the other. Even when the chateau was well under way, Francis was busy working and lecturing, and Annie was busy raising children and managing the house. Everything accelerated once they began packing and moving, and Francis decided he would keep the secret a few more weeks to surprise Annie with a French Chateau in the middle of the wilderness. He could barely contain his excitement!

∼

Edward thought San Francisco no match for New York. It smelled differently. The people weren't as friendly. The Palace Hotel, although newly built and quite luxurious, was stuffy and noisy. The floors seemed to amplify every footstep and the clattering of young Wrightson feet was constant throughout each long, boring day. Father seemed to have abandoned his idea of instruction and exercise for the family now that their train journey had ended. Annie was so tired from the long journey and the difficult pregnancy that she just wanted the children out of sight and hearing. Nanny was overwhelmed. Louisa and Margaret yelled at the younger children, Arthur curled up on his bed with a book and refused to move, even when Edward and Harold pummeled him with pillows. Alberta made a complete nuisance of herself wanting to hang around with Edward and Harold. It was a miserable time.

The hotel was vast with over 700 rooms, Edward learned. However, the children were not allowed to go off exploring on their own, as they had on the ship bringing them to America. They had several adjoining rooms to house the family, which gave them plenty of space. They were escorted by Nanny to the dining rooms and expansive center court-yard, which towered over them seven stories high. Edward found it very boring! The front of the Palace Hotel opened onto a busy street full of carriages and people everywhere. It didn't have the same vibrant atmosphere he'd loved in the big eastern city, with its smiling faces and bustling activity. He wanted to be settled somewhere. He was sick of traveling and moving and trying to be polite to his brothers and sisters. Father was away much of the day, busy doing some-thing to do with land, so Edward was stuck with his family in waiting mode.

It was rainy sometimes, other times misty. The mist clung to the city like wet steam, making everything smell even damper. It was Tuesday and Father had been gone since Saturday. Robert cried and cried because he was teething.

Harold and Edward were given the task of cheering him up. Nanny told them to practice his walking. Robert would totter between them on his fat little legs, as they held out their arms, then fall flat with a squeal. Edward wanted to run down the street away from the family, away from Robert and Harold, away to board a ship and sail as far away from California as possible.

WILD HORSE VALLEY

On Tuesday afternoon everything changed.

Francis arrived in a flurry of excitement. He ran into the hotel calling to Annie that all was ready. Annie frowned in disbelief. After being gone for four days her husband arrived to tell them "all is ready." What was she supposed to do?

"Francis," she scolded. "We cannot be ready to leave whenever you show up. We are not prepared. We will need help to pack everything again. I do wish you would give us some idea of your plans." She sat down with a sigh, looking around at their belongings scattered around the adjoining rooms.

"My love," exclaimed Francis, "Take all the time you need. We will hire extra help to pack and manage the move. The children can all lend a hand; the older ones are quite capable." As usual, he managed to smooth out her worries. His enthusiasm never failed to raise her spirits and ease away her cares.

With the help of Helen and Mary who worked in the hotel as

maids, Nanny supervised the packing. The children helped where they could, although they seemed to slow the process down with their "help." Edward was so happy to be on the move that he packed with a wild abandon, throwing clothes, shoes, and books into his trunk, until Nanny came to rescue the growing pile of possessions. Poor Edward had to take everything out of the trunk and repack under Nanny's supervision. What a waste of time!

Goodbye Palace Hotel, and onward to Napa, thought Edward as he climbed aboard the coach that would take them to the San Francisco Bay ferry crossing. Edward loved ships of any kind and he thought back to the Atlantic crossing a few weeks ago —it seemed like a long time ago now. The ferry was a paddlewheel, which filled all the children with awe, watching the huge wheel propel them through the water. Edward watched it until he felt sick, then he chased Harold around the decks, dodging the people lining the railings, enjoying the sunny, breeze-filled air.

The landing dock was a chaos of people, carriages, porters, trunks, carts, horses, large and small packing cases. It took some time to load the children and possessions onto the waiting array of horse-drawn vehicles, but finally they were underway.

"It seems Napa is very far," said Edward quietly, as he gazed out on the expanse of rolling hills. "Will we be there soon?"

Nobody answered him because they were all thinking the same thing.

The road was dusty and dry with many bumps and dips, making the journey inland unpleasant at best. Annie felt each jolt as they bumped along, and prayed the baby inside her would remain there.

Francis couldn't contain his excitement as they neared the ranch on the land he had bought in Wild Horse Valley so many years ago.

As the carriages drew up behind each other at the front of the building, Francis hopped out quickly, throwing his arms open wide to display "the castle." Nobody moved or spoke. Annie fell back against the seat cushions. Francis, red faced, hopped from foot to foot, nodding and smiling until he could contain himself no longer.

"Say something!" he yelled "Somebody, say something!"

Everything exploded into bedlam; the boys burst from the carriage as one, tumbling over each other as they piled onto the ground. The girls screamed, whilst holding their hands to their ears and staring at their mother with wide eyes. Robert cried at all the commotion. Annie was still sitting very still with her eyes on the building, not quite believing what she was looking at.

"Darling Annie. It is for you. It is a French chateau for you." Francis grasped her hand and helped her out of the carriage, putting his arm around her shoulder and leading her up the stone steps, under the archway, to the huge wooden doors. Annie remained trance-like as her husband led her through the vast entrance way into the dark, cool vestibule. The children spilled into the house, filling the space with laughter and noise.

"Francis," Annie finally gasped. "What is this? How did you do this? Why did you not tell me?"

"It is our new home. I did it because it was my dream, and I love you. It has taken many years - too many for me to bore you with the details. I wanted to surprise you."

All the answers came quickly. Unrehearsed because they were true.

"Do you like it dearest?"

Tears now flowed down Annie's cheeks. How dearly she loved this man! The chateau was like a dream. She couldn't believe it was real.

"Give me some time please, Francis," she whispered. "It's all so new - so unbelievable."

The children ran all over the house. Edward was always ahead of them, racing into all the rooms, noticing everything and retaining nothing. He galloped up the staircase two at a time and ran down the long corridor with doors on each side.

Which one was his room? Father had told them that rooms had already been chosen and furniture put in place. The first three doors were definitely not "boys" rooms. With pink furnishings and frilly curtains - yuk! The fourth door revealed a more promising space: Two beds on opposite walls, with brown check coverings to match the drapes. Two desks, two dressers, two bookcases. *Very plain and appropriate for me and Harold,* Edward thought.

"Harold," Edward yelled. "I've found it. We are in here."

Harold came to the door, red-faced and sweating. He tended to be a little on the chubby side and found keeping up with Edward very taxing.

"Wow! It looks great, Ed! There is room for all our things in here."

This was it, the final destination. The two boys unloaded their trunks into the cupboards and drawers, being careful to keep things tidy because they knew Nanny would be "inspecting" things later. Lastly, Edward placed his captain right beside his bed on the small table with the lamp. It would be the last thing he would see at night and the first thing he would see in the morning. Like a security blanket, the captain of the Prussian army made Edward feel safe.

They lived in a castle!

STAFF

ℒife in Wild Horse Valley was an adventure from the very beginning, with no butler, valet or housekeeper to run the house. Instead, Annie was introduced to the new staff by her beaming, always optimistic husband.

"Annie, please meet Ah Sam, Ah Fong and Chung. They are farm labourers, but will also help in the house."

Annie stared at the three Chinese men who bowed low, each of them smiling.

"Do they speak any English, Francis?" she whispered.

"Not much, I'm afraid dear. But they will learn quickly. They are excellent workers. You will get used to them."

Ah Sam, Ah Fong and Chung remained bowed and smiling.

"Thank you," was all Annie could utter, which made them smile more and bow lower.

Francis ushered them out of the room and into the kitchen,

waving his arms about and miming eating, so that they would get the idea to cook something.

The house was comfortable and cozy and Annie was happy not to have to furnish it herself, knowing another baby was due and the eight she already had were enough of a handful. She prayed whatever the "help" was cooking was edible and recognizable, then sank onto the sofa in the elegant sitting room and put up her feet; she had never felt this tired.

Francis took control of the children, informing them that they were to begin lessons the next day. In addition, they would have chores to do around the house, which was a new thing for the privileged offspring of the famous Dr. Wrightson. They learned quickly that their three Chinese servants worked very hard in the fields with their father and had little time for work in the house. Father worked out duty rosters and responsibilities for each of the children: the older girls would dust the downstairs rooms, help with the dishes and table setting, and even learn to iron after the clothing was washed by Chung. The boys would sweep the porch, carry in wood for the stove, feed the chickens, and keep their rooms clean. Nanny took care of Lucy and Robert as well as supervising everybody else.

Nanny also lovingly tended to Annie's needs, knowing she was so uncomfortable, both physically and emotionally. Having no personal maid made life very difficult for Annie.

After only one week of struggling to maintain the castle, it was obvious more help was needed. This was no ordinary house and there was too much work for Chung. The help the children gave was limited at best and at the end of the week, the kitchen was in chaos, the bedrooms were a wreck and the living areas showed signs of abandonment to dust. In desperation, Dr. Wrightson called on his neighbour, Christoph Reimer, to ask for help.

The area around Napa was bustling with new settlers, many looking for work. Christoph asked his housekeeper, Mrs. Penner, to look for a suitable woman to help the Wrightsons. She found an ideal couple, with a teenage daughter, living in a small rental room in Napa. They had arrived by wagon train from the east several months before, hoping to begin a new life and maybe find work. But the gold rush days were over and there were very few domestic jobs to be had. They had placed an advertisement in their church and Mrs. Penner, who had also put the word out to her friends, was told of their situation. She visited them the next Sunday afternoon and thought them most suitable.

George and Ida Conner and their sixteen year old daughter, Kathlyn, went out to the castle the following day in the carriage Dr. Wrightson had provided. As Mrs. Penner predicted, the Irish couple suited the Wrightsons very well and Annie welcomed them warmly into their family home. Rooms off the kitchen were cleared for their living area and their few possessions were sent for and quickly installed. Ida had worked in service in County Cork as cook and house-keeper. George had done gardening and livery and odd jobs. Kathlyn had worked for the past two years as a scullery maid, but wanted to improve her position by working as a lady's maid, or children's nurse. Nothing could be more perfect.

"Thank you m'Lord." said Ida with a curtsy. "You'll not be sorry you took us all on."

"Yes, yes. You will make life easier for my wife. She will meet with you and let you know what is expected." Francis never liked dealing with domestic matters and quickly left them to Annie's care.

What a change for the household. In only a few days order was restored.

LIFE AND DEATH

*I*da's breakfasts became legendary. Fluffy biscuits and eggs, sometimes canned ham and an array of fruit tempted the pickiest eaters. Food was plentiful and Ida, with Kathlyn's help, enjoyed cooking for the big family. Even Lucy, who was known to eat like a bird, began to try the unfamiliar delicious fruit grown in the fertile valley where they now lived.

Study time was not optional, but Edward found it a chore as he watched the blue sky through the window, waiting for the three hours to slip by when he would be outside in the sun. Francis took the children's study time very seriously, knowing the importance of continuing their education, even though they lived in a new country and a strange land. With his background in chemistry he leaned heavily towards teaching the sciences and mathematics, assigning history, geography and English literature projects as an afterthought. Of course, Annie would ordinarily have made sure they were reading the best books and studying languages, but she didn't have the energy to be involved with the children's education.

Edward soon learned to concentrate on the science subjects to gain his father's approval and praise.

The afternoons were filled with wonder, especially for the boys, who roamed the vast area around their new home, looking for adventure. Arthur, Edward and Harold soon had the hang of riding the horses, with Father's help. The western saddles were tricky compared with English saddles, but once mastered proved to be more comfortable and easier when guiding the spirited horses. The boys were soon galloping across mile after mile of Wild Horse Valley, watching the great land before them being prepared for planting. The Chinese workers, busy on every property, worked long hours planting seedlings of fruit trees and vines into the soil.

As he rode, Edward pretended to be the Prussian Captain, dressed in his blue uniform and leading his army into battle. Each day, after lunch, he would go to his room and take the captain from his place above the bed and tuck him deep into the pocket of his trousers. He never left him behind.

Dr. Wrightson was much in demand in the valley. He set up a workshop in the grounds of the house to test soil samples gathered from the various ranches and vineyards. He was excited with his findings and would try to explain to the family at dinner what great components were in this particular soil, making it unique for growing fruit, particularly grapes. The older children joined their father in the workshop on many mornings, to watch and help with the experiments and write out and understand the formulas as part of their chemistry classes.

Annie never really recovered from the journey and rested a great deal. There were no stories at bedtime, which the children missed terribly. She was pale and thin and even Ida could not tempt her to eat more than a few mouthfuls.

Francis was worried about her and the baby she carried. He asked Dr. Goldstein from Napa to examine Annie.

Dr. Goldstein drove out to the ranch in his carriage one bright Thursday morning and, after visiting Annie, met with Dr. Wrightson.

"Your wife is very undernourished. She is weak and I am worried she will not deliver the baby alive at this point."

Edward was grave and concerned. "What can we do for her?"

"I have left a tonic, but other than that, she is doing all the right things by resting, giving the baby a chance to take what it can from her." Even as he explained the situation, Dr. Goldstein shook his head. "I will come out to see her in a week's time, but if you should need me before then, please send for me."

He was sent for two days later, when Annie collapsed onto the floor of her bedroom and was found by Nanny in a pool of water and blood.

By the time Dr. Goldstein had returned, a tiny baby and its mother were both struggling to survive. Nanny stayed with Annie and the baby, leaving Louise and Margaret in charge of the younger children. As Annie gained strength, the baby became weaker. The day after the premature birth, the baby boy died in his father's hands as he held him gently, willing him to breathe one more breath. Dr. Wrightson registered the birth in Napa and buried the tiny body beneath the first grape vine planted on the property.

All the children gathered around, along with the three Chinese servants, Nanny and the Connor family. Father read from the Bible the passage about Jesus gathering the little children around him. Father cried as he read, as did the children, Nanny, Ha Sam, Ha Fong and Chung. The baby was wrapped in a blue blanket and placed into a wooden box brought from England to hold Annie's silk undergarments on the journey. Ha Fung dug a deep hole. The children scattered flower petals into the bottom of the hole, then Father placed the box onto the petals and filled in the hole.

~

This wasn't the first baby they had lost.

Annie thought back to the winter of 1863 at Nine Elms. The winter was hard and cold. It seemed their three small children were hardly ever outdoors because of the frigid temperatures. There were fires built in every room of the house to keep the cold out, but even so the cold crept in through every small crack around the windows and doors. Layers of clothing were worn to fend off the chill, the three children were wrapped in their warmest leggings and cardigans. Even so, the little ones seemed to go from one cold to another, the nursery was always full of steam kettles to relieve the congestion and Dr. Armstrong visited frequently to check on sore ears and wheezing chests.

One Friday in February, at the peak of the winter, Richard's cold morphed into a fever. Then into serious illness. Annie sat beside her eldest son's bed plying his forehead with cold cloths, trying to force tiny sips of water between his cracked lips. Dr. Armstrong came several times that day, his concern ever increasing. Richard was not responding to the care and nursing he was receiving from both Annie and Nanny. The three-year-old boy didn't open his eyes anymore and his breathing was raspy and shallow.

There was little they could do except be beside him. Annie

dreaded each minute. Francis came into the little room late in the afternoon and put his arm on his wife's shoulder. No words would come to him. He looked at his little son and knew they would lose him soon. How would he comfort Annie? How would he be able to be strong when he felt so wretched and sad?

At 8:07 that evening Richard shuddered and opened his eyes really wide. He saw nothing, but his mother took him in her arms and whispered her love, and he stopped breathing. Annie wondered how her world could have ended so quickly. How the happiness they had known for five lovely years could be so easily swept aside.

She held her little boy in her arms, wanting time to stop so that she could stay holding him forever. Frances held both of them tightly as he came to the chair where he had watched his wife nurse and hold their baby.

~

As Annie lay in bed in the beautiful castle in Wild Horse Valley, she mourned the loss of her infant son. After some weeks, she was downstairs for breakfast one morning when Edward ran into the dining room.

"Mother," he greeted her, throwing himself into her arms, but gently because she still looked so fragile. "You are better!"

"Yes darling, I am. I have so much to catch up on and want to hear everything about each one of you."

Soon she was bustling around the house, adding her touch to everything again. Pots of flowers made the rooms come alive with colour and perfume. Francis was elated and beamed from ear to ear as he watched his wife return to her family.

She continued to think about the baby boy, but mourned the loss quietly this time and with a sense of resignation.

The other children needed her. They once again gathered at Annie's feet to hear bedtime stories and bent over her to have her kiss planted on their heads and cheeks. Life was beautiful again for the Wrightson family.

GRAPES

*D*r. Wrightson's reputation preceded him. Several landowners in Napa, of German heritage, knew of his work. He had studied chemistry in Germany under the famous Professor Bunsen at the University of Marburg. He lived in Germany during his years of study and loved the country almost as much as his homeland. He wrote several books in German. He travelled there often to give lectures and meet with other scientists. The talk always turned to the new world and what opportunities there would be for men of science, as the new continent expanded and developed. Francis was captivated by the stories he heard of this wild world across the Atlantic Ocean.

Francis' friend, Conrad Peters, had taken the plunge and in September of 1850 he boarded a ship in Hamburg heading for New York. Francis had helped him load his chemistry equipment into a secure tin trunk and accompanied his friend to the Hamburg dockyard.

Conrad promised to keep up a regular correspondence, giving Francis every detail of his adventure into the unknown. He planned to travel west with a wagon train. Francis almost jumped on board ship with him; the very thought of such an adventure gave him goosebumps.

For almost thirty years Francis had communicated with his friend, who encouraged him to buy land and helped supervise the construction of the "castle." Older than Francis, Conrad's health was declining and he rarely left his home in Los Angeles, but he was overjoyed that his old friend had finally brought his family to Napa where the house of Francis' dreams was waiting.

Francis had expert help from the landowners around him who advised him on wine production. He had all his grapes transported to Bohm's vineyard, where the winery equipment converted the heavy, delicious harvest into fine wine. All of the properties in the valley were covered in fruit trees or vines and the harvest was abundant. Year upon year the harvest grew and multiplied and the wine industry, in particular, produced fine quality wines known for their sweet, fruity flavour.

All the work Francis had done on the soil samples, all the advice he had given to the vineyard owners, had been invaluable and now they all profited.

As the harvests grew, so did the children. Four years after losing the baby boy, Fanny was born. Healthy and strong and a pure delight to her parents and siblings, she would be the last of the children born to the Wrightsons. Edward was twelve years old when Fanny was born and was already taller than his brother Arthur, who was eighteen. Arthur was going away to college in San Francisco in August to study chemistry. Louisa had taken a trip back east and was enrolled in the University of Pennsylvania as one of the first female medical students. Both students profited from their father's tutoring in the sciences and achieved the highest marks in the entrance exams.

Living in California had changed the pale, slender family into a suntanned, robust one. Their faces glowed with good health. Nanny no longer wore her laced corsets or her high-necked, long-sleeved gowns. The children ran around without shoes for most of the day, only getting on their boots to ride, or their dress clothes and shoes to visit neighbours, or to go into town.

Ah Fong, Ah Sam and Chung loved their family and the love was returned. Francis had a cottage built, close to the chateau, for the three faithful servants, where they gathered their own possessions around them. The children were always welcome to explore the cottage, fascinated by the trinkets from the far east, which were displayed proudly in the small cottage.

Ida and George Conner became as much a part of the family as Nanny. Kathlyn married a young man from Napa, who worked with the blacksmith, and moved to a tiny house on the outskirts of town. She visited the castle often and helped out when there was a dinner party, or with spring cleaning. Ida replaced Kathlyn with a young girl from the same church they had attended in Napa. She was part of a family of eleven and was delighted to move to the Wrightson house to assist Ida in the kitchen and help keep the house clean and tidy.

Cooking was often a family affair, with the children helping Ida prepare the recipes she loved to make. Laughter filled the kitchen after meals as the family helped clear the table and wash the dishes. All class lines seemed to blur in this new land; they would never have even been allowed to set foot in the kitchen at Nine Elms, nor would they have wanted to. Here was different! Plunging their hands into the hot soapy water in the huge sink, where three of them could stand side by side and still have space, Ida supervised and called out instructions.

"Scrub those pots, Master Edward. Be careful with the plates, Margaret - they are fragile. Alberta, you are spraying water everywhere. You won't need a bath tonight."

The servants were such an integral part of the family and Francis and Annie encouraged the interaction. Edward and Harold ran down to the cottage as the sun set to prepare a warm bath for Ah Fong, Ah Sam and Chung. The men took turns to wash away the grime of the day in the fields; they kept careful track of whose turn it was to go first, so they had a fair share of the cleanest water. A cool drink was placed into each eager hand as they wrapped themselves in the thick towels after their baths. All three nodded and smiled at their new family with great affection. Wong still cooked some special dishes; he made the best soup in the world! Even Ida had to admit to it. He also baked sugar cookies that filled the whole house with their aroma - everyone knew it was Wong's baking day, just from the smell.

When Fanny was a year old, Dr. Wrightson became increasingly worried and spent many hours in his workshop. The neighbouring vineyard workers had noticed some of the grape vines were showing signs of distress. Leaves at the bottom of the vines were curling at the edge and turning brown. He visited the homesteaders, taking soil and leaf samples. Edward was no longer allowed into the workshop to help Father with the samples, but was told not to bother his usually easy-going father.

Francis called a meeting of the vine growing community to give them his thoughts and findings. It was not good news. The vine pest phylloxera was the culprit. It was difficult, if not impossible, to treat and could spread quickly and cause devastation for the vine crop. Francis advised burning the affected vines immediately to try and halt the spread of the pest.

It did, indeed, slow down the spread. The area celebrated the fact that they had lost only a small portion of their lucrative product. However, Francis remained cautious. His sampling and careful monitoring continued. He would inform each plantation owner if he found evidence of the blight so that they could burn the infected vines.

Without the intervention of Dr. Wrightson, the entire grape production in the Napa Valley would have been at risk.

SAD TIMES

The following year, as Dr. Wrightson turned sixty-seven years old, he struggled with the options for the future of his family in California. Annie never gained back her full strength after the journey to America. Francis watched her smile her way through the days in the beautiful chateau he had built for her, and knew instinctively that it was a mask for his and the children's sake. He saw the tired eyes and hidden tears, the small appetite, the pale cheeks. Over the years, they had not discussed Annie's health. In fact, the brave lady of the house refused to admit to a problem and brushed her husband away with a soft laugh if he mentioned how tired she looked, or how pale she was. Francis was convinced that doctors at the university hospital in Birmingham would have Annie feeling better in no time.

Returning to England was not an easy decision for Francis. The chateau was his life's dream. He had, however, never given up the house in England. Nine Elms had been maintained throughout their years in America. For some reason,

Francis had kept the house as insurance. For some reason, he had maybe known they would return one day.

As for himself, Francis didn't want to begin again replanting the property. He would leave it to a younger man. He still saw the evidence of the grape blight continuing its hold and advised the local grape growers to uproot their entire crop and plant with Vinifera varieties that could be grafted to American rootstock, which were immune.

Francis didn't have to look far to find a buyer for the castle. Mr. Vorpe, a wealthy landowner in San Fransisco, had made several offers to buy the property. He was a flamboyant figure in the bay area, well-known and admired. Francis discreetly arranged to meet him for lunch in Napa to ask if the offer still stood.

The entire family was shocked. Nobody wanted to move back to England, least of all Edward. This was his home. This was who he was. How could Father make this decision? Even Annie, who had taken so long to settle into the new life, was upset about the decision to leave. She loved the house and the beautiful weather. She never guessed that part of the decision to move was due to her own health. The free and easy life they now lived was in such contrast to the restricted, straight and narrow way they were expected to live in England. To go back to that seemed impossible.

However, Francis was determined. He had been offered an excellent position with the University of Birmingham, which was a big part of his decision to move. With the money from the sale of the property in the valley they would lack for nothing. He had moved his wife, eight children and Nanny here when the children were but babies, and this journey back would be so much easier now that the children were grown.

Louisa and Arthur decided they would stay in America and finish their studies. Arthur never returned to his homeland.

Ah Sam, Ah Fong and Chung walked around in mourning, once they heard their family was leaving. They cried all day, every day. The children hugged them and cried with them. The sale of the property would include provision for the three faithful servants to be allowed to stay in whatever capacity they decided. All three wanted to go back to England with their family, but that wouldn't have worked on so many levels.

Francis asked Ida and George to go with them. They would find a good home at Nine Elms in England. But Ida and George had already made the move from the British Isles to California with their daughter years before and wanted to stay in their adopted home. Kathlyn was pregnant and they were to be grandparents for the first time. They had saved some money and knew they would have no difficulty finding good positions with another family after serving at the castle for the Wrightson family. It would be a difficult parting for them all.

Edward decided not to talk to his father again as long as he lived! He felt the decision his father had made was unforgivable. He plotted with Harold how they would ride away into the hills and hide rather than return to England. They smuggled food up to their room and stashed it into a strong saddle bag.

"We could hide out in the cave on the south side of the valley," whispered Edward, in the darkness of the bedroom. "Remember, Harold, the cave where we lit a campfire once. There's a stream close by, so we'd have constant fresh water."

"Great idea, Ed," agreed Harold, as he sat up in bed and

leaned closer to his brother. "We could each take a blanket, tin cups to collect the water, matches for the fire."

As they lay back on their pillows in the quiet of the night, questions popped into their heads. How long would they be able to stay in the cave? What would they do once the family had left? Would they become wild? Would they ever be accepted into society again? After going over all the problems, they decided to eat the food they had smuggled. There were too many unknowns, and Edward felt responsible for Harold. If it was just him, he would go in a minute. But with Harold along, well...

The boys settled into a dull, quiet, miserable attitude. Watching their Chinese friends cry was awful. Watching Ida and George get quieter and quieter was worse. Watching their mother gathering the family's precious possessions together to ship to the other side of the world made their hearts sick. The objects gathered during their seven years in Wild Horse Valley were memories of time spent in a new world, and now they were returning to the old world.

It seemed the only constant in Edward's life was the Prussian Captain. He packed him carefully with his personal belongings to ensure he would travel safely and be beside him during the long journey "home."

Edward couldn't even remember Nine Elms very well. He remembered he had just gone into his own bedroom the year before the journey to America. He couldn't remember much else about the house or grounds or staff. He remembered never going without shoes and stockings, wearing layers and layers of warm clothing that restricted every movement. He remembered rain pouring down the windows and soaking everything outside, it was an "indoor" kind of place, where being outside doing anything took effort and planning because of the weather.

Two other properties owned by Dr. Wrightson remained in his possession. One in Russian River and one near Santo Rosa, Sonoma County. He never quite closed the door, but left it just open a crack, so that there would be an opportunity ahead. Maybe one day one of his sons would return and the land would be waiting.

The journey back to the eastern seaboard was tedious and miserable. Edward hated every minute. No games and fun this time, just miles of nothing.

Francis had classes every morning for the six growing children. He noticed Edward's hostile manner and treated him with no disdain. Francis realized the boy was struggling with the move from California and left him to his struggles, knowing that time and distance would be the healer.

Edward, however, never really forgave his father. Although he did heal and his life continued on its course, the memories of California haunted Edward. He knew his father had made the wrong decision to sell their home and move back to England and he never changed his mind.

SCHOOL

Nine Elms became vibrant and full of life again. The rooms were all opened up and aired when the family arrived. New staff were hired on the family's return, but Mrs. Brookes remained as housekeeper, training each new servant in the ways the house was to be run. The bedrooms were shuffled and made ready for the grown children.

The nursery was needed for only Fanny, who was still attended by Nanny. Dear Nanny, who was so much a part of who they all were, never flinched at Francis' decisions. She would go where she was needed. She would be with them no matter what. She only made one condition— she would never wear corsets again.

Most of the children didn't know the house, of course, and the first few days were spent exploring the rooms and settling into their oh-so-different surroundings. No warm kitchen to run barefoot into in the morning, to help Ida with the breakfast, sampling the fruit as it was cut and piled onto the platters, sipping the lemon tea in big yellow mugs as they worked and laughed. No! They were up in the morning to dress in stockings, shoes and layers of clothing. Then down to the dining room, so formal and cold, with its long polished table and twelve straight-backed chairs. The table was set with white linen tablemats and napkins, silver cutlery and crystal glasses. Breakfast awaited in silver dishes on the sideboard, steaming and ready to eat. Somebody named George, standing by the sideboard, helped serve the food and pour coffee or tea. Unlike "their" George, always joking and making them laugh, this George never talked to them other than to offer his help. He never smiled either, his face looked like a mask.

I wonder what Chung is doing now? thought Edward, as he sat down at the table with his civilized breakfast of scrambled eggs and toast and marmalade. He looked around the table at the serious faces of his siblings and knew their thoughts were much like his own. *No laughing here! No bowing and smiling Chung bringing in jugs of fresh milk, patting the girls on their heads as he passed by. Nanny used to be fat and happy in her loose fitting gown, telling her silly stories about when we were babies. Now she is dressed up to the throat and down to the wrists in a dark coloured gown, rigid as a pole, picking at her breakfast with no fruit.*

Margaret, Alberta, Edward and Harold were to attend the new preparatory school in Kings Norton. Francis had registered them all after inspecting the school for himself and interviewing the headmaster. This was good news for Edward, who wanted to spend as little time as possible in the house. He would throw himself into his studies to make the time fly by so that he could leave Nine Elms to attend University.

A governess, Miss Marshall, was hired for Lucy and Robert, who would not benefit from Father's tutoring in mathematics and science.

Time and distance did heal the longing for California. Edward settled into life in Kings Norton. He was a good student and popular with the other pupils. The boys school was separated from the girls school by a high brick wall. As a prefect, you could stand at the top of the stairs in Block Six, the science building, to supervise the students as they went in from the playground. From this vantage point, the girl's sports field was well visible, so it was a prime location that the prefects fought to be posted to. At fifteen and sixteen years of age, it was the highlight of the day to watch girls of the same age run around in knee length navy blue skirts and short sleeve clingy shirts. At least Edward thought so.

Edward was particularly good at cricket and was chosen for the school's first eleven. He practiced his bowling skills at every opportunity and could hit the wicket almost one hundred percent of the time. The school won the divisional championship that year and Edward was the hero, bowling out the opposition's best batter for ten runs. The silver cup they won took the place of honour in the showcase in the main hallway, which Edward passed every day on his way to classes. Yes, California was slipping further and further away.

Only when a letter came from Arthur or Louisa and was read at the dinner table, did the old pangs of longing come back. Then Edward would think about Ah Sam, Ah Fong and Chung and smile as he remembered the three men he loved. Of course, they never wrote, but they would always be a part of Edward's memories of his life in America.

Ida and George wrote about their new grandson, William. They wrote about their new family and their new house, a big house with many rooms close to Kathlyn in Napa. They wrote of how much they missed "the castle" and the family; how the new people didn't come into the kitchen to help with the dishes; how the class line seemed to be drawn firmly and they were not encouraged to cross over it.

OXFORD

"*E*dward, I would like to talk to you after dinner," Francis said. "Please join me in my study will you?"

Edward was seventeen and in his final year of preparatory school. He joined his father after dinner, taking the seat opposite him on the other side of the large mahogany desk.

"Edward, what are you planning to do after school?" Francis came straight to the point.

"I plan to go to Oxford to study engineering," answered Edward without hesitation. "My marks are high, due to the tutoring I received as a boy from a highly educated scientist." Here, Edward couldn't keep the glint of humour out of his eye as he looked directly at his tutor.

Francis smiled slowly. He had felt a distance from his son since California and knew Edward still held a small grudge for the decision to leave that great land.

"Then we must make sure the paper work is all in order. The

entrance examination will be difficult. You must not take it lightly, thinking you know all there is to know. Much study will be needed if you are to do well. I will work with you during the next several months to ensure your best advantage."

It was unusual for his father to offer tutoring at this time. Francis had devoted his time to his job at Birmingham University and had decided to leave the teaching of his children to the schools. However, he wanted Edward to pass the entrance examination if that was his desire, so must offer him every advantage for doing so. They discussed the best times to meet and study, so as not to interfere with cricket of course. They began to meet three times each week for two hours to go over previous entrance exams and fill in the gaps of Edward's knowledge.

The entrance exam, although challenging, was completed by Edward in the designated time allowed and the result was his acceptance into university the following August. Edward was leaving Nine Elms. He was headed for Oxford.

Annie was proud of Edward but didn't want to see him leave home. As with all mothers at such a time, her heart was torn between him becoming a man and remaining a boy. She thought back to the first years at Nine Elms, when the house was filled with babies and had never imagined the day when the babies would grow and be gone. Edward was the tallest of the children, only two inches shorter than his father. He was slender and had lost the robust colouring and vibrant countenance of California long ago. He was good looking, with steel grey eyes and dark hair, and a smile that won the hearts of everybody he met, especially the young ladies. Annie knew he would do well at Oxford and, as she watched him go, she blew him a kiss and smiled through her tears, knowing he would only be back to visit during vacations from now on.

Edward shared rooms with two other young men, Cecil Carmichael from Bristol and Frederick Walters from Southampton. The three of them were green as grass and knew nothing of life in Oxford, a beautiful town with spires of white stone everywhere, and bells ringing the hour from every tower. Everybody worked, lived, or studied at the University. The town existed because of the University. It was an exciting place to be for Edward! He fell into the relaxed, easy atmosphere of the camaraderie of his fellow students and the fierce competition of the classes he attended. Engineering was not an easy degree by any means - nothing at Oxford came easily and every mark had to be fought for. Edward soon learned that revelling with the other students cost dearly at exam time. He adapted quickly, enjoying his leisure and working hard at his studies.

He joined the cricket team, where he was welcomed with great enthusiasm, once they had watched him bowl. He tried out for the rowing team, thinking himself fit and strong, but failed miserably against other young men with greater upper body strength than himself. Cricket was a summer sport, so he took his rooms for the whole year instead of for eight months, knowing he would likely not make it home very much during the good weather of the summer. Dressed in his whites, he looked very dashing, a magnet for every young lady with an eye for a handsome, single man. He had no shortage of female company, which he enjoyed immensely.

His Prussian Captain was now hidden in a drawer beside his bed. Edward saw him every day when he reached for clean socks. It was his connection with the past, a reminder of New York and California, where he had felt so free.

KATHERINE

*E*arly in the first part of Edward's first semester at Oxford he lost his virginity. The chance of any romantic adventure with girls at his Prep school was pretty well zero, but at university he was independent of his parents' or teachers' supervision.

Katherine Brennar lived in rooms in the same college as Edward. The female students' building was across the quadrangle from the males.' On Mondays and Thursdays Edward noticed her hurrying along in front of him as they left their quadrangle to attend class in different colleges. Soon they were exchanging nods, then smiles and then a "good morning."

Katherine had the most beautiful smile! She was tall and slender and had dark hair and eyes. Edward plucked up the courage to ask her to join him for afternoon tea at the tea shop in the high street and she agreed. They were soon studying together in the common area in their quadrangle buildings, despite the fact that Katherine studied English

Literature and Edward studied Engineering. From the study hall to Edward's private room was more risky.

"No member of the opposite sex will be allowed in rooms" was listed as number three on the great list of rules in the foyers of the resident houses. Of course the students were very creative when it came to smuggling members of the opposite sex into their rooms.

Edward's good friend, James, helped out. Katherine, dressed in a borrowed man's long coat and hat, was placed between Edward and James and the three of them, linking arms, boisterously entered the building. Looking like they were helping their friend in the middle back to the dorm after a night of too much ale, the doorman glanced at them briefly before shaking his head and waving them inside. It helped that it was raining hard outside and the three friends had their coat collars up and their hats pulled down, as well as being pretty much soaked through.

Edward laughed as he opened his door, "Thanks James, you were a great help."

He waved his friend away and closed the door, helping Katherine off with the soaking coat and hat, then sitting her down and removing her equally wet shoes. He lit the gas fireplace and set the kettle full of water onto the gas ring, and soon they were toasting their toes and drinking their tea. Katherine knew that agreeing to come to Edward's room would include an expectation on his part that they would *not* be studying. She looked up at him shyly, not knowing quite how to behave. She wasn't in the habit of accepting such invitations.

She had no experience of even kissing a young man. She

naively thought that the kissing was what they could practise in Edward's rooms.

Edward realized early in the tryst that his plan was thwarted. Katherine was lovely, she was so desirable it hurt, but she was innocent - that was the issue. Edward hadn't anticipated her innocence. He hadn't given it very much thought, only thinking of his own unquenchable desire which kept him awake at nights, thinking about Katherine in his bed. That girls did not act out on their desires had never occurred to him. He thought she would be just as game for jumping into his bed as he was. As soon as he began to kiss her, his hands touched her breasts and hastily began to unfasten the buttons down the front of Katherine's gown. She jumped back, with a face of such horror that Edward stopped in his tracks.

"I'm sorry!" he muttered, catching his breath in gulps as he drew away from her. "I assumed too much. I thought this was why you had agreed to come."

"How could you think that, Edward? I came because I thought I could trust you and that you were a gentleman and a good friend."

"A good friend?" Edward sputtered. "Katherine, this is much more than a friendship for me. You are everything I have ever dreamed about. You are beautiful and I want you more than I've ever wanted anything in my life. Please, Katherine, don't turn away and shut me out. I promise I will not hurry you, or force you to my bed."

"Edward, please let's forget this happened. I want to be with you, of course I do. I love our times together. I never imagined that accepting the offer to come to your room would mean we would go to bed. I know I must appear naive, but I have lived a very sheltered life at home, with no experience of boys or men. I don't even have a brother, only three sisters. Give me some time."

Edward, always the charmer, held her close and assured her he would give her time, with no expectations.

"Only, don't accept an invitation to my room again, will you," he whispered. "Not until you're ready, I mean."

Something about leaving Katherine with all the control in the situation worked like magic. Only two weeks later, after a rainy tea in the high street, Katherine asked to be invited to his rooms. Edward had to make sure the other fellows were out that evening and would help with the plan to sneak Katherine into his room. They were happy to comply. Cecil and Frederick would engage the door man in a complicated question about receiving parcels from home and where should they be addressed etc., and Edward and Katherine would sneak past them and up the stairs. It worked like a charm, although Edward thought that the doorman probably knew what they were up to, after many years supervising the men's dormitory building.

This time was different. Although they were both nervous and inexperienced, they didn't take their eyes off each other while they took off their outer clothing. When Edward was down to his underpants and Katherine her undergarments, they cuddled into Edward's single bed under the covers. Edward knew enough to be careful and gentle with this lovely girl. Although he wanted to rush ahead and satisfy his craving quickly, he showed great composure, as he kissed Katherine tenderly on her lips, her neck, her arms and finally her breasts. He struggled for control then, taking deep breaths to dampen the surge of passion. More wonderous than Edward could have imagined were the delights he explored with Katherine. More beautiful, soft and moist than his fantasies. She moaned and sighed with each caress, touching the soft skin on his back and down to his hips, then around to touch the very essence of his desire. Surprising for both of them to see and feel their bodies in such a way, it delighted them both. When Edward finally entered her, Katherine didn't feel anything but pleasure. It seemed so right. So warm. So lovely. They were making love and all other life seemed to fade into the distance. It was the first time for them both and they treasured the memory of their love-making forever.

Katherine confessed as they dressed afterwards, that she had sought the help of an older woman in her dormitory. She knew enough not to risk a pregnancy and the older woman had given her a precautionary product called a diaphragm, which once inserted properly prevented pregnancy. Edward confessed he hadn't given it a thought.

"You are the most wonderful girl in the world." exclaimed Edward. "You not only make love with me, but take care of all the practical aspects. I find you amazing."

It was the beginning of an affair that would last for two years. They met frequently to make love, adding to their knowledge of each other, and finding new and exciting ways to please each other. They spent every available moment together, either studying, punting on the river, walking the beautiful streets of Oxford or drinking tea in the tea shop.

Katherine went back to Kings Norton with Edward for Christmas and Easter breaks and he went with her to visit her family in Essex. Her three younger sisters thought him a novelty but her father looked on him with furrowed brow and suspicion - rightly so!

Katherine graduated a year before Edward. She took a position in Oxford at the Easton House Girls school as an English Literature teacher. She would be close to Edward in his final year at Oxford.

Edward was uncomfortable with his reaction to Katherine staying in Oxford. He had thought she would return to Essex. Had he secretly hoped she would? He found himself making excuses why he couldn't meet her for tea after school - studying hard you know, for finals! He avoided running into her on the high street when he knew she was at the bookstore. He had moved into private rooms, outside the campus, which had been so much more accessible for their rendezvous. Now he decided to take in a roommate, Jonathon McIntosh, who became a close and dear friend and who made it difficult for Katherine to visit as often. Edward had to admit to himself that, although the affair had been remarkable, the time to end it was drawing near.

Katherine felt it too. She enjoyed her work at the girls school, but had recently heard from her father that there was a position at the elite Essex County Girls school opening in the spring for an English Literature tutor. Katherine didn't want to belabour the affair with Edward, he was the most handsome man she knew and the most charming, but lately her thoughts had turned to writing her own novel. She spent more and more time at the great literature library in Oxford researching one of the colleges, with a view to using it as the background for her literary work. She wrote to her father asking for details of the position mentioned and when she received the school's address and the contact name for applications, she forwarded her resume.

GRADUATION

*L*ife without Katherine was exceedingly dull for Edward. She had left in March to take up her new position in Essex. There were no tears, just a feeling of sadness for them both as they parted ways. Their two years of friendship and love-making would be treasured memories. How fortunate they were to have found each other.

For Edward, graduation couldn't come quickly enough. His father and mother and four of his siblings arrived for the ceremony, all duly proud of Edward.

Now what would he do?

As he packed his belongings into the trunk for the journey back to Nine Elms, Edward picked up his worn Prussian Captain from the drawer by his bed. They had lived together for a long time, ever since Edward was eight years old. The captain had never been far from Edward in all that time, staying by his bedside wherever that bed had been. Now Edward was a man and heading who knew where. To Kings

Norton first though, where a great feast to celebrate his graduation was to happen on Saturday.

Nine Elms was ablaze with light and music. Everybody they knew had been invited to the celebration and Edward was the guest of honour. Speeches were made, honouring his degree and his prowess as a cricketer. Toasts were drunk, wishing him well in his future endeavours. His mother glowed with pride, as her tall, handsome son took it all in his stride with his usual effortless charm. He presented Nanny with a first edition of Alice in Wonderland to say "thank you" for all the years of love and care she had given him. The day was his and yet he wrestled with a decision about his future.

As with all wealthy families of the day, Edward would be presented with an inheritance by his father. He was expected to use this large sum of money to "make his way in the world." Francis expected his son would follow in his footsteps and pursue a master's degree, then a Ph.D in Engineering and finally teach at the university level. Edward had other plans.

After the party, Edward closed the door of his room and stood for a moment in the dark silence. He walked to the bed in the dark and sat in the armchair by the window, staring out into the night sky. He reached out his hand and took the captain from his bedside table and held him for a few moments. How often had he done this very thing over the years. *You have been with me always, on the train crossing America, in "the castle," in my pocket for wild horse-back adventures across the valley, on the trip back to England, beside me at Nine Elms and at Oxford. Now where will we go?* thought Edward. California drowned out all others memories. Edward pushed the visions of America into the back of his mind. *I might try traveling through Germany, where I spent so much time as a boy.*

Maybe I should retrace the steps Father took when he was a young man. But what about America? Edward closed his eyes tightly and forced himself to think of something different. *I could seek a position as an engineer and work for a few years to begin an independent life. I could return to University for post graduate studies, as Father wants.* But his thoughts went once more to Wild Horse Valley, to New York, to America.

He spent a sleepless night considering possibilities. He didn't want to disappoint his father. Maybe he should choose the path expected.

BOSTON

*E*dward did not choose the expected path, he chose a different path. An adventurous, uncertain , path that he announced at breakfast the morning after the party.

Father did not approve of his son's decision.

"Edward, I am disappointed," Francis said as he walked into his study ahead of Edward. "Your memories of America have influenced your choice. You were just a boy and your head is still filled with the excitement of New York through the eyes of an eight-year-old. All you see is yourself galloping across miles of open land on horseback when you think of California. I am concerned you will not find the country of your childhood when you return as an adult."

"I have given this much thought," said Edward, facing his father across the desk. "I have weighed all my options, but am convinced I must go to America once more. I am no longer a boy, Father, and my heart will never be settled until I go back to the land where I was so happy. I would like your blessing."

"Edward, please reconsider. Take some time. Stay here at Nine Elms for a few months and really think it through. You may arrive at a different conclusion."

"No I will not," said Edward with determination, giving each word the same emphasis, as he met Francis' steel grey eyes with his own. Then, turning on his heel, Edward marched out of the study, ignoring the stares of the family as he ran upstairs to his room.

Before leaving for America, Francis Wrightson presented his son with the promised inheritance, but could not give his blessing on what he considered to be a frivolous adventure.

Edward sailed on the Arizona from Liverpool in April 1893, and arrived in New York thinking he would take this new country by storm with his good looks, education, and wealth.

His first idea was to travel back to California, but he decided to stay on the east coast instead, drinking in the exuberant life it offered at every turn. He loved New York, but after spending a month there visiting the places he remembered, he travelled north to Boston.

Boston was the city for Edward, he decided, and he set himself up there in rooms above First City Bank, very well appointed, with a view of the harbour and the bustle of the city below. He furnished his apartment lavishly, finding a wealth of willing helpers in female form who, attracted by his money and good looks, advised him on everything from red velvet drapery to monogramed towels. With hardly a thought on his part, his new lady friends hired a housekeeper and cook for him, and of course he simply had to have his own carriage. There was money enough for everything Edward desired, and he found himself surrounded by his new acquaintances, enjoying their company and lavishing his generosity upon them.

His fortune was large and his Boston home, with all its decadence, hardly dented the bank balance. Edward was advised by the young men in his circle of friends to invest his money. After all, he was a gentleman and not expected to actually work. There were a myriad of schemes in the new world waiting to be funded by the right backer. Word travelled fast that a newly arrived "rich" English gentleman was willing to invest in just about anything, and within a short space of time much of Edward's fortune was tied up in schemes he knew little about.

He loved the high life, dining out at the best hotels, accompanied by the most beautiful women. He smoked the best cigars and drank the best brandy. The women in his life had expensive tastes and he loved to please them with gifts of jewelry and furs. He loved women. He stood six feet two inches tall and was wickedly handsome. He had a smile to melt hearts and eyes that sent shivers down slender spines. He was a considerate and ardent lover. Touching, caressing and kissing all the erotic, secret places to send women wild, which in the nineteenth century was a rarity indeed. Knowledge of his ability as a lover spread like smouldering grass among the society women, who knew from heresay, if not experience, that the men of their acquaintance were lacking in such skills. In fact it would have been unrefined and indeed vulgar for a society lady to even acknowledge her own body in such a way. Edward was very much in demand.

In August, after being in Boston for only three months, Edward received unexpected news from England that his father had died. He had been in splendid health when

Edward left, although the relationship between them was strained after Francis learned that his son would not be staying in England. He had expected more of Edward after the engineering degree and was shocked to realize that the dream of America was still burning in his heart.

The will of Dr. Francis Wrightson left the two properties in California to his sons, Arthur and Harold, sending a clear message to Edward that his decision to go back to the new world had displeased his father greatly.

Mr. George Gross was Edward's saving grace. He had become the manager at the First City Bank in 1894, and had made it his personal goal in life to rescue Edward from the mess he was in. A year of poor investments and high living had left the fortune sadly diminished and Mr. Gross shook his head as he poured through the financial history of one of his most prestigious clients. He could see, from his quick thumb through the file, that without intervention, the life Edward had created for himself was about to end.

Edward sat across the desk from Mr. Gross and listened intently to the older man's advice. He thought about his privileged education and background and how he had left his family and their expectation that he would "make good." He'd wasted so much of what his parents had given him and here was the proof, in this file sitting on the old walnut desk in the bank manager's office.

Why was Mr. Gross so interested in Edward's file? Maybe he saw something in the young man, who had led a misguided year of folly, that touched a nerve from when he was in his twenties. He was from a much different background, but, given the same advantages as Edward, would Mr. Gross have chosen any differently? Maybe not.

The advice was sound, yet risky. Pull his money out of the get-rich-quick schemes, where possible, and invest everything into the railway, snaking across the huge plains of America to the west. Many subsidiary lines were being developed to link cities. Edward liked the risk and Mr. Gross liked Edward's courage, and the deal was done. His fortune stabilized, as the railway came to life and branched out to more and more communities. The railway became the main artery of America. Life was just about near as perfect as it could be for Edward.

Edward didn't marry. He loved the women of Boston and loved making love to them, but he never fell in love. He enjoyed riding, reading, lunch at the club with his male friends.

With his major investment in the railway came his introduction into corporate life, sitting on the railway board, which he surprisingly enjoyed. His life was full and beautiful. He moved to an elegant house, where he had a small staff of people to take care of his everyday needs. He was just about the most eligible bachelor in Boston, top of everybody's list for dinner parties and sought after at every society function the busy city afforded.

Edward decided to celebrate his twenty-fifth birthday with a lavish party, surrounded by his many friends. The house was draped in lights, shimmering from the pillars at the front door and twinkling in the trees lining the driveway. It was a spectacular night. The best people in the city were all there. Extra staff had been brought in for the occasion; preparing sumptuous dishes of quail and pheasant and salmon, a never-ending table of side dishes and the most elegant lemon torte, Edward's favourite, with chocolate sauce and strawberries for dipping. Silver trays covered in petite fours, cream puffs, chocolate truffles accompanied the coffee and brandy. People mingled and danced to the music of a group of talented musicians, laughing and talking until the early hours. What a wonderful host Edward Wrightson was. Quite the best in Boston!

EVERYTHING LOST

*E*verything stopped the following year. Stocks in the railway began to fall, slowly at first then helter-skelter. Nobody could stop it. Nobody knew how. Edward had some money, but the fortune was gone. Everything happened so fast. He moved from the house into "rooms" again, with only two people to look after him: his long-time valet Jim Pinkleton and his wife Janet, who cooked and cleaned. They were loyal servants and lived in two cramped rooms at the end of the hall, willing to put up with the lack of privacy and space just to be of service to their dear Edward.

Edward talked to everybody he knew to try to get onto a corporate board, or serve in some capacity in the city. A position as an engineer would have been suitable, but suddenly there were no vacancies anywhere. It seemed the whole country was plunged into financial ruin. The friends who had surrounded him for more than three years were conspicuous only by their absence, becoming urgently entangled in their own lives, or with important details that couldn't be delayed. Boston was increasingly, for Edward, a cold and unwelcoming city.

Uncomfortable with his life and prospects, he left his two trusted servants in his meagre home and boarded a train west, to find out for himself where all his money had been invested, and if it had all been for nothing.

He had done this before when he was just a lad, and the memories flooded back as the smells and sounds of the train surrounded him. This time he travelled third class in a straight-backed seat. He bought sandwiches when the train stopped at stations. He used the only public toilet at the end of the carriage.

The country was as vast as he remembered. It went on forever. He spent days sitting staring at the expanse of land before and around him. Losing most of his money, as many men had done during this time of depression, he found some consolation that it had not been for nothing, but had contributed to the exploration and settlement of this great country.

He was dirty, dusty, bearded and very tired when he departed the train in a small wooden town at the foot of the mountains. He had money for a room at the dingy hotel and for a bath and shave at the only bathhouse in town, where he shared a room with six other men, attending to their own layers of dirt and grime. No valet to shave him today and only lukewarm, not overly clean water to bathe in, sitting with his knees under his chin in a wooden barrel bathtub. The soap was carbolic—strong smelling. It stung his eyes and nose and turned his skin red, but it got rid of the grime and grease of the days on the train and killed all the tiny crawlers which had, no doubt, invaded the cracks and crevices of his skin.

He put on a clean white shirt from the bottom of his bag, where he had saved it for the day he was clean. His trousers, jacket, and waistcoat had been brushed and sprayed with cologne by the bath house girls and he had clean hose. Even his boots had been shined. He felt like his old self again.

He strolled out of the bathhouse, turning the heads of everybody who encountered him as he made his way back to the cheap hotel.

CLARA

*E*dward didn't intend to stay in this run down, shack of a town long. He was just passing through. He was used to the city and the good life and not used to dirt roads, wooden sidewalks, saloons open all night, people carrying guns. He would have moved on in a couple of days, but for the beautiful widow who invited him to stay for a while.

Clara's husband had died the year before. He had owned most of the town, and she had stayed on because she didn't know where else she would go. Edward's arrival turned her world inside out. Like many women before her, she loved the look of him. His gracious manners, his aristocratic voice and tall poise, his confidence and debonair spirit. She spotted him going into the hotel the morning after he arrived and made it her business to find out who he was.

She was past the point of caring what the townspeople would say and, after only one week of wooing him, she openly invited Edward to stay with her in the one decent, non-wooden structure in town. Being Edward, and being short of cash, he was easily persuaded and moved into Clara's house. His few possessions were stored in a wooden chest under the bedroom window. The Prussian Captain was placed on the table beside the bed. Clara raised her eyebrows slightly when she saw the toy.

"He's an old friend," smiled Edward.

No matter what happened, it seemed Edward's life was charmed. From disaster, he was transformed to another phase of his life of leisure, where all his basic necessities were provided for and he had little to think about except to enjoy his life.

Clara adored him and showered him with every imaginable luxury, and Edward reciprocated by giving her his undivided attention. How could he fail to fall in love with this sensitive, lovely woman? He had never experienced anything like the sensation of warmth and joy Clara gave him. She lit up his life like no other had done, making him feel safe and loved. Other women disappeared for Edward, he never even noticed them anymore. This was a once in a lifetime kind of love, which had happened accidentally for Clara and Edward. Out of loneliness on her part, and desperation on his. They understood how lucky they both were.

The town grew quickly as people moved from the eastern seaboard to join the pioneers settling the west. First a church, doubling as a school, then a bank, then another hotel, a doctor's office, a lady's shop, a lumber yard, stables, a sheriff's office. Houses sprung up, increasing the size of the town tenfold. Within three years the town had mushroomed and was thriving.

Edward had taken over much of the management duties of

the various rental properties Clara owned. He enjoyed being busy and meeting people. He enjoyed helping the town grow. It was a good place to live. Edward had long given up his rooms in Boston and Jim and Janet Pinkleton had joined him and become part of Clara's staff at the big house. To Edward they were his family and he wanted to keep them with him forever. In fact he wouldn't have minded if life could have continued the way it was. But life isn't like that.

Edward was aware of Clara's cough. She had developed a "tickle" in her throat, as she explained it, making excuses of the dust from the streets, or not enough to drink. She laughed it away mostly, but began to retire earlier and earlier in the evening, exhausted by the day's activities. She had three pillows in bed, sleeping almost upright to stop the coughing. Edward was concerned for her, but she brushed his concerns away with a smile and told him not to fuss.

Edward awoke one morning to find the bed beside him empty, Clara was sitting by the window gazing out into the garden. It was a beautiful autumn day, and as he watched her, he thought she was the loveliest woman he had known, with the soft morning light falling on her auburn hair and the white nightgown falling off one shoulder, her skin soft and creamy, exposed. As he watched her she turned to look at him, large tears rolling over her cheeks.

"What is it?" He was beside her in less than a second. Clara leant against his strong chest.

"I can't hide this from you, Edward. I have to prepare you to continue your life without me." He felt a strong pulse slamming inside his head and his chest. What was she saying? What life without her? Clara sighed and looked up into his worried eyes.

"My love. We have been so happy together. You have made my life so complete. But I can't stay with you. I have consumption, Edward, and you know what that means." He heard the words, but didn't comprehend them. She would be the one to beat this. She would be the one who was cured. Clara would be with him forever.

It was eleven weeks of gradual decline, where her strength left her and she moved from the sofa in the morning room, to the day bed in the sun room, to the bedroom. She never complained. She loved Edward until her last breath. For his part, he thought he would die. He wanted to die with her. He was twenty-eight years old and felt ninety. He lay beside her on the bed, as she took her final breath, and held her gently in his arms, kissing her hair and eyes and lips, trying to breathe life back into her.

Jim came and gently helped him to his feet and led him out of the room and down the stairs. It was a tragedy like no other in Edward's life. All he had known was fun and laughter, wealth and luxury and he was totally unprepared for this twist of fate which took his love from him and left him to face his future in bleak despair.

Jim and Janet tried to help him recover, good and faithful friends that they were. He would never be the same, he would never love anybody the way he had loved Clara. With these two thoughts in his mind, he began slowly and carefully to think of what the future held for him now.

Clara's money and property had gone to her husband's niece, who lived in Georgia. She wasn't interested in seeing the house. but left instructions with her attorney to sell everything off. Jim and Janet decided to buy a little place in town. They had made a home there and wanted to stay.

Edward decided to pack his belongings and get back on the train east to Boston, where he would settle his affairs and take the boat to England.

JOURNEY HOME

*E*dward turned twenty nine-years-old on the ship.

Looking out over the grey water back towards America, his heart ached for both the country he had adopted and loved, and for the woman he had lost there. *Oh Clara, I miss you so,* Edward murmured into the wind. *I will love you forever. I feel your presence wherever I am and expect to look up and see you walking towards me, your beautiful red hair blowing in the sea breeze. Why? Why dear God? How could you take my love away from me?* He dissolved into sobs, putting his head onto the cold railing and letting the tears run through his fingers and into the ocean.

He was returning to England without having "made good." Without a fortune. Without a wife and family.

What would he do?

He wasn't experienced at anything except being a gentleman. He did have a degree in engineering, which he had never used. He would go back to Nine Elms. His Mother and three sisters still lived in the old house. He would find work nearby and begin again. If he had inherited one thing from his father, Francis, it was an optimism that rose above the most daunting of problems.

He kept to himself on the Atlantic crossing, having his meals alone and spending much of his time walking the decks. He discovered keeping a journal gave him comfort, writing, sometimes for hours, the thoughts and feelings spilling onto the page along with the tears that flowed freely, covering the pages which nobody would read. The Prussian Captain stood on the desk as he wrote, an anchor of familiarity for the distressed young man. Edward continued to write, almost daily for the rest of his life, always throwing the journals away once they were full.

Liverpool was the usual bustle of activity as liners deposited and picked up passengers. Edward stood on the dockside with his trunks around him, watching the other passengers being greeted by family and friends, exchanging hugs. No such homecoming for him him. He hailed a porter and gave instructions for his trunks to be held in the luggage office until his return. He walked away from the dockside and the throng of people scurrying for handsome cabs, and found himself in a maze of warehouses. It began to rain and he quickened his step.

At the first mail box, he mailed a letter to his mother, Annie, telling her he was in England and would see her soon.

He remembered now, just north of the dockside, where the city really began, were some decent places to stay. He ducked into the first entrance he saw.

"Traveller's Gate" read the sign above the door. Then, underneath in small print, "Lodgings fit for the gentry." Edward opened the door onto a cozy, warm, slightly frayed-around-the-edges foyer. He was soon settled into an adequate room, with all the necessities. A cheery fire burned in the small fireplace, and with the added touch of a plush red velvet armchair and a deep piled rug under his feet, Edward felt almost human again.

The Traveller's Gate proved to be a comforting home for Edward during those first weeks back in England. Mrs. Freeman, the proprietor, was friendly, yet discreet and somehow sensed Edward needed to be left alone with his thoughts. He went for long walks in the crisp, salty air. Immersing himself in the smells and sights of England! Trying to connect with the country he had left as a young man and desperately fighting to relieve the aching for the adopted country he had left on the other side of the Atlantic Ocean. Slowly his soul began to heal. He could remember Clara without feeling the sickness in his throat. He carried her picture in his waistcoat pocket, next to his heart and swore it would always be there.

It was time to move on. With his strength, spiritually and mentally, partly restored, Edward said his goodbyes to Liverpool and to Mrs. Freeman and headed for Birmingham. As his mind had cleared, he remembered names of old friends from Oxford who had gone to work in the Birmingham area. He intended to trace whoever he could find. He would use his engineering degree, to seek work. At least it was a plan of sorts.

NINE ELMS

*L*ouisa had returned to Nine Elms after their father had died. She had a medical degree from America, but was not allowed to practice in England. She enrolled at Birmingham University, challenging the courses she had already completed with honours in the new world. She gained her English MD two years after her return and was now practicing medicine in the women's hospital in Birmingham. She lived with her mother and younger sisters, Margaret and Fanny, at the family home.

After such a long absence, how would they greet him? Would they be happy to see him? Would they welcome him back to the home he had left so long ago?

The carriage from Birmingham drew up in front of Nine Elms and the driver unloaded the two trunks, placing them at Edward's feet. Edward looked up at the double doors at the top of the stone steps, nothing seemed to have changed. He hesitated for a few minutes before striding up the steps two at a time and knocking loudly. The first time he had ever knocked at the door. It was opened by a stranger, who peered out at Edward suspiciously.

"Yes, sir," he spoke, in a low voice. "How can I help you?"

Edward explained who he was, stepping inside as he spoke.

The servant hurried off to the drawing room, with Edward close behind him, even though he had been asked to wait in the hall.

Edward didn't wait for an introduction, but pushed open the door and covered the distance between himself and his mother quickly, pulling her up from her chair into his arms.

Annie had been waiting for her son to arrive since the day she received his letter. Every day she expected this would be the day he would come. Although she was prepared, she was still surprised to see him. So handsome, with his hair now greying at the temples.

Annie held him close for a long time. She was a lovely woman still. Dressed, as she always was, impeccably. Her smile lighting up the room, even though Edward detected a sadness deep in her eyes.

"You are so like your father," she murmured as she held him closer, as if she would never let him go.

His sisters, Louisa, Margaret and Fanny, were waiting in line for the next hugs.

"Edward, we have thought of you so often and wondered where you were," Louisa said, leaning against his broad shoulder, as the tears spilled freely. "We couldn't believe it when Mother received your letter to say you were on your way home."

Edward embraced his two older sisters, then grabbing his

sixteen year old sister Fanny into his arms, spun around and around.

"Look at you, Fanny!" he shouted, delighted with his youngest sister. "Look how you have grown. You were a baby when I left, now you are a young lady, with long skirts."

Fanny laughed, breathless as Edward lowered her to the floor. How good it was to have a brother around again. With Robert away at University, the house had been too quiet.

It was good to feel the warmth of human contact again, especially from people who loved him. It would take a few hours to tell them all about America and Clara. He knew they would understand his heartbreak. Fanny sat beside Edward, not wanting to leave his side. Mother sat in her armchair facing her son. Margaret and Louisa rang for tea and busied themselves with the pouring and serving, as they listened to his stories of adventure in Boston, then crossing the great plains to the midwest.

"I fell in love, mother," Edward's voice lowered and his eyes clouded as he held his mother's anxious gaze. "Her name was Clara. We lived in a growing town in the west and adored each other. Clara was beautiful and clever and vibrant, but she became ill." Edward choked on his words and covered his face with one hand. Louisa poured him a brandy and after a sip of the fiery liquid, Edward continued, his eyes fixed on his glass.

"She died in my arms, a moment frozen in time, and I was not ready to let her go. I held her and tried to warm her, but it was no use."

Annie rose and went to her distraught son, taking his face in her two hands and kissing his forehead. The three sisters dabbed their eyes and tried to think of words of comfort they could say, but none came.

"Edward, my dear," Mother spoke for them all. "You came home to us, which was a good decision. We cannot take away the hurt you feel, or even know how to comfort you, but we are your family and we will love you and try to help you recover."

The four women sat quietly while Edward gained his composure. He would overcome this tragedy, here with the people who loved him.

His room was ready and he was happy to climb the familiar staircase and close the door. He was home. Not the home he remembered, with Father larger than life in the middle of everything, and children running everywhere with their noisy chatter and clatter. But it was home. Familiar rooms, familiar smells and sounds, loving mother and sisters downstairs, happy to see him and comfort him. *Yes, I have made the right decision,* he murmured.

MAC

Jonathon McIntosh, a great friend of Edward's at Oxford, had been in Birmingham for several years, working as a successful barrister. It was the one person Edward had occasionally written to when he was in America. Although Jonathon didn't know Edward had returned to England, Edward thought contacting his friend should be the first step.

Early Wednesday morning, Edward headed for the address he had kept, easily finding the offices of Antwerp & Sons. It was the largest building in the small street, close to the city centre. Marble pillars and an impressive staircase led to the oak doors and Edward was greeted by a uniformed doorman. He was given directions to Mr. McIntosh's office on the second floor and, with his stomach in a knot, he climbed up the winding stone staircase slowly. Maybe this wasn't such a good idea. Why would Jonathon even remember him? Why would he want to see him? After all they had been at school together a long time ago. Things changed. They probably wouldn't even like each other now!

The door in front of Edward was dark mahogany with "Mr. Jonathon McIntosh Q.C." written on a bronze plaque across the middle. The hallway was so quiet. Maybe he wasn't in. He was probably in court. Before Edward could knock, the door flew open and Jonathon McIntosh almost collided with his Oxford chum.

"My God, Edward? Is that you, old man?"

"You look just the same, Mac" Edward smiled.

"What are you doing in England?" asked Jonathon, grabbing Edward by the shoulders and spinning him around. "You look old. Sorry! You're still really tall. Oh God help me, I'm not making any sense. It's just such a shock to find you outside my door like this." As he talked, Jonathon pulled Edward into his office and backed him into a chair by the desk.

"It's a long story, Mac. No regrets though. I thought we might have dinner and do some catching up. What do you think?"

"Yes. Yes, of course we'll have dinner. You must come to the house tonight. You have to meet my wife, Constance, and our three children."

Mac's house was near Russell Square. Edward appeared at the front door at the expected hour of seven. It was a well appointed, large house, facing the usual square of park, surrounded by wrought iron railings and enclosing the usual mixture of trees, grass, a pond and benches scattered around. The house was three stories and a basement for staff. Everything one expected for a successful lawyer in the city. Edward considered his own position and thought it more and more a poor idea to be here, visiting his old friend, when his ulterior motive was to ask advice on how to secure a paid position of some kind.

As he paused to consider his options, he reached out and pulled the bell cord. He had no other option. The door was opened by Drange, Mac's "man," who took his coat and escorted him into the drawing room. Mac hurried to meet him, smiling and drawing him into the room. It was spacious and well furnished with a roaring fire and the bustle of small children.

"Come in, Edward. My dear, this is one of my oldest and dearest friends. We were at Oxford together many years ago and he has recently returned from America. Edward, this is my wife, Constance."

Edward gazed into a perfect oval face, with grey eyes surrounded by the longest lashes he had ever seen. Constance was small in stature, feeling even more so against Edward's tall frame. She held out her tiny hand, lace encircling her wrist for Edward to grasp.

"You are so welcome to our home, Edward. Jonathon was very excited about your showing up so unexpectedly. We are looking forward to hearing all about your adventures."

"You are so kind," replied Edward, feeling very much at home. "My adventures in America may be more boring than you think, but I can probably come up with a trumped up version to amuse these little people."

He turned to the three small McIntoshes, two girls and a boy. They each gave a small bob as they were introduced.

"Isabella, six years old." Bob!

"Elizabeth, four years old." Bob!

"James, three years old." Bob mixed with bow!

"I am honoured," said Edward, from his great height, taking each little hand and giving it a squeeze as he bowed low to look into each face.

He had never had anything to do with children and was delighted with them. He saw them as small people and didn't talk down to them or try to adapt his way. He talked to them as he talked to everybody, and they loved him. He told them about the great country he had lived in, the huge prairies and mountains. The trains, the cowboys with guns and horses. He told them about Boston and the boats coming and going in the harbour, and the carriages and fine ladies, dressed so splendidly. Their eyes were wide as they listened to his great stories.

Constance interrupted the stories with the feared words "Bed time."

She was greeted with the usual response from youngsters who are having too good a time. "No Mama. Please, just five more minutes."

Constance looked at Edward with pleading eyes.

"I will pack those five minutes with an hour's worth of story," Edward told his three new little friends. "Then you must do as your mother says." Then in his best American accent, "Do we have a deal?"

The children fell about laughing and yelling. "We have a deal," trying to copy Edward's accent. He loved this. Why had he not had children? He didn't know he'd missed out until now. He should have been a father. He felt his throat tighten and a stinging behind his eyes as he remembered Clara—the years he would have fathered children would have been with

Clara. He moved on quickly to his five minutes filled with wild encounters with bears and wolves, which he'd never seen, and the mountains covered with snow all year round. He described the hot dusty summers, with rattlesnakes around every corner. He ended with his departure from his much loved adopted country, as he described the ship which had sailed from Boston to bring him home to England.

The children's faces were rosy with excitement and Mac and Constance knew that sleep would be difficult after their encounter with Edward. Sally, the nursery helper, came to gather them up and, along with Constance, they guided them to the door. To Edward's great surprise, they all three turned together and ran back to him, throwing themselves at him with hugs of thanks. He picked them up and planted them all on his lap, giving each a kiss on the forehead and hugging them close.

"You are the best grown up we've ever met," Isabella whispered.

"Yes, you are," agreed Elizabeth.

"You are," joined in James.

"And you are the best children I have ever met," affirmed Edward, with one more hug.

They scampered off to join Sally and their mother at the door, laughing and squealing with delight at the stories they had heard.

Edward looked at his friend with envy. Mac had everything and Edward wondered how differently things might have been had he not gone to America. But then he would never have met and loved Clara. No, there would be no regrets.

"Come into the dining room, Edward. Constance will leave

the children in Sally's tender care. I am certain there will be no sleep for some time tonight. You have quite turned them on their heads with your stories. I had no idea you were so talented with toddlers of this age. It's rare for them to be so forward with a stranger, but they loved you."

"I have absolutely no experience with children of any age, Mac. Unfortunately children have not been part of my life. I really didn't consider them, until tonight when your three delightful offspring were suddenly thrust upon me. My word, I have missed out, I think." Edward again looked misty-eyed and Mac didn't miss it. He hurried on to cover up any awkwardness from the emotion that absolutely no man ever showed.

"Please Edward, sit down here," Mac said, guiding him towards a comfortable dining chair at the table, set elaborately for the three of them.

Constance joined them, telling them of the antics upstairs, trying unsuccessfully to get the children settled down for sleep. With a tinkle of a small bell at the side of her plate, Constance summoned dinner to be served. It was suitably elegant, a clear chicken soup with tiny bread sticks, a tomato salad, roast pork with apples and French beans, ending with a chocolate soufflé drizzled with raspberry sauce. Two very good wines accompanied the meal and an excellent coffee and brandy with dessert. The meal reminded Edward of the years of plenty when he dined like this every night.

Afterwards, back in the drawing room, Edward broached the subject of finding a position.

"Mac, I'm not going to beat about the bush. I wanted to see you as an old friend, of course, but also I am in need of a position in the city. I have returned from America with little of the fortune I left with, and find myself having to encroach on your good nature. I would be forever in your debt if you could advise me on seeking, and securing, some form of employment, very soon."

Jonathon looked at his friend. He saw the lines around his eyes and the sad look inside them. He knew he didn't have the whole story of Edward's years away. Something had happened to him that he couldn't share, at least not now. Jonathon didn't want to be too hasty in his reply.

"As I remember, your degree was engineering, Edward!"

Edward nodded his agreement.

"But I haven't used it, Jonathon. I doubt an engineering company would seriously consider me after all this time out of the field."

Edward sat back and let his friend think it through. He wasn't expecting a quick and easy reply. He wasn't expecting a quick and easy fix. He didn't want to put Mac into the position of having to work out his problems for him.

"Look, Mac," Edward started to say. Jonathon held up his hand to silence him and kept up his steady pace up and down the carpet in front of the fireplace. When he stopped walking, he looked Edward in the eyes.

"You are still a young man, Edward. I am stating the obvious, I know, but the city is a young man's city these days. I have some contacts in the city. Let me talk to a few good people and get their input and advice. Give me a couple of weeks and we will see what I have come up with."

"I am forever indebted to you, Mac. I have no contacts in this country but yourself, and after all the years I have spent away, I am at a loss to know where to begin."

Edward was walking on air as he left the McIntosh house. He didn't hail a cab, he wanted to walk through the streets of Birmingham for a while and reflect on his good fortune. To have such a friend.

Clara, I'm still alive down here, he murmured to the dark night sky.

WORKING LIFE

*H*e met with Jonathon, at his club, in two weeks as planned. His friend had been busy contacting business associates. One company, based in Birmingham had shown great interest in Edward.

"They are looking for a mechanical engineer with experience," explained Jonathon, "But are willing to meet with you on my recommendation. They are an old established company, who hold your father in high esteem, which doesn't hurt your situation."

Edward met with James Morrison and Douglas Hinton the following Monday at ten in the morning at their impressive offices in Spruce Street. The two men welcomed Edward with a handshake, and the interview proved to be intense and thorough. They both spoke highly of Dr. Francis Wrightson, with whom they had been acquainted. Although Edward had never actually been employed, nor used the knowledge gained in his degree years earlier, his charm and enthusiasm shone, and Morrison's Engineering Company became his employer.

He was to join a team of engineers working on developing public transportation for the city of Birmingham. He was the junior member of the team, having to learn and refresh the knowledge he had once studied. Edward was, as always, friendly and quick to learn, becoming a valued addition to the transportation department of the company. He worked long hours trying to learn all he could.

Such a different life, challenged him in every way. He began each day with a quick breakfast at Nine Elms, before heading into the city to begin his workday. Mother arranged for William to drive Mr. Edward each day, so, in some ways, privilege was still part of his day. Edward would inform William if he needed to be picked up, or if he was staying in town for the evening, which he often did, dining with friends, or attending a concert.

Edward enjoyed this new life. He dined frequently at the McIntosh household, revelling in the company of Isabella, Elizabeth and James. He was Uncle Edward now and had progressed from storytelling to wrestling on the floor and helping tuck his adopted nieces and nephew into their soft beds, all of them smelling as only very young children can, a sweet mixture of soap and young skin that sent Edward's head spinning. He loved them dearly and felt it was the closest he would ever come to having a child of his own.

Clara, though still a part of his soul, became a treasured memory.

Edward's friends, including Jonathon, all had a motor vehicle. Edward rode in this new invention with envy, admiring the leather seats and shiny chassis. He longed to be able to afford to sit behind the wheel and drive around the city, but his salary only covered the necessities of life, which for

Edward were silk shirts, Italian leather shoes and money in his wallet to dine out when he liked.

Annie and the girls lived quietly at Nine Elms. They enjoyed having Edward around, bringing them stories about the city and the McIntosh children. At the weekends Margaret, Fanny and Edward went riding through the damp country-side, remembering their childhood and the wild rides in Wild Horse Valley. It seemed so long ago. Robert came up from Oxford to spend a few weekends, joining in the fun of riding and reminiscing, laughing as Edward recalled the horrid week in San Francisco trying to teach Robert to walk in the vast solarium at the Plaza hotel. Nine Elms was reborn somehow. The spirit of the old house was revived.

Edward remained a bachelor. He changed his employment, working as a consultant engineering agent. It gave him more free time and a wider experience of the largest companies in the Midlands. He was at the top of every hostesses list for dinner parties, dining with the best families in the Birm-ingham area. He was acquainted with several eligible women, who bribed and begged the hostess for a seat beside Edward at dinner. He charmed them all, inviting one or two of them for a carriage ride or tea at Nine Elms. Among them was Amy Gent, who he had known slightly before leaving for America. Her family's home was close to Nine Elms and her father had been acquainted with Dr. Wrightson. Edward gave her little attention as she was several years his senior. However, she had never married and now, in her late thirties, she attended the various social functions with her aging father, her mother having died several years before. Amy was a regular guest at the same dinners and balls as Edward. She made it obvious that she enjoyed Edward's company. She was well past the age for marriage, but often broached the subject with Edward.

"Do you think you will ever marry, Edward?" she asked one summer night as they strolled in the garden of her father's house, where they had just finished dinner.

"Maybe, one day," answered Edward flippantly.

"Surely you would not marry a very young girl, as most men of your age seem to these days?" she continued.

"Who knows. It would have to be somebody very special. I am not the marrying kind. Life is uncomplicated being single."

Edward always managed to steer clear of Amy's prying questions, but he had the impression she was pushing him in a certain direction, as she smiled up at him and took his arm.

After living with his family for three years, he moved out of Nine Elms and into fashionable rooms in the city. The years that followed saw Fanny go to finishing school in Essex and from there to Oxford to study Mediaeval History. She met and married a young man from Bath and never returned to live at Nine Elms. Robert too was well established and living in London with his wife and two small children. The two eldest girls remained at the house. Louisa absorbed in her hospital work and Margaret supervised the running of Nine Elms as their mother aged.

Edward was bored with his life. He had filled his life with pleasantries. He was never short of female company and still in high demand as an escort in society. He had a good job, but it didn't generate the income required to support a motor vehicle or a trip to Venice or Rome. He began to feel trapped, something he had never felt in America. He borrowed money to buy the latest automobile, keeping pace with the gentile society he lived in. He borrowed more money to take a particularly glamorous and discreet woman to Italy for two weeks of luxurious travel and love-making. He lived beyond his means, going further and further into crushing debt.

Edward had plenty of experience taking risks. He remembered his investments in America turning sour, but he now saw an opportunity to put everything right. Andrew Mills, who owned a small engineering company in Wolverhampton, had approached Edward several times about becoming a partner in his business. Edward thought the company had great prospects for future expansion. Maybe it was worth the risk. If Edward could borrow enough money to buy into the company, he was sure it would save him from financial disaster. But where to borrow the money? He was already up to his limit at the bank.

He only had one option. Not an option he would have chosen, but one in which he was willing to risk everything. He drove out to Nine Elms early on Saturday morning, before the family were up, and went into the dining room helping himself to coffee.

"Good morning, sir," said Barclay, the footman. "Can I serve you with breakfast?"

"Just the coffee, thank you," replied Edward.

He gazed out of the window at the sunbathed lawn stretching to the tree line. His mind drifted back to his father striding into the dining room for breakfast, full of energy, greeting the children and helping himself to a pile of food. Father never liked being waited on by a footman for breakfast.

"Edward, what a nice surprise, darling," Annie greeted her son. "What are you doing here so early on a Saturday morning?"

"Hello Mother," Edward rose to kiss his mother on her cheek. "I came to see you."

Annie was served with her usual breakfast of scrambled eggs and toast, with a cup of tea of course. Edward waited until she had finished eating, making small talk about the lovely weather and asking after his sisters. He suggested they move to the veranda with their coffee and tea, where they could enjoy the sun-filled garden.

"Lovely idea," agreed Annie, taking his arm and indicating to Barclay to carry their drinks outside.

"Mother, I came to discuss a business proposition with you," Edward said. "I know you have no head for business, so I won't bore you with the details. I have been offered the chance to buy into a small engineering company in Wolver-hampton. It's a splendid business and the chap who owns it, the very best of men. He needs capital to expand and I really think it's just the thing for me to invest in." He paused for breath, trying to assess his mother's feelings about what he'd just said.

"I would need quite a large sum of money for the investment. More than I could raise on my own. I wouldn't ask you for help if I wasn't absolutely convinced of the merit of the investment. You would see your money returned with high interest from this venture. Will you consider it?"

Annie never took her eyes off her son's face as he spoke. She trusted him completely. She realized he would not have come to her if he had any other option.

"Edward," she smiled. "However much is needed for this investment is yours. Of course I will help you. It sounds very exciting. I will make arrangements with my bank to have the money made available to you. How much do you need?"

"Mother, thank you. You will not regret your decision. I will talk with Andrew Mills, the company owner, about finances and let you know the amount, if that meets with your approval. He is a fair man and will not ask for more than is required for the partnership."

Edward's step was light as he left Nine Elms. He would drive to Wolverhampton to see Andrew on Monday morning. His life was about to turn around and his future looked suddenly very bright.

Andrew Mills was delighted with Edward's decision to invest in the company. The finances were arranged with Annie's bank and Edward became a partner in The Montrose Engineering Company.

Over the next six months, new machinery was purchased and three new employees were hired. Edward attended a regular weekly meeting with Andrew for updates on the business. All was progressing very smoothly, although the large loan at his mother's bank, and the debts at his own bank, weighed on his mind.

Andrew bid on several large projects, but was not successful. There were larger companies winning the tenders who could undercut the smaller company's quotes every time. Business dried up, and the newly hired men were let go. Edward poured more money in, but was over his limit and desperate. It was his worst nightmare. Even worse than America, when it was only his money he lost and only himself suffering for it.

The inevitable happened—the small engineering company failed.

Edward was lost in a world of debt and remorse. He couldn't tell his mother the news. His bank called his loan. His mother's bank wrote to say the manager required an immediate meeting.

"Edward, how are you old man?" Jonathan asked, bumping into his friend crossing the square outside the town hall. "Haven't seen you in ages. The children miss you terribly. We all do. Your visits were the highlight of our day."

"Sorry old chap," Edward replied, aware of his friend's searching look. "Busy you know - working all hours. But, no excuse for my absence. How about I call on you tomorrow evening?"

"We will expect you for dinner," Jonathan said, eager to find out what his friend had been doing and concerned about the anxiety that showed in his face.

The following evening, after a day at the agency not really achieving much, Edward made his way to the familiar house in Birmingham.

The children were all over him in a minute.

"Uncle Edward," the three of them chorused. "Where have you been?"

"I've been to London to see the Queen," he rhymed back.

"Are you the pussy cat in the nursery rhyme then?" laughed Isabella.

"Maybe I am. Meow, meow."

Edward chased the three children around the room on all

fours, until his knees could take no more and he lay on his back, legs kicking in the air. The children piled on top of him laughing and squealing.

Jonathon and Constance laughed along with their children. It was good to see Edward again. He was unlike anybody they knew, particularly with the children.

As always, it took the better part of an hour for Constance to settle her brood down and get them up to the nursery before dinner.

Jonathon handed his friend a whisky while they waited. He sensed something was bothering Edward. The tired lines around his eyes. Hair a little too long. Finger nails not manicured. All the little things that Edward was usually fastidious about.

"Do you want to talk about it now, or after dinner?" Jonathon asked.

"What? Are you assuming something is on my mind?"

"I know there is. I can see right through you."

"You have known me too long, Jonathon," sighed Edward. "After dinner would be better if you don't mind."

Dinner was always superb at the McIntosh house. They had a great cook—even better than Nine Elms. Edward ate with relish, washing down the food with fine wine.

"I couldn't eat another bite," he finally said. "Thank you Constance for such a delicious meal. Please pass on my compliments to your talented cook."

"I will, Edward. She has been with us from the beginning and we know how lucky we are."

Constance excused herself to check on the children while the men sat with their brandy. She knew they needed to talk and would take her time upstairs.

Edward hadn't told anybody about his financial problems. His bank knew of course and so did several other institutions he had borrowed money from. He had been a fool. He found it extremely difficult to divulge the extent of his debts to his good friend who had found him a job when he returned from America.

"Jonathon, you are a good friend. I feel I have abused that friendship." Edward held up his hand as his friend tried to contradict him. "No, let me get this out. I am a foolish man. I don't learn from my mistakes. I think more of keeping up with social expectations than using common sense. I have put possessions before everything else, wanting to appear affluent to my peers. I have lived far beyond my income and now find myself so deeply in debt I can see no way out. The worst was persuading my mother to fund an investment which has totally failed, leaving me in an intolerable position. The company has already filed for bankruptcy. That cannot be avoided. It's the debt I owe my mother I cannot leave unanswered."

Silence stood between them like a veil. Debt was a stigma no man of honour wanted. Jonathan knew what it would mean to Edward's family should this come to light. The good name of the Wrightsons would be tarnished forever. The scandal of such debt reached beyond just Edward.

"How can I help?" was Jonathan's first reaction. "I know you to be a good man, my friend."

Edward sat with his head in his hands, fighting the emotion that threatened to overtake him. He knew his next words to his friend would probably not be accepted lightly. He had spent days and nights pondering his future. He decided his future lay in the hands of a woman.

"Jonathon, I have only one solution, and you are not going to like it. I know you will think I am the worst kind of cad, but I beg you to not judge me too harshly."

Jonathon filled Edward's glass with more brandy. Then filled his own glass, thinking he was going to need it if what Edward had just said was true.

"There is a way I can repay all the money borrowed from my mother, as well as pay my own bank loan. I will agree to marry Amy Gent. She has indicated she would not be adverse to a proposal on several occasions, but I had never thought it an option, until now. Don't look at me with such distain, Jonathan. It would be a match suitable for both of us. She a spinster, with no chance of a social life without a husband, now that her father has died. Marriage would allow her a place in society."

"Edward, think clearly before you take such a step," Jonathan finally spluttered. "You have heard the rumours, surely. You don't want to end up in a worse position than you already are, with a wife you cannot love and a marriage in name only."

"I have heard the rumours," Edward said, "And am willing to risk all to put things right with Mother and end the money worries. Amy is not unattractive and she is extremely wealthy. I will be completely honest with her, and confess that her money is the foremost reason for the union on my part."

"Then, good luck to you Edward. I cannot pretend I approve of your decision. Life with Amy will be difficult I would imagine. You have many years ahead of you to regret your foolishness."

This said, Jonathon shook his friend's hand with genuine affection. His own life was so blessed compared with the life his friend had lived and was about to embark on, and he felt sorry for him, despite the fact that Edward had caused most of the problems for himself.

AMY

Two weeks later on Christmas Eve 1908, the Wrightson family was invited to dine at Amy Gent's house. Her father had died in October, leaving Amy heiress to a sizeable fortune. At forty-five years of age, she faced a future with no financial worries, but a social stigma of being a spinster would exclude her from the hostess lists. Edward, his mother and two sisters were greeted warmly by Amy, and they joined four more dinner guests in the drawing room. The house was beautifully arrayed in Christmas garlands, with bunches of holly and ivy cascading from the mantel and the tables around the room. Amid the lively chatter, drinks were served before dinner was announced by a grave looking servant.

Amy led Edward in, making sure he was seated beside her. The meal was sumptuous. Leek soup, braised turkey with chestnut stuffing, tiny roast potatoes, carrots, beans, peas, asparagus served with bread sauce and gravy. The footmen were kept busy serving the food and topping up the wine glasses as the guests talked and laughed. Lemon sponge pudding with vanilla sauce to finish, the ladies retiring to the drawing room to leave the men to their brandy and cigars.

Throughout the meal, Amy had given Edward her undivided attention and this time Edward smiled back at her and encouraged her. She was a good looking woman. Taller than average and slender. Not much of a figure, but impeccably dressed. Her best quality was her hands, with long slender fingers and perfectly manicured nails. She drew attention to them by wearing several rings, displaying expensive jewels set with artistic precision.

He felt sure that a proposal would be met with affirmation and from then on there would be no money restrictions. He could have it all. Women married for money all the time— why not a man? He would be a good husband. He didn't love Amy, never could, but he could be her escort, companion, lover.

Edward arranged to visit Amy again on Boxing Day for afternoon tea. There would be a lull of several days before the festivities began again to celebrate the new year.

"Thank you again, Amy, for a wonderful Christmas Eve dinner," Edward greeted her as he was shown into the drawing room. She rose to meet him from the armchair beside the roaring fire, holding out her hand and giving Edward a wide smile.

"It was a lovely evening. I enjoyed having your family here. Your mother and sisters, all such charming women. I never tire of their company."

Tea was served in response to Amy's pull on the bell cord. An array of pastries, cakes and scones with cream were placed on the low table between Edward and his hostess.

The footman discretely withdrew and closed the door behind him, leaving Amy to pour the tea and offer the sweets. Edward waved his hand at the offer of the sweets, but took the tea and sipped it thoughtfully.

"Well, Edward, is something on your mind?" Amy asked. "You are very thoughtful."

"I am pondering how to say something important," Edward replied, looking into Amy's eyes. "I want to be sure to say the right thing in the right manner."

All of a sudden, he was nervous. He had gone over and over what he would say to her when the time came. Now, his practiced words seemed weak. He was afraid Amy would turn down his proposal, leaving him to face an uncertain and difficult future.

"Amy, will you marry me?" he said quickly. "But before you answer, I need to be completely honest with you, because I don't want your answer until you know what you would be taking on."

Edward sprang to his feet now and paced up and down between the window and the fireplace. Amy sat quietly, realizing he needed time to explain himself.

"I can offer you my companionship, my friendship, my devotion. I know that your position in society changed when your father died. With me beside you, every door would be open to you, to us. The circle of society we have had the pleasure of being part of would remain intact. I promise you I would be beside you to escort you to every event in the social calendar. To every dinner, every ball, every concert. It would be my greatest pleasure to escort you and be seen with you."

Amy started to speak, but Edward rushed on.

"For my part, I cannot hide the truth. I returned from America without fortune. I invested badly and the money I inherited from my father was lost. Since then, I have not been able to establish a footing financially. A recent partnership venture has failed. In fact the bankruptcy is already filed and will probably be reported in the newspapers very soon. This is an intolerable situation, of which I am highly ashamed. I will not pretend that the marriage, should you accept me, would come at a price."

He had said what he came to say and he choked now, turning away from Amy so that she wouldn't see the emotion in his eyes.

"You would be saving me from disgrace, Amy," he said quietly and when she didn't speak, he turned towards her. She was still sitting rigidly in the arm chair. Her face white. Her eyes on his.

Edward crossed the room and went down on his knees in front of her.

"Knowing all of this, Amy, I ask again—will you marry me?"

She didn't answer immediately, but sighed and looked into the flames.

When she did speak, her voice was very calm.

"You have been very honest, Edward. We both know I have no chance of marrying at my age, and you described my situation as a spinster in this society correctly. Your debts are insignificant to me. I am happy to take care of every pound you owe. I accept your proposal, Edward Wrightson, but always remember what you have promised."

She rose from her chair and kissed Edward's lips to seal their promises to each other.

Edward was quite a catch! She would be the envy of all her friends. So handsome and distinguished. She threw herself into preparations for the wedding. It would be small, because of the circumstances, and being a woman of mature years she couldn't flaunt herself, but it would be exquisite. Edward was happy to listen, as she reported on the details of the ceremony and dinner for close friends afterwards.

They were married in a small side chapel in St. Paul's Church of England in Kings Norton in February 2009. Amy wore a cream silk dress and matching coat, with mauve and white flowers in her hat. "Lovely," Edward murmured to her as she joined him in the chapel. There were six of their closest friends present, along with Annie, Frances, Margaret, Fanny and Robert. The McIntosh children carried baskets of flowers and walked in front of Amy as she made her way towards Edward. The children didn't like Amy and she didn't like them. Edward would always be "Uncle Edward" and would always visit them on his own.

Married life wasn't what Edward expected. Of course he now had a beautiful new automobile—a Wolseley, built locally in Birmingham. Amy thought it was ridiculous that he didn't want to use the chauffeur-driven Daimler, but Edward loved driving and never used the bigger car unless Amy was with him, when she insisted he would not drive. What would people think? Driving themselves around like commoners. There were silk shirts enough for six men in his dressing room, along with suits, ties, shoes and silk undergarments. He lacked for nothing.

The money returned to his mother's bank, his debts cleared, he devoted himself to Amy as he had promised. There was no more attentive husband in society than Mr. Edward Wrightson.

Their first few nights together were a foretaste of what the future would hold. Edward did not have difficulty making love to a woman. After all he had had a great deal of experience. He was not repulsed by Amy. She wore a long white silk gown to bed, and did not flinch when Edward moved to lie close beside her. As he leaned over her to kiss her mouth, running his hand gently along the inside of her thigh through the gown, he felt the pleasure seer through him. There had been occasional women to make love to since his arrival in England, but they had been for his convenience and none had been permanent. A man just needed a woman sometimes, that was all. Amy was his wife and even though he hadn't fallen in love with her, the intimacy of that relationship was not lost on him. As his lips touched his wife's lips, he was met with a firm, tightly shut mouth. He cautiously wet her lips with the tip of his tongue, easing her lips apart, but the lips remained firm. Amy didn't push him away, she just didn't respond. Edward left the lips and kissed her cheeks, her nose, her ears, urging her to relax as his hand slipped upwards to her small breasts.

How could she not react? thought Edward, as he caressed her.

The love making was a biological act. Edward did eventually open Amy's legs enough to perform the act but she didn't move or participate in any way. The whole pathetic deed was accomplished in less than five minutes, and when Edward withdrew from his wife and lay back on the bed beside her, she had nothing to say and neither did he. Amy believed it was her duty to endure this part of marriage, but it certainly didn't need to be a frequent occurrence, and she wanted Edward to get the message loud and clear that this would be a very rare treat for him. He got the message when, two nights later, he tried to touch her and she responded with, "Not again, so soon."

Were the rumours true after all?

Since the consummation of their marriage on their wedding night, they had made love only once in six weeks, when Edward had stayed in town all week and on his return plied his wife with enough red wine for her to not deny him.

He continued to go to the city to work as an engineering agent. He would have gone mad in the big house alone with Amy. He enjoyed the comradeship of his colleagues at the agency, as well as meeting the representatives from the companies he visited. Amy was content to continue her daily routine, visiting friends, hosting afternoon tea, managing the house.

The next two years drifted by with Edward leading his own life, with his own friends. His home was with Amy, but he spent much of his time in the city. He had moved into his own bedroom after just six weeks of marriage It suited them both. Amy was content with her handsome husband as escort when needed, which seemed to be the only responsibility he had in the marriage.

Edward had moved to a new company, Braithwaite and Hobbs, where he represented the company at meetings with prospective clients. He travelled often, so was away from home frequently A suitable arrangement for both husband and wife.

ALICE

Amy invited her good friend Alice Bridgewood to stay. Alice had attended finishing school with Amy when they were very young, and had remained her closest friend. Edward welcomed his wife's friend graciously. She was much shorter then Amy, with a sallow complexion and brown hair. She was a kind woman and, like Amy before marrying Edward, had remained a spinster. When Edward came home at the weekends, it was to find his wife happy and talkative, telling him everything she and Alice had done that week. A pleasant atmosphere reigned and Edward was thankful for the friendship his wife had with the quietly spoken woman.

As the visit neared its end, and Alice prepared to go back to her own home, Amy approached her friend.

"Alice, please consider staying here with me permanently," begged Amy. "Edward is always away and I am lonely much of the time. When he is home, he is busy with his own friends and we rarely do anything together. This has been the best month I can remember in many years. Please say you will stay. You have nothing to stop you."

Alice didn't have anything to stop her. She had lost both her parents, as they were elderly when she was born. She had a decent income and a small house near Oxford, but Amy was the closest she had to family. They were such good company for each other, enjoying the same activities, the same music, the same lady's clothing stores. Edward was open to the suggestion, seeing it as a perfect solution to his wife being alone. She was happy when Alice was there. In fact, Amy preferred Alice's company to Edward's.

Alice moved into the house at Kings Norton as soon as she was able to sell her home. Amy encouraged her to furnish her own room as she chose, with her own possessions around her. For weeks, the two women were busy with plans to refurnish and redecorate different parts of the house. Amy persuaded Edward, with no objection from him, to move from his adjoining bedroom, to a "suite" of three rooms, newly and elegantly furnished by herself and Alice.

Happiness poured through the house, and none was happier than Edward, who delighted in the peaceful life he now had at home. His allowance was generous, allowing him to live a life of privilege. The best of food, wine, clothing and his superb motor vehicle. Servants to tend his needs and the freedom to come and go as he pleased. All Amy asked was his attendance at several important occasions each month, as her escort. Mr. and Mrs. Edward Wrightson looked to all outsiders like the perfect couple.

As the years passed, Edward was well aware that Alice and Amy were more than friends. As he was quietly leaving his suite very early one morning, he caught a glimpse of Alice as she left

Amy's room. He was aware of the looks between them and the touching of hands as they passed each other, the obvious pleasure of each other's company. Far from it distressing Edward, he embraced the arrangement. He understood why his wife appeared to be frigid. He was happy that Amy had a romantic relationship. He wasn't short of female company when needed.

The rumours about Amy Gent were indeed true.

TRAVELLING

The only time Alice didn't accompany the married couple was on journeys abroad. Amy loved to travel and she enjoyed touring in Europe, especially Italy and Germany. Edward was her happy companion on these occasions, playing the devoted husband, escorting his wife to every social function in the cities they visited. They always stayed in separate rooms, an accepted practice in their day.

"We should take a journey on one of the new liners to visit Arthur," suggested Amy one day, as she joined Edward in the morning room.

Edward's brother, Arthur, had stayed in America when the family had returned in the 1880s. He had inherited the farm at Los Guillicos, near Santa Rosa in Sonoma County, California in his father's will and, for a time, had cultivated the land and enjoyed several harvests of fine grapes, increasing the value of the land greatly. He sold the farm at a good price to a family from Italy, who continued to develop the vineyard into one of the most successful wineries in the Napa Region.

Arthur followed the advice of a group of friends from his University days and bought property on the island of Trinidad in the Caribbean, sinking his money into cocoa farming. It was a lucrative endeavour, making Arthur very rich in the space of a few years.

"It would be a long journey," remarked Edward.

He didn't know if he could act the part of attentive husband on such a long sea voyage.

"Would you not like to see him again?"

"I would. I'm just thinking of you, dear."

Amy was determined to take the journey. She wanted to see the islands of the Caribbean. She also wanted to see New York, after listening to Edward rave on and on about his America.

"We could take the new ship to New York, then travel to the islands from there," Amy said. "What is that new ship called? It is to be launched soon—it has been in all the papers. Ah yes, Titanic, the unsinkable ship. That's it."

Amy was impatient to be underway and the new ship wasn't being launched on time. It wasn't to be launched until April. Amy was very disappointed.

Edward went along with the plans and let Amy and Alice make the reservations. This time Alice was to accompany them, in her own cabin of course. Edward and Amy were to have a suite comprising two bedrooms and a sitting room. They booked passage to New York on the new RMS Olympic, the largest passenger liner in the world. After spending Christmas in New York with Edward's sister Lucy, now Mrs. Swinnerton, they would travel to Trinidad on the Saramacca and stay for an extended visit of twelve weeks.

Edward resigned his position with Williams Brothers in Birmingham. He would find another position, on his return, if he so desired.

They left Southampton on a bleak December twelfth, wrapped in their warmest clothes against the damp mist of the English Channel. The Atlantic Ocean in December was a heaving grey monster, confining many passengers to their cabins for much of the trip. Edward had always been a good sailor, but Amy lay in her cabin, sipping water laced with bicarbonate of soda. Alice, acting as nurse, stayed close beside her to supply wet towels for her friend's forehead.

It took courage to walk the promenade deck in the stormy weather, but Edward breathed in the salty air with a relish and strode through the mist at a great pace. He dined on the finest foods and explored the beautiful ship, with its grand staircase and opulent dining rooms. He swam in the indoor swimming pool and enjoyed the sauna and steam rooms, after which he lay on a padded bench listening to classical music while a firm-handed masseuse worked his magic on tight shoulder muscles.

Christmas with the Swinnertons was wonderful. Lucy had married well. Her husband, James, was an investment banker, devoted to his wife and three sons. The house, on the outskirts of the city, was large and comfortable. Amy understood, within days of them living there, why Edward was so enamoured with New York. Despite the cold and snow, the city was ablaze with lights and the entire family went to watch the Christmas tree being lit in Madison Park. The energy of the city was vibrant. Life was lived on a different level here than in England and the English visitors found it very exciting.

Lucy was a wonderful hostess and, along with her two eldest

daughters, she paraded Amy and Alice through the best lady's outfitters in New York.

"Edward," laughed Amy as she came into the cozy sitting room from the blowing snow outside. "I should not have packed any of my clothes in England. Indeed, I think I may have to donate all of them to a charity. I have bought the most beautiful outfits this afternoon. I shall wear one of them tonight to dinner to show you."

"I will look forward to it, my dear," Edward said. "I am delighted you are having such a good time shopping with my sister."

"I may abandon the idea of going south to the islands. New York is too wonderful."

"You may change your mind when the winter takes a hold. I believe it can be terribly cold during January and February."

Edward was overjoyed to be back in America. He felt at home in the new country and enjoyed walking around the city streets drinking in the atmosphere. He visited the toy department in Macy's, thinking back to the first time he was there, when Father bought the Prussian Captain for him. He smiled to himself as he thought about the captain, stowed away in his black leather bag, along with his shirt studs.

By mid-January the snow was piled deep in the streets. Edward, Amy and Alice were not disappointed to be on their way to warmer weather in the Caribbean.

The Saramacca was no match for the Olympic, but Amy had booked three separate cabins for the journey to Trinidad, giving them all their privacy and independence. It took three days to sail out of the cold weather, but as the sun broke through on their fourth day at sea they could put away their winter clothing and open up the trunks carrying their Island clothes.

Arthur was at the dock to meet them with horse drawn carriage in tow. The trunks were carried to a cart, drawn by two donkeys, waiting behind the carriage.

After greeting Arthur warmly, Edward introduced his wife and Alice to his brother, and they set off along the coast for Arthur's estate, feeling the warmth of the sun and the wonderful smell of warm rope and salt air mingled together.

The plantation was splendid. The twelve weeks spent there were lived mostly outdoors, under the shade of the vast, canopied courtyard or the waving palm trees. The three English visitors walked, swam and relaxed in the warm sun. The cocoa harvest provided endless chocolate-based desserts to tempt even Amy.

Arthur's island paradise gave Amy and Alice ample opportunity to be alone, walking the long white beaches, swimming in the turquoise Caribbean Ocean or sleeping on the day beds on the verandas outside their bedrooms. Although they would rarely allow the sun to shine on them directly, they soon became deeply tanned by the filtered rays.

All too soon it was time for the journey back to New York and England. Arthur had enjoyed his brother's visit immensely, spending time talking about the family times. Laughing, they remembered climbing into the life boat on the SS Egypt to watch the beautiful girl bathing.

Arthur's wife had died several years before, leaving him childless. He sympathized with Edward, perceiving the situation between him and Amy and the relationship between the two women. He also guessed Edward had married for money. He didn't judge him, but felt sad that his younger brother lived a lonely life, void of affection.

It was springtime in New York when they arrived. Ellis Island was the usual buzz of activity, as they left the ship to register. They soon realized it was not the usual buzz, but something much more serious, making the people scurry around with frowns, questioning everybody they met.

"Any news?"

"Did you hear any more?"

"Do you know what happened?"

As Edward gave his name and particulars to the clerk, he pieced together the fragments of information he was hearing all around him.

The Titanic had sunk.

The very ship Amy had wanted to travel on from England.

People were saying it had hit an iceberg.

It could have been them.

James Swinnerton picked them up and confirmed the rumours. The day before, as Edward, Amy and Alice had travelled north from Trinidad, somewhere out in the Atlantic the unsinkable ship had sunk. James didn't know if there were any survivors.

For the next week, the people of New York could talk of nothing else. Relatives and friends of the passengers of the Titanic poured into the city, anxious to find their loved ones. Anxious for any news of survivors. As the tragic news reached them, they mourned the lost or celebrated the saved.

Out of twenty two hundred passengers and crew on board, only seven hundred had survived.

After a short stay with the Swinnertons in New York, it was with heavy hearts that the three travellers boarded the Mauritania bound for Liverpool. All the passengers on board were well aware that only a few short weeks before, on the same sea route, fifteen hundred people had lost their lives and lay at the bottom of the Atlantic somewhere.

THE LAST GENTLEMAN'S WAR

*E*ngland was buzzing with rumours of war with Germany. Some said it could never happen, especially when the royal family had such close German ties.

Edward had worked sparingly during the two years since the trip to Trinidad. He enjoyed the contract work of an engineering agent and worked for a few months here and there as it suited him. He listened to the gossip about Germany, but knew it would never happen. He knew Germany almost as well as he did England. They were England's closest allies.

England went to war with Germany in 1914, just as Edward was coming up to his forty-fifth birthday. All the young men were joining up before the call-up began, eager to be part of the action and defend their country against the Hun. Edward was too old, but how he wanted to be a part of it. Then he heard from several gentleman at his Birmingham club that regiments were looking for officers. Men who were well bred, from good families, who could command the respect of the troops and had leadership qualities. His good friend, Thomas

Sinclair, told Edward he had been successful in acquiring a commission with the Worcestershire Regiment. Edward left the next morning to drive to the headquarters of the regiment to find out if they would consider a commission for him.

He arrived in his splendid car by late morning. Unannounced and without introduction, he found doors closed to him. The army base was buzzing with activity. Edward's beautiful clothes and elegant manner were nothing to the sergeant who barred his way at the gate.

"Sorry sir," he barked. "Nobody enters without a pass."

Edward seemed to have little choice than to drive all the way back to Birmingham to seek out Sinclair for a letter of introduction. What a waste of time. He wasn't used to being turned away. His aristocratic tongue alone was usually enough to give him an edge that most common men lacked. This time it wasn't working for him.

Thomas Sinclair did better than a letter of introduction, and returned, with Edward, the following day to the barracks in Worcestershire. His pass at the gate admitted them both. Thomas took Edward into the command office, where they waited for a short thirty minutes to see Colonel Abraham Walters, who greeted Thomas warmly.

"Well, Thomas, what a surprise. I'm devilishly busy, old man, but can spare a few minutes. It must be important."

The Colonel was short compared with Edward. He had the most amazing twinkling blue eyes and ruddy complexion.

"Colonel Walters, may I introduce Edward Wrightson, a good friend," Thomas began. "I highly recommend Edward for a commission in the regiment. He would make an excellent officer, being born and raised to command. He has the respect of all who know him."

Thomas paused. The Colonel shook Edward's hand and smiled.

"Well, well. You have a nerve coming here on such business!" he declared. "Not the correct procedure at all. But I am confident Thomas would not have taken this action if he were not convinced of your ability."

Colonel Walters rang a bell on his desk and his adjutant came in, saluted, and awaited orders. Within minutes, a mass of papers were handed to Edward and he was ushered into the adjoining room and given a desk, a pen and ink to begin completing the forms before him. He was told to return the next day at two o'clock, where he did indeed sit down with Major John Barker to talk to him about becoming an officer in the regiment. At forty-five years of age, Edward was really out of the age group, even for officers, but Major Barker liked him immediately and thought he would make a good officer.

Captain Edward Wrightson took up his duties on October 3, 1914. He was part of the Mediterranean Expeditionary Force, serving in Gallipoli, Turkey from June of 1915.

The Turks were unexpectedly good soldiers. Edward's men were picked off during the night whilst on sentry duty, despite being protected by the deep trenches. They were picked off in the middle of the day, as they went about their duties, making it impossible to know where the next sniper fire would come from.

The biggest fear was gas. The Germans had offered to supply Turkey with gas, so that they could use it against the British, French, Australian and New Zealand troops on the small peninsula. With gas, the war would be over quickly with few survivors. Edward, like all the men in his regiment, carried his gas mask with him everywhere, hoping he would have time to put it on when the gas was used. Turkey, however, refused the offer and gas was never used in the conflict, leading to the label "The Last Gentleman's War" by the newspapers of the day.

The trenches were so close together it was possible to hear the enemy talking a few yards away. Nobody knew who began the exchange, but suddenly there were missiles of brown, strong cigarettes tied by strings to rocks, arriving by air into the trench. The British soldiers reciprocated and projected an occasional milder cigarette into the Turkish trench. With a ration of only two cigarettes per man each day, giving up one for the enemy was not an insignificant gift. Sometimes the Turks attached notes to their missiles, but nobody could read them.

After a particular bloody battle, with casualties on both sides, a truce was called and the two armies buried their dead. Men looked into their enemy's eyes for the first time and, seeing another man face to face, wondered why they were killing each other.

The battlefield was a disgusting place for any human to endure. The trenches were their home for months of fighting, when neither side gained ground, but killed and maimed each other at every opportunity. Trenches were full of wet sand and blood. The troops were either dry and baking hot, or cold and soaking wet. The daily ration of thick dark rum, dished out in tin mugs, was the only relief as it trickled down throats and warmed from the inside for a brief time.

Edward was horrified with his life and the lives of the men in his command. There wasn't enough food, or water, or basic necessities of life. They killed a horse and ate horse meat when they were really desperate. There wasn't enough food for the horses anyway and some of them died from malnutrition. The stench was the worst. Edward never quite removed it from his nostrils He would recall the smell for as long as he lived, whenever the memories of Gallipoli would engulf him. The blood, gall, sweat, dirt, horse shit, unwashed bodies, vomit, all mixed together. It seemed they would live in those God forsaken trenches forever.

The lack of nourishing food took a great toll on the regiment. Dysentery made the lives of the soldiers a living hell, for those suffering with the ailment and for those living with the effects of it. Unbearable conditions of human distress beyond endurance. Edward struggled with every aspect of trench life, particularly the lack of privacy and the degradation of having to empty a watery bowel in the tin container in front of others doing the same thing. The abhorrence of not washing body or clothing, leaving the dried-on leftovers from the dysentery covering both skin and clothing.

Through it all Edward's Prussian Captain stood on guard. He stood in a hollowed out hole in the mud wall, sometimes riding in Edward's pocket out into the field where the noise of the battle surrounded them. The captain's coat was worn and faded, so were his shiny black boots, but Edward still treasured him and found comfort in him being near, even though he was a middle-aged commissioned officer in the middle of a war.

Edward himself was dizzy and sick most of the time. His gums were infected and his teeth were loose. His hair and finger nails were falling out. His uniform, dirty and stinking, hung off his frame.

At the beginning of December 1915, after seven months of

intense fighting with great losses on both sides, the allied forces quietly began to withdraw their troops. It was evident to the commanders of the British and French armed forces that they were slowly losing the battle in Gallipoli. The evacuation of troops was done in secret, the Turks believing their enemies were only moving positions to renew the battle, although many believed the Turkish troops knew exactly what was happening.

The Worcestershire regiment had orders to begin the evacuation on December twelfth, and to destroy all equipment, leaving nothing of benefit for the Turkish troops. Edward awoke to a frigid landscape, covered in freshly fallen snow several inches thick. Unbearable pain filled his mouth as the cold seeped in through his cracked lips. He sipped some of the rationed water from the rusty water can, pushed the Prussian Captain into his pocket and called for Lieutenant Fellows, his second in command, to muster the men. The soldiers, stiff from cold, bravely destroyed what was left of their arsenal, before hobbling along the maze of trenches, their breath forming a mist around them. Each step taking them away from the fighting and closer to the ships that would take them home.

The snow made the going tough and it took much longer to reach the sea than expected. Edward encouraged them with pats on the back and a crooked half-smile as they filed past him.

"Keep going," he murmured. "Soon be home."

A bedraggled, beaten army of sick and injured men, who would remember the trenches of Gallipoli in their worst nightmares, were tendered to the ships by a never-ending stream of small boats. It didn't matter to them that there was no food on the ship, or a place to sleep. They sat on the decks next to each other, not speaking, each with his own private memory of hell.

Edward stood at the railing, looking out onto the misty sea and longing for a whisky and a warm bed, in that order. The whisky would numb his aching, raw gums and melt the cold inside him. He closed his eyes and thought of Clara for the first time in many months. He saw her laughing, with her head back and her hair cascading down—drawing him to her and wrapping her arms around him, pressing her lovely, soft body into his.

England! Home! The ship docked and the men staggered onto dry land. They were greeted by a multitude of volunteers, who threw warm blankets around their shoulders and gave them hot tea and buttered scones. Edward couldn't eat or drink anything and was now shaking and weak-kneed. He was escorted quickly to a warehouse converted into a medical centre where he sat on the floor waiting his turn for medical help. It was a long wait. Edward was low on the priority list. Men with visible traumatic wounds, bleeding, crying out for help were taken first, some not making it any further than the waiting area. These were the lucky ones, who were not injured or sick enough for the hospital ships and had been able to survive during the evacuation without medical help.

The doctors and nurses worked through the night to see every man. Edward was close to the last to be seen. One look into his mouth told the doctor the story of malnutrition and decay and Edward was transferred by horse-drawn carriage to the hospital in Southampton immediately. His teeth were removed and his gastritis treated. His gums slowly healed enough that he was able to drink the thick protein-filled potions the nurses brought to him. He began to regain his strength but he would remain unfit for active duty for the rest of the war.

Amy's house in Kings Norton was a welcome retreat after the chaos of war and the overcrowded hospital ward. Amy and Alice were attentive nurses, feeding the undernourished captain until his loose skin filled out again and the drained, tired eyes began to lose some of the horror. Dr. Blenkinsop, eminent dental surgeon, worked on Edward's mouth once the gums were completely healed, fitting him with teeth that looked almost as natural as his own. The army had given Edward a time of convalescence after which he was posted to a Yorkshire regiment—at a desk job instead of the front lines. Edward didn't complain, but his war experience in Turkey was etched in his mind forever, and would continue to haunt him throughout his life.

The armistice was signed on November 11, 1918. The war to end all wars was over.

MOVING NORTH

*A*fter the war, picking up the pieces of his life in Kings Norton wasn't easy for Edward. Amy welcomed him with a smile and a kiss on the cheek and, although she enjoyed being seen with him, their life together was a matter of routine. Edward occupied his own suite, as he had before the war.

Edward reported to the company office, where he had worked as an engineering agent before the war. They asked him to set up an office north of Birmingham in Staffordshire and he jumped at the chance to move somewhere different and explore a new society.

He was still in easy access of Kings Norton, where he could spend the weekends in Amy's house. The arrangement for his allowance and all the perks of being Amy's husband continued as before, and his salary easily covered the costs of a small house in Alsager, a country town in North Stafford-shire. Edward employed a housekeeper to take care of his needs, and he slid into the new life with ease. Although the war was behind him, the memories were still with him. Clara was also there in the background, haunting his rare and beautiful dreams.

The McIntoshes were still in the same house in Birmingham. The three children were growing up, but were still the apple of Edward's eye. They adored him in return and Uncle Edward's visits were always the highlight of their week. The stories of war would never run out it seemed, although most were fiction, full of adventures and heroes, with none of the death and destruction.

The Duck and Dragon pub in the centre of Birmingham was a frequent port of call for Edward. Many of the soldiers who had been lucky enough to survive the war gathered there on Friday nights. Out of a need to be with others who had survived, they shared their stories and their fears. They shared their disconnection with the world around them and the lack of understanding from everybody who hadn't been fighting. Although Edward was the only commissioned officer at the pub on Friday nights, he found it a great comfort to be with the soldiers and they accepted his presence with none of the usual class rules of being on their best behaviour around a toff. The "toffs" were expected to drink in the lounge part of the pub, not the bar, or even at a different pub. There were pubs for the toffs and pubs for the working class.

As in all things, time heals the soul. The memories, like those of Clara years before, faded and became recalled less frequently. Friday nights at the pub became a monthly visit, instead of weekly. Then every couple of months, when there were less and less of the brave soldiers turning up. Edward felt the memories slipping away, like an old friend. Not really wanting to give them up, but watching them evaporate, against his will, until they were just an occasional dream or a chance meeting on the street with an old comrade.

Amy, Alice and Edward settled down into a routine which suited them all. The couple was seen together at the theatre and at dinner in the city frequently, and on the weekends at church services, and various country homes, where they were in demand as dinner guests. Edward drove a Daimler car, which was very sleek and new. His work in Staffordshire paid enough to supply his money for cigars and drinks at the club on the weekend and to entertain an occasional lady, very discreetly.

His weekly life in North Staffordshire was dull and disinteresting. He was assigned to a new mechanical engineering company in Biddulph, as consultant and advisor. The people of North Staffordshire were not cultured people. Their language was coarse and their dialect difficult to understand. There were few good restaurants, or theatres, or parks, or even interesting company. The factory owners made up the wealthy of the area and they had one thing in common—making pottery. The area was clouded in black smoke from coal- fired kilns, which covered all the buildings in soot and turned Edward's silk shirts a dull grey colour.

Mrs. Bennet was Edward's housekeeper. She didn't want to live in, but preferred to come to the house daily, to cook and keep house for Edward. She didn't want to work on the weekends, which also suited the situation, as Edward travelled to Birmingham on the weekends. He usually went back to his house in Alsager in the evening, enjoying the drive away from the grime of the Potteries to the small village, where he could breathe and see trees and sky. He drank too much whiskey and smoked too many cigars. He read books, building up a good library of his own. He walked in the surrounding countryside and stopped to talk to the farmers and the people in the village, who he found to be more friendly and trusting than the folk in the city.

He lived for Friday afternoon, when he headed south to Birmingham, called at his club for a wonderful meal and afterwards visited with Jonathon McIntosh's family, before heading home to Amy.

GERTRUDE

*A*my and Alice were going to London for the weekend, so Edward wasn't needed as an escort. Would he go to Birmingham anyway and visit Mac and his family? Or would he stay cooped up in North Staffordshire and walk the country roads around the cottage?

The decision was made for him when William, a local man who helped with the garden, stopped by on Friday evening to ask about the new rose bushes Edward had ordered. They had been delivered to the cottage that morning and would need planting. Did Edward have a plan? William enquired.

"Great news," said Edward. "Rose bushes. Just the thing. I'll stay here this weekend and, if you can come early tomorrow, William, we'll plant them together."

"Very good sir," said William, doffing his cap. "I'll be along about eight o'clock."

Saturday morning was bright and sunny for a change. The North Staffordshire weather was rarely bright and sunny, with days of rain coming off the Irish Sea to the west, or the wildness of the Pennines to the northwest.

William was earlier than expected, laying out the dozen rose bushes, wheelbarrow full of black soil at the ready, spades and watering can on the path. William loved the outdoors and made a good living gardening for the locals who didn't have the time or inclination. Edward was different from most of the gardener's clients. He loved roses! They reminded him of Clara—soft and scented, yet strong and courageous. Able to survive, even in harsh conditions and poor soil. He wasn't afraid to get his hands dirty and do a bit of digging, and William enjoyed the older man's company as they prepared to plant the bushes.

They selected the best position for each bush, making sure the light was good and soil moist. The roses would be spectacular, William assured Edward.

Mrs. Bennet left Edward a sandwich for his lunch, but he had told her he would eat out for dinner. He had made arrangements with a colleague to meet at the North Staffordshire Hotel, where the food was adequate and the atmosphere lively.

At seven o'clock he went into the hotel and sat at a table, ordered a half pint of beer and waited for his friend. He would have preferred a sherry before his meal, but beer was the drink of the people in the area and he preferred not to be the centre of attention, by drinking what would have been considered a lady's drink.

Edward had been into the hotel several times to meet business acquaintances. The food was influenced by its location, offering pastry and meat dishes, which the people of the Potteries seem to favour.

On this particular evening, he was meeting with Gordon Wilcox, who worked for the same company. He was younger than Edward by ten years and married with two grown children. He enjoyed Edward's company and they occasionally met at the North Staffs, as it was known locally, on Fridays after work.

Gordon arrived and waved as he saw Edward. They ordered their food and more beer, talking over the plans for the new bridge they were working on.

As Edward enjoyed his beer and conversation with Gordon, his attention was drawn to a small table tucked at the back of the dimly lit room. Facing him, talking to another girl, was the most beautiful girl Edward had ever seen. Not just the oval face, or the halo of dark hair, or the slender figure. There was something else. A magnetism he had only experienced once before. She met his gaze with rich dark brown eyes, smoke from her cigarette swirling around her. She didn't look away, Edward dropping his eyes before she did, as he continued talking to his friend, although he really hadn't heard anything for a few seconds. When Edward glanced back at the dark-eyed girl, she was looking straight at him, and this time she broke the gaze, but blushed in the process, which Edward thought charming.

PART II
BORN INTO POVERTY

IT'S A GIRL!

ongton, City of Stoke-on-Trent, North Staffordshire. It was the year 1901. In the middle of England, in a dark, dingy, smelly tenement house, lying on newspaper to soak up the fluids, Emma gave birth to her first child, a girl she named Gertrude. The birth was difficult, long and painful. There were no luxuries here. Only the smell of poverty, the gas lamps, the grime of industrial England at its worst. Mrs. Hodges, from the next street, helped out as midwife. Doctors were expensive and were never involved at the birth of a baby in 1901. If the baby or the mother died, the response was, "That's just life, isn't it duck?"

Emma didn't die, nor did Gertrude. Mrs. Hodges stayed with Emma, teaching her how to latch the baby to her breast and how to change her nappy, such as it was; just a few thread-bare pieces of rag a neighbour had given her. There was one nightie and two little coddling shirts from the same kindly woman and Mrs. Hodges had brought along a blanket to swaddle the newborn. Folks around the streets dropped off baby things to the midwife now and then to use as she saw need, and this was need. A dresser drawer was removed to make a crib. Not the crib of choice, but of necessity in this town. Mrs. Hodges lined the drawer with more newspaper for warmth and folded a woolen sweater of Emma's into the bottom, placing the new baby gently onto its folds. She put the dresser drawer on a wooden crate, used for fruit and vegetables, beside the couch.

"'How ya doing, duck?" Mrs. Hodges asked as she bustled into the dingy front parlour, used just for visitors, or for having babies, or for laying out the dead.

"Don't even ask," whispered Emma, tears starting down her cheeks.

"I know, duck, I know," the kindly midwife said, patting Emma on the head and wiped her tears away with the back of her hand. "Ya've got a luvly little babbie, anyroad."

Emma pulled down the blanket from the new baby's face, a tiny wrinkled little creature appeared with a shock of black hair and a troubled frown.

"Eee, she's grand," cooed Mrs. Hodges, stroking the tiny face gently.

"Don't know what he'll say when he knows it's a lass," choked Emma.

"Never you mind duck. He'll be too drunk to care any'ow."

Mrs. Hodges continued to bustle about the room. Cleaning up all the soiled newspaper and placenta and placing it into a cardboard box, which she'd drop into the dustbin on the way out.

She made Emma a cup of tea in the kitchen, where the fire had burned throughout Emma's confinement, heating the kettle on the hob, providing the hot water needed. She heaped two spoonfuls of sugar into the strong tea and added cream from the top of the bottle of milk. She cut two slices of bread from the left-over loaf wrapped in a cloth on the table, and toasted it in front of the fire, spreading lard on the hot bread and sprinkling it with a generous amount of salt.

"Get this into ya, duck," she said kindly as she placed the steaming cup of tea beside Emma on a chair seat and handed her the toast.

"Thanks missus," mumbled Emma, her mouth already full of toast and fat and salt.

Tom reeled into the parlour and squinted at his young wife through bleary, bloodshot eyes.

"Whar is it then? Betta not be a bloody girl." Mrs. Hodges looked up at him in disgust.

"Well, Tom, you've got a lovely little lass," she said, trying to be bright and cheerful.

"I'm goin' upstairs," was his only reply.

He hadn't wanted to marry Emma Thursfield. He loved Joan who worked at the pub. The trouble was, he could never stay sober long enough to wait for Joan to get off work and, well, he had a room at the Thursfield house. He rented the small back bedroom for sixpence a week. It was cheap and clean, which was all he needed - he was saving up to buy a horse.

Tom had left school at twelve, like most lads, but had avoided the pits and the pots and struck out on his own. His Uncle Ralph had an allotment behind the gas works, where he grew all kinds of vegetables. Tom helped him out, digging over the potato patch and weeding the tomatoes. His uncle was a quiet man and Tom enjoyed being outside, so they got along well.

Uncle Ralph came up with an idea that would change Tom's future.

"Hey Tom," he said one day while they were both working in the drizzling rain. "We should build you a barra. You could go 'round the streets selling me veggies. I bet we'd make a few bob. What d'ya say?"

Tom thought it was a grand idea, and he nodded in agreement, a broad smile filling his face. He could earn a few bob selling the veggies.

Uncle Ralph begged two old wheels from Johnny Filbert, who fixed old bikes in Market Street, and went to Longton Market to talk to a mate of his, who fixed him up with a couple of wooden crates. Tom found nails in the rubbish tip at the back of Bould's Furniture factory in Fenton and the old man and young boy worked on a wobbly barrow, using an old pram handle to pull it along.

The first load Tom took out was just carrots and potatoes. He walked up and down the streets of Neck End yelling "Come get your taters here." He was surprised and more than a little excited when his small load of vegetables were snapped up, and Tom was back at the allotment garden showing Ralph the ten pennies in his hand.

"You did good, lad," said Uncle Ralph, giving Tom two of the pennies for himself. Tom went home to his mother and sister in Jones Street, stopping to buy a penny loaf and a pot of pickled red cabbage with his tuppence.

What a feast for our tea tonight, he thought.

Soon the barrow was loaded down with two more crates, carrying beetroot and cabbage. The women of Neck End were happy to buy from the barrow instead of lining up at the market, having to drag babies and kids with them. Tom always sold out of everything in those early days and Ralph planted more and more produce to keep up with the demand.

Tom worked for five years just for Uncle Ralph, but as he built up his trade, he expanded his supplies to include Joe Robert's garden and Bill Copeland's apple trees. He saved his money to buy materials to build a much bigger barrow, which he put to good use expanding the business and making a good living.

At eighteen, his mother remarried and Tom looked for somewhere else to live. Mr. Freeman, his stepfather, didn't like Tom, and Tom didn't like him. There were one too many men in the small house.

That's when Tom went to board with Mrs. Thursfield. That's when beer became his pleasure and his passion. He put away money for a horse, but there was always some left over for the pub. That's when he fell for Joan.

She was a buxom, dimpled girl, with a quick smile and blue eyes. Tom loved her from the moment he saw her. His mind was full of Joan and what he would do if he ever got her on her own. The trouble was, she was always working in the pub at night and weekends. The other trouble was her dad owned the pub, and kept a watchful eye on young would-be suiters like Tom.

Joan never agreed to actually meet him after the pub was closed, even though Tom asked her many times. He would wait around in the entry beside the pub after closing time, just in case she changed her mind and turned up to give him a kiss, but it never happened.

One Saturday night, he wandered back to his digs to find Emma, the landlady's daughter, standing outside the house. Tom swayed a little from the night of drinking. He was still thinking about Joan, but Emma was right here in front of him. She had a thin frock on, which clung to her legs from the drizzle coming down in a mist around her. She wasn't a bad looker, just a bit thin.

"Mam's made a sugar and butter cake," Emma said as Tom walked past her to go into the house.

"Do ya want some?"

"Aye, all right," said Tom.

Emma followed him into the house, through the parlour, into the kitchen where the cake stood on the table covered in a white cloth. She cut a big slice of cake and put it on a plate.

"Here, sit down and have some then," Emma offered.

Tom ate the cake with relish. The beer always gave him an appetite. Emma propped her bum on the edge of the table, looking down at him as he ate. She scooped some of the sugar and butter filling from the cake with her finger and sucked on it, never taking her eyes off Tom.

Tom licked his lips, then wiped his mouth with the back of his sleeve before getting up from the chair to go upstairs to his room. Emma didn't move. He would have to climb over her outstretched legs if he was going to make it to the stairs.

That was all it took. He clutched her into his arms, pressing his lips heavily onto hers. She didn't resist.

Asking for it, she is, thought Tom as she followed him upstairs to his room. They heard Emma's mother snoring softly as they passed her bedroom. Joan was in his mind, but Emma was in his arms. What was a man to do?

Tom didn't want Emma or any wife and he certainly didn't want a baby. But you did what was right in 1901 and he "had" to marry Emma.

Mrs. Thursfield arranged with the landlord for her Emma to get number twenty seven when old Mr. Blenkinsop died, and Emma and Tom moved in, with their meagre possessions, four months before the baby was born.

The money for the horse was spent on provisions for the house. They had to buy a bed, a table and two chairs and some pots and pans. The horsehair sofa in the kitchen was left by Mr. Blenkinsop's family, when they knew a young couple, expecting their first baby, had rented the house. The sofa in the parlour was a gift from Tom's Uncle Ralph.

"You'll be needing a sofa in the parlour for the birthing," he'd said to Tom when he came to the house, delivering the sofa on the back of the coal wagon, courtesy of Arnold, the coal man.

Now Tom would be a barrow boy his whole life - he'd never get his horse.

EDWARD STREET

When Gertrude was almost two, Sarah Ellen was born. Gertrude went to her grandma Thursfields for the day, as the parlour was put to use again as the birthing room, with the same missus from the next street tending to the birth. Gertrude was taken back to Emma when it was all over, where she was lifted up by Aunt Sarah to see the new baby tucked into the dresser drawer. Emma lay in bed crying and Tom was at the pub.

The new baby was never called Sarah Ellen, always Dolly. Gertrude now drank her milk, when there was milk in the house, from an old tin cup, and the baby was the one at Emma's breast. Sometimes, in the night, if Gertrude woke from her sleep at the bottom of the couch where Emma lay, she would crawl up to her mother's breast and help herself to the warm, sweet milk. Emma, too tired to notice, would only stir briefly and Gertrude suckled away, taking her fill before creeping back to her spot.

The nightly milk was short lived for Gertrude. As soon as Emma was able to leave the parlour after her confinement,

Gertrude slept on a straw mattress on the floor of the second bedroom. She was scared and lonely and cold, but knew already at her tender age, that her life would be much worse if she cried or called out to her two parents, who didn't care.

Tom was as unhappy with the second child as he had been with the first. Another girl! He never touched either of them, or even looked at them, and he blamed Emma if they cried.

Dolly slept beside Emma so that the milk was in her mouth before she could cry and disturb her beer-soaked father. The days were spent in front of the kitchen fire, Emma sitting at the table, drinking tea and minding the two little girls. Emma didn't speak to them or play with them. She was just there. She fed them a mixture of bread soaked in warm milk, called pobs, and mashed bananas, if there were any left over from the barrow. She changed their nappies now and then, when the smell became too bad, but the two little girls both had raw bums most of the time. The curse of poverty and depression hung over the terraced streets like a plague, contaminating all who were unfortunate enough to live there.

Neck End was the area in Longton where the miners and potters lived. The working poor. Street after street of brick terraced houses, shrouded in damp and mold from the ever constant rain prevalent in the Midlands of England. No trees grew here. No blade of grass pushed through the black bricks in the yard or on the curbside outside the front doors.

Edward Street, built on a hill, was lined with terraced houses. All the same, with two up and two down; a kitchen, with a black fireplace and warming oven taking up an entire wall, a small wooden table and two chairs under the only window, an old well-used armchair squashed into the corner by the fireplace, never to be sat in by anybody but Tom, and a horsehair sofa along the back wall. Two large oval portraits of Queen Victoria and Prince Albert hung on two of the walls. Tom's great aunt had given them to the couple and Emma was very proud of those portraits. The parlour, where Gertrude and Dolly were born, held a horsehair sofa and one chair and a fireplace, polished black, which never had and never would be used. Up the wooden stairs off the kitchen were two small bedrooms; one containing a double iron bedstead with a kapok mattress, a cot for baby Dolly, handed down from eight different babies on the street, and a chest of drawers. The other bedroom had the small straw mattress where Gertrude slept and a wooden box where her clothes were kept. The two bedrooms smelt of old dried urine from all the times the kids had wet the bed, the chamber pots that were too full, and the times Tom hadn't made it through the night. Urine soaked sheets and blankets would be hung around the fire to dry, the smell of the pee drying permeated the house. Washing sheets and blankets was a low priority as hot water was precious and hard to come by. It was saved for washing bare necessities like undergarments and baby's stuff, once a week.

The back kitchen was separate from the house, and contained a brown stone sink with cold tap and a gas ring for cooking. Also in the back kitchen was the round tin washtub which served for the laundry and for bathing the kids once a week or thereabouts, and only if the weather wasn't too cold. The adults went to the public baths at the end of Bath Street by the railway station once every few weeks. Men went less often - some only once a year.

The lav was up the yard and consisted of a wooden plank with a hole, dropping to infinity. A tin bucket, filled with water, stood beside the plank, with an old pot sitting in the water to wash down the solids. It was Emma's job to empty the chamber pot, kept under the bed, every morning. Some mornings she couldn't be bothered, so the pot-full of urine stayed where it was, waiting for the following night's pee. To clean up there was newspaper cut into squares and threaded onto string, hung on a nail on the inside of the lav door. It never did the job, and the printer's ink was left smeared across the bums of the users. What didn't get cleaned off left a smear of brown on the underwear, joining the previous smears. At least there was newspaper in Emma's lav. Gertrude had been to the lav at her friend, Gladys', once and they used a bum rag. Washed every couple of days, when nobody could find a clean patch to wipe with.

The household rubbish was thrown into a small alcove outside the back gate. The city rubbish collectors came once a week in a horse-drawn wagon to shovel up the garbage and take it to the local dump. The flies and smell from the piles of open garbage were an accepted part of life in the slums.

Oh yes, and don't let's forget the coal cellar, the access door placed between the two downstairs rooms. Steep steps disappeared into the dark hole where the coal was tipped from an outside grid. The trips up and down those stairs, to fill the coal buckets several times a day, brought more dirt tracking through the tiny home; boots and clothes were covered in coal dust as the heavy loads were hauled to the side of the fire grate in the kitchen.

Cockroaches were a big problem, thriving heartily among the dirt. Emma would put out a saucer of beer each night and several of the large black beetles would be found belly up the next morning drowned in the beer—at least they died happy!

Mice had free run of most houses. The large gaps under the doors gave them easy access. Families kept a small crumb brush on the kitchen table, which they used to sweep away the numerous mouse droppings before they ate. The only time there was a bit of panic was if a rat was spotted, then the rat catcher was called in to lay down traps, giving the children days of enjoyment checking for trapped rats.

Such was life in Neck End and numerous other poverty-stricken, working class towns in England in the early twentieth century.

FAMILY

*I*t was a miserable existence. Gertrude was always cold, hungry, dirty and unloved.

The only time she could forget about her surroundings, and even have a laugh or two, was when she went to grandma Thursfield's, her mother's mother. Otherwise Gertrude was stuck at home with Emma and the baby, and she rarely left the confines of the tiny terraced house. Emma's younger sisters would sometimes come for a visit and play with the baby and, as Gertrude grew, they would often take her back to the Thursfield house with them and keep her for a few days.

Gertrude was aware there was a wider family than just Emma and Tom and Dolly. Emma had a mum called Grandma Thursfield, who lived just a few houses away on Edward Street. Gertrude knew from a young age that Grandma's house was where she wanted to be. Aunties and uncles lived at Grandma's house, who picked her up and kissed her. There was always warm milk and home-made cookies at Grandma's. Grandma sang songs to Gertrude and brushed her tangled hair. Grandma had a real dolly with a china face and curly hair for Gertrude to play with.

The house was on the corner and had three bedrooms and a large kitchen, with a table and six chairs. It was always clean and always smelled of bread. A carpet square covered the linoleum floor in front of the fire - a wonderful cozy island where Gertrude could rock and sing to her dolly. Grandma always wore a starched white apron. Her hair was pulled back into a bun. She had large hands, always busy with baking or knitting. She had a hearty laugh which shook her generous belly and wobbled her chins.

There were three of Emma's younger sisters living at home, Sarah being Gertrude's favourite. Sarah was the one Gertrude would sleep with when she stayed over, cuddling up to her in the warm covers and smelling the freshly washed sheets and thinking she was just about in heaven. It was always worse to go home after visiting Grandma's and there were always tears. Emma didn't appreciate the sulky, sniffling girl who came home and a hand across the head would be dealt out within minutes of her return.

Tom Bryan made a meagre living selling fruits and veggies from a horse-drawn cart in the streets. Most of what he made went directly to the corner pub, the Brown Duck. He came home only when the money ran out, often sending Emma and the two children into hiding, so that they wouldn't feel the back of his hand as he lashed out at anything that annoyed him, mostly his family. They would hide across the street in Minnie Powell's parlour until they saw the bedroom candle go out, the signal that he had passed out, and they were safe to sneak home. Emma would often spend the night on the kitchen sofa for fear of disturbing her drunken spouse. She became a bitter, miserable woman, with no love for anybody, including her children. They were more of a nuisance to her than a joy and she couldn't wait for them to be out of her sight. She began to seek refuge in black bottled stout and at every chance would take money from the food budget to buy a bottle or two from the Brown Duck, leaving even less money for food. There was never enough money to buy meat or fish. Emma wasn't a cook anyway. She seemed to destroy the taste of everything by frying the hell out of it over the coal fire.

Everything was fried in lard, sausage being the usual fare, fried until it was black. A penny-worth of chips and a bowl of sloppy peas from the chip shop was the main diet at tea time, namely dinner to the rest of the world. The Bryan family had one good thing going for them, which was the fresh fruit and veggies from Tom's cart. They got all the left-overs. Dinged oranges and apples, blackened bananas, soft fleshy tomatoes, the left over cabbage leaves, turnips and potatoes. A neighbour showed Emma how to boil and mash potatoes and turnips together, with plenty of lard and salt. Most of the time she couldn't be bothered, but on special occasions the turnips and mash were a welcome change from the chippy.

RULES

When Gertrude was almost five years old, a man came to the house from the school board. Handing Emma a letter, he told Emma to take her daughter to Edensor Primary School on August 28th, 1906. Fortunately for Gertrude, Minnie Powell's boy was the same age and was starting to school on the same day, so Minnie took them both. Emma had no intention of walking Gert to school with Dolly to drag along. Minnie Powell was rough but not unkind and even gave Gert's hand a small squeeze as they arrived at the entrance of the big black building, with a stream of skinny, dirty children pushing their way inside.

A stern looking, tall, thin man, with thin grey hair and large glasses, greeted the new students. "Stand by the wall. Don't talk. Don't fidget. Feet together. Heads up. Hands out in front," he boomed.

He walked down the line of five-year-olds, inspecting each pair of dirty hands, back and front. His eyes taking in each pair of shoes, each pale face, each head of matted hair, each frail body clothed in a variety of hand-me-downs and cast offs from the chapel jumble.

"Disgusting!" he said, his nose wrinkled as if smelling day-old fish. "You are to attempt to wash your hands and face before school. You are to rub your boots with newspaper to get rid of some of the dirt. You are to beg or borrow some kind of brush or comb to detangle your hair. This is a school and now that you are a student, you will follow the rules."

To Gertrude, the rules were all over her head. *Who washed their hands and face EVERY DAY?* She thought. *Where will I find a brush or comb? Maybe Aunt Sarah would give me one. I remember seeing two brushes at Grandma Thursfield's house, and I always have my hair brushed when I stay there.* She could use one of the bum sheets of newspaper for her shoes. She didn't want to be singled out as not following the rules, so she followed through on her plans and did indeed get an old brush from Aunt Sarah, which she hid in a hole in the floorboards beside her bed, so Emma wouldn't know about it.

Sarah soaked Gertrude's hands in warm soapy water for a long time at the weekend when she was at Grandma's house. Then she gently used a small brush to ease the dirt from under and around each finger nail. Finally, Sarah clipped the tiny nails, until they were all smooth and even. Gertrude's little hands had never looked so lovely.

Of course, Emma never noticed the small differences in her girl's appearance; she never really looked at her anyway. She was just happy to have her out of the house and away at school - one less for her to look after was the way she saw it.

UNTIL ELEVEN

Gertrude loved going to school. She was away from home. Away from Emma. She was popular with the other kids and in much demand as a "best friend." Gladys was her really best friend, and they played together every playtime and walked to and from school together. Gladys lived in the next street and was just four weeks older than Gertrude. The two girls would stare through the railings of the St. Gregory's Catholic School playground and jeer at the uniformed girls in the "girls only" school.

"Right little snobs, you are," they would call out.

"Go away, horrid, nasty brats," the "girls only" girls would snap back.

"I bet your shit dunna stink," Gertrude was brave enough to shout as she and Gladys ran down the street to Edensor School, where all the kids wore a uniform too - the uniform of poverty.

Clothes were too big or too small, cast offs from others, or from the jumble sale at the chapel. Socks, if worn at all, were full of holes and stiff with dirt and foot sweat. Boots—well, it was anybody's guess where they had come from; they had belonged to somebody else, and always had holes in the bottom. Pieces of cardboard were cut to fit inside, so that the water didn't seep in, but it still did. Hair was dirty and lice ridden. Lice were a big problem. Gertrude stood in line in the playground before classes started, and watched the lice jump up and down and run in and out of the girl's hair in front of her. The school provided each child with a bar of delousing soap, which was supposed to be used each week for hair washing. Gertrude took hers home, but at five years old she still relied on Emma to help her and Emma didn't feel so inclined.

"Aunt Sarah'll wash it for thee," she said.

Gertrude put the bar of soap under her rag pillow and hoped the smell of the soap would kill the crawlies running around her head.

Gertrude was one of the clever kids. She revelled in the attention from the teachers, who praised her for the good marks she achieved. She learned quickly and was one of the first in her class to read, which vexed Emma to no end.

"I'll knock that bloody book outta your 'and if you dunna put it down. And git out of his chair, he'll half kill ya if he catches ya," she yelled, coming into the room and finding Gertrude curled up on Tom's chair reading a book the teacher had lent her. Emma snatched the book from Gertrude, threatening to throw it in the fire.

"It's teacher's book," Gertrude said, jumping up and snatching it away from Emma. "You'll be the one in trouble if ya burn it."

Always defiant, Gertrude dodged out of Emma's way, as the arm came up to hit her.

Miss Arnold was Gertrude's favourite teacher. She was the one who lent her the book to take home. She was softly spoken and smelled of lavender. She wore long black skirts with different coloured blouses, always attaching a round cameo brooch at the neck. Gertrude thought she was very elegant. She wanted to be just like her. She wanted to wear clean clothes that smelled nice and talk in a refined voice and have her hair swept up into a bun held with a fancy comb. She blossomed under Miss Arnold's supervision, learning how to write down her thoughts and learning to read great adventure stories, which opened up a world she didn't know existed. She enjoyed learning about the country she lived in and the world beyond it, learning the history of the British Empire and how powerful it was. Almost a third of the entire world belonged to Britain. Gertrude crammed her head with every bit of knowledge she encountered in her short years of school.

Gertrude and Dolly lived for Friday nights, when Emma allowed them out after tea to go to the chapel for Children's Hour. From six o'clock until seven o'clock the girls joined dozens of neighbourhood kids at the Methodist Central Hall. They met in the big hall behind the chapel where they were greeted by Mister and Missus Maddox and several teenage helpers. They played oranges and lemons, being caught in the "chopper" and then picked to go behind the "orange" or the "lemon," until there was a great long line of children behind each fruit, and they could end with a tug of war. They played hide and seek, Mister Maddox going over the rules of where they could hide in the non-church part of the chapel. The rooms were always dimly lit and scary and a ton of fun, with kids screaming and laughing as they were found. There were games set out on tables, like snakes and ladders, checkers and happy families. They were fed lemonade and sugar cookies at the end of the hour. Then back to reality. They would walk home to Edward Street, with their tummies full and thinking how long it seemed before next Friday night.

The only other time they went into the big hall at the chapel was for the monthly jumble sale, when Emma would equip her brood with "new" clothes and boots.

Twice during the years at Edensor School, Emma cleaned the parlour. Both times, Gertrude and Dolly were sent to Grandma Thursfield's out of the way. Both times the girls were told "Your mam's having a baby." Both times the girls waited to return home to see the new baby and both times there was no baby to see. Instead they went home to a darkened parlour, with a small shrouded figure, covered in flower petals, in a box laid across two kitchen chairs. Emma lay on the couch looking pale and sick. They didn't talk to her, nor she to them. They were made to kiss the dead baby on the forehead, then ushered through the parlour and into the kitchen.

Over the next three days, family and neighbours paraded in to see the dead baby. An assortment of food made its way onto the kitchen table, for which Emma, Gertrude and Dolly were grateful. Once Emma was over her confinement, the family led the procession, following the men carrying the baby in the coffin, first to the Central Hall, where Reverend Johnson said some prayers, then on to the cemetery, where more prayers were said and the tiny casket was put into the hole in the ground.

Over and done with. A dead baby was nothing new.

During her last year at Edensor, when Gertrude was eleven, she came home from school to find Emma cleaning the parlour again, putting a thin blanket on the horsehair sofa, a pile of newspaper on the floor beside the sofa, two old towels in a bucket.

"What's going on, Mam?" Gertrude asked.

"Ya'll find out soon enough, nosey cat," replied Emma.

"Are ya having another baby, Mam?" persisted Gertrude.

"What does it look like?"

"That's the only reason ya'd clean the parlour," Gertrude observed.

"Cheeky sod, you are."

"Will this one die?"

"Shut bloody up, you," yelled Emma. "If it dies, it dies."

Emma opened a small bag and laid out a baby wrap vest, a tiny nighty and a ragged cloth and safety pin for the nappy.

"You and Dolly go to Grandma's, and don't come back until you're told," were Emma's final words.

Gertrude went through to the kitchen, where Dolly sat at the table eating one of yesterday's dinged apples. The girls gathered their few things together and walked past their mother and up the street to Grandma's house.

"Mam's having another baby today," explained Gertrude, as they joined Grandma in the warm kitchen.

"Come on in then. Kettle's boiling. We'll have a nice cuppa shall we?"

Grandma poured mugs of steaming tea and added milk and

sugar, giving the girls thick slabs of homemade bread and jam to eat. She had a frown between her eyebrows, not hiding her anxiety. Gertrude, at eleven years old, noticed everything and wondered if she should worry too.

Mam's already birthed two dead babies. Will this one die too? If it lives, where will it sleep? Will it have to sleep in with me and Dolly? Now we have a double mattress, Mam will surely say there's room for three. What will Tom do if it's another lass?

At nine o'clock Aunt Sarah came to get them.

"Come on you two. Come see your baby brother."

"A boy then," Grandma smiled. "He'll be pleased about that."

In the parlour lay Mam, looking smug and pink, drinking her tea and eating her larded toast. In the chest drawer lay a wrinkled, red faced, hairless baby. He lay very still and Gertrude worried he was dead and nobody had noticed. She touched his tiny cheek; he felt soft and warm. His mouth opened slightly moving towards her finger, so she knew he wasn't dead.

"What's his name then?" Dolly asked.

"William, after me dad." Emma said. "Now up to bed you two, before your dad comes home."

Finally a live baby. A boy. Tom was delighted and spent the next three nights celebrating at the Brown Duck. Wetting the baby's head, they called it. Everybody in Neck End knew Tom had a son at last.

BIG SCHOOL

Gertrude went to the big school at eleven years of age. She was one of the youngest and there was no Miss Arnold there. The teachers were more severe and seemed to hate all the kids equally. They carried canes around with them, using them frequently on any talker, chewer of gum, or cheater. Students lived in fear of their teachers, who used their positions of supreme power not to teach, but to discipline. Very few children learned well in the atmosphere of fear and hatred. They were so scared of doing something wrong, that they soon learned not to take any risks. They played it safe, disappearing into the background and becoming invisible. Gertrude was no exception and she progressed very little in her years at Cook Street School. School was much the same as home. Rules, beatings, disapproval.

If she could have expressed how she felt, it would have been a feeling of hopelessness and helplessness, which embedded itself deep inside her very being.

Gladys cried all the way to school Monday morning. Gertrude tried to comfort her.

"Come on, Glad," she cooed. "It'll be all right, duck. The test wunna be that hard. I know you'll pass."

Gladys struggled with her school work, and Cook Street was a nightmare for her. She was at the mercy of Mr. McLeod, a great giant of a Scotsman, with fat hands and bad breath. He would tolerate no F's in his class. It wasn't an option. To get an F was to die.

Gladys had never had an F, but there was always a first time, and she couldn't bear the thought of another test, which may bring the dreaded result.

"You're clever, Gert," she blubbered. "You'd never get an F."

Gertrude put her arm around her friend's shoulders as they walked against the bitter cold wind. It didn't help that it was January, with wind whipping through the layers of inadequate clothing. It didn't help that Christmas, the season of joy and peace, had been miserable.

~

Christmas for Gertrude meant parents at the pub celebrating, leaving the children at home, looking after younger siblings, listening for the sound of singing voices, as the adults rolled home, then scattering to their beds like little mice threatened by a cat. They huddled together under the covers, shivering against each other and pretending to sleep, as the noise from downstairs continued, and the carols of good cheer were sung with slurred voices.

William fell asleep against Gertrude's shoulder. She lay

awake, listening for the creek of the wooden stairs. Her father was in fine form tonight. Neighbours had returned from the pub with him and Emma; Christmas Eve was one of the few nights in the year when the women were welcomed at the pub. Tom was shouting for bread and cheese and sour pickles.

"Good Christian Men Rejoice," sang Tom, the other men joining in with him, as they waited for their food.

What a joke, thought Gertrude, listening to the words and cringing at the hypocrisy.

"Deck the halls with boughs of holly. Tis the season to be jolly," floated up the stairs.

Tears stung Gertrude's eyes. *Who had written the words? Whoever it was had never been near north Staffordshire.*

As the voices stopped and the party ended, she drifted into a half sleep, still holding William against her frail body. She heard the stairs creak, as Emma and Tom ended another joyful Christmas Eve. She heard the bed creaking in a rhythm in the next room and a low moan as the creaking stopped. Merry Christmas.

There was an orange each for the children on Christmas morning. There was a gift each from Grandma, wrapped in tissue paper and red ribbon. Gertrude tore open her gift; two books. *Jane Eyre* and *Wuthering Heights*. How wonderful; she would read all day. *What a Christmas this will be. Oh thank you Grandma!*

There was left over bread from the night before, which Emma toasted with lard for breakfast. They were each allowed a mug of tea to wash it down with milk and sugar; A treat indeed.

The day after Christmas, Tom took *Jane Eyre* and *Wuthering*

Heights to the pawnshop in exchange for drinking money. He'd overspent the night before.

~

The test wasn't near as bad as Gladys had thought and she breathed a sigh of relief as she met Gertrude after class in the playground.

"Told ya," said Gertrude. She linked arms with her friend and they walked over to stand by the wall so that boys couldn't jump on their backs from behind. As they leaned against the wall, stamping their feet up and down to stop them from freezing, Gertrude felt a nagging ache at the bottom of her stomach, even down into the fronts of her thighs. She felt a little sick and had the strange feeling that the blood was draining out of her head.

"You all right, duck?" asked Gladys, as she saw her friend change colour.

Gertrude slid down the wall and sat on the dirty, frozen ground.

"Feel funny," she whispered. She put her head on her knees. A sudden warm gush came out between her legs. "I've peed me self," she croaked to Gladys. "Get me to the lav."

Gladys helped her friend to her feet and they scurried into the back house on the playground. It was big enough for several girls, having three holes in a row.

"Oh my God! I'm dyin.' I'm bleedin.'"

It was the way most girls found out about their period. Nobody ever told them ahead of time. Such things weren't discussed! Gladys ran to get the nearest person to a human on staff, Miss Finchley, the music teacher, who accompanied Gladys back to the back house in a calm, controlled manner, as was her nature.

"You have started your menstruation cycle, Gertrude. Stop that crying. Every woman begins their cycle around your age. You are not going to die. You are not going to bleed to death. Here is a rag for you to put into your undergarments between your legs."

Miss Finchley, prepared as always when she was summoned to the lav, handed over a wad of grey rag and Gertrude pushed it between her legs.

"Now, run along to your class. No more dawdling." Miss Finchley hurried back into the school without a second glance back.

Shaky and tear-streaked, the last thing Gertrude wanted to do was go back into class.

Gladys looked as bad as her friend as they stood looking at each other in the back house.

"What'll we do?" she said.

"Go home," Gertrude replied. "Come on."

They crept into the cloak room to get their coats and sneaked around the edge of the old brick building so they wouldn't be seen and ran along the deserted streets to Gladys' house. Her mum was at the chapel ladies meeting, her dad was working and as Gladys was the youngest, her siblings were either at school or work.

Gertrude lay down on the sofa with her eyes closed. "Menstrual cycle" Miss Finchley had called it! "Every woman had one!" "Nothing to get in a state about!" The rag between her legs felt sodden and uncomfortable. Now what would she do? Other rags?

"I need more rags, Glad!"

Gladys went into the rag bag in the corner cupboard and pulled out an old piece of towel. "This'll be good, duck. It's thick and soft."

Like a mother hen, Gladys fussed around her friend, rolling the piece of towel up into a soft sausage shape and giving it to Gertrude.

"What do I do with the wet one?" asked Gertrude.

"Dunno!" replied Gladys, her eyes wide at the thought of the blood soaked rag between Gertrude's legs. She was glad it wasn't her this was happening to. *But Miss Finchley had said "Every woman," hadn't she? That meant it would happen to her too. Oh not yet, please not yet,* thought Gladys.

Gertrude went to the lav up the yard and threw the old rag down the hole and put the new one in place. She would never tell Emma about this, nor anybody except Glad. She would deal with it herself. It probably would only happen once anyway and that would be that. *The bleeding will probably stop later today,* she thought, *then I'll have finished with my "menstrual cycle" and won't ever have to worry about it ever again.*

LONGTON MARKET

*G*ertie was thirteen years old when the first world war broke out. Suddenly everybody was excited, and all the young men were in uniform. Emma's brothers, Edwin and William, both joined up. Edwin at 30 years of age, and William at only seventeen, were both proud to serve and fight for their country against the Hun. All the children from Edward Street would go to the bottom of the street where the saffruck was and scramble over the endless piles of rubble and chipped pottery from the potbanks, shouting and screaming and "killing" each other. It was a great game. The war was supposed to last only a few months, but after three years it was still raging, with thousands dead and more thousands returning home terribly injured.

Gertie left school the year the war began to work at Deakin's Pottery. There was never any question about where she would work. She'd work in the Pots like everybody else. She had no regrets about leaving Cook Street School and she was ready to earn sixpence a week mould running for the mould maker. It meant carrying heavy moulds made of clay on her head or shoulder to and from the kiln for ten hours a day, which for a thin, undernourished thirteen-year-old was strenuous indeed. She often fainted at work, usually during "menstrual cycle" time, which had not just happened once as Gertrude had expected, but had made a regular appearance once a month. She recovered from each faint with the help of Miss Marshall and her smelling salts, and was sent back to carry on running moulds. She never had enough to eat and all her money was given to her mother, who bought more black stout with it. Gertie hated her life.

The parlour was put into action again, as Emma produced another son. Thomas, born just two years after William. He was welcomed with less enthusiasm than his brother, all the adults being preoccupied with thoughts of war. What future was there? What kind of life was ahead for this new baby?

Gertrude and Dolly seemed trapped in a cycle of work and watching the babies. The only positive thing coming from the nightly stout Emma drank was the rich milk she produced from the dark brew. Thomas was well fed with Emma's beer-soaked milk. He was a content baby, which was fortunate for the whole family, especially now William was toddling around and needed more watching.

Saturday night, after six o'clock, Gertrude, Gladys and a stream of other young teens, would make their pilgrimage to Longton Market for the last hour of shopping, which was cheap-deal time. Emma would give orders to Gertrude about how to spend the few pennies entrusted to her: "Broken biscuits, fatty scraps from the meat, dry bread (don't matter if there's some mold - it can be cut off), pigs feet or ears, keep your eyes open for fish heads as well." The market was a seething mass of kids and adults alike, all grabbing for the last of the damaged, unwanted food.

Gertrude usually did well; pushing her thin body between people and getting to the front of the line to grab a few fish heads from the bucket and throw a penny into the fishmonger's fishy hand. Broken biscuits were the hardest to get, with smaller kids crawling on all fours between legs to reach up and grab the paper bags full of the remnants of the week's biscuits. Fights often broke out. The swearing would have made a sailor blush. Every Saturday the same. If you wanted to eat, you'd better be ready to do battle for the food.

War, war, war, was all anybody talked about. Longton was full of troops.

The North Staffordshire Regiment was stationed close by, taking up the fields at the bottom of Longton Hall Lane with their tents and roughly made huts. Most of the boys from the local area joined this regiment including Gertrude's uncles. They couldn't wait to fight the Germans. Anything was better than their lives working down the pit or on the pot banks.

For the first time in their lives they had clothes that fit them, albeit woolen and itchy. They were supplied with undergarments. What were they? Most didn't know. Some had seen their fathers in combinations, a single garment with long legs and long sleeves, but they were only worn by old men, who couldn't stand the cold. Each old man only had one pair, which were washed usually once a year. Most men had a ring around their necks and wrists where they washed their faces and hands, but never their bodies.

Gladys and Gertrude would go down to Longton Station some Friday nights and wave the soldiers off. Gertrude bought a lipstick and the two girls smiled at the soldiers with their red lips, thinking they were the most glamorous young women in town. The soldiers responded with whistles and waves and sometimes a daring young man, knowing he was on his way to war, would even risk a kiss.

Of course it was strictly forbidden for Gertrude or Gladys to be seen with a member of the opposite sex. But could they help it if boys were walking to Longton Park at the same time? Or going to the market to buy broken biscuits? Or eating their lunch on the same wall outside the pot bank? Gert learned at an early age that men liked the way she looked, and she liked the way they looked at her.

SARAH'S WEDDING

*O*n a cool, rainy day in May, when Gertrude was sixteen years old, Emma's sister, Sarah, married Felix Marshall.

It was a wonderful day for Gertrude. It was the one time she remembered Tom in a starched white shirt, tie and jacket and Emma in a flowered frock. Tommy and Billy were dressed in the best Emma could find at the chapel jumble sale. Gertrude wore an almost-new blue skirt, which she had saved for weeks to buy along with a lovely white blouse, borrowed from Aunt Lena. Dolly scraped together an outfit from Aunt Sarah's cast-off clothes—they were the same size, although Sarah's clothes fitted a little snugly on Dolly's rounder figure. Gertrude and Dolly each managed to buy a hat, complete with flowers, at the thrift stall in the market and shared a small bottle of Evening in Paris perfume, bought at Woolworths with their pooled money - just a dab behind each ear. Tom actually shined his shoes, and went to the bath house the night before, to scour away the grime of months without bathing. Emma's sister, Lena, curled Emma's hair the morning of the wedding and let her borrow a quaint little blue hat. The hat didn't match the flowered dress, but Emma felt like a queen even so.

They walked, as a family, to the Longton Central Hall Methodist Chapel for the ceremony.

The only time the whole family had ever been together in public. Gertrude felt she was in a dream as she sat in the vast chapel between her mother and Tommy. She looked down at her feet, dressed in patent boots two sizes too big for her - they looked so beautiful! The massive pipe organ scared her at first until she became used to the loud, amplified sound. Gertrude had heard the organ from a distance before. She went to kids night at the chapel every Friday night for years, and she helped cook the sausages on Sunday in the hall, but it was in a different part of the building and the sound was muffled and distant. Now she heard the full effect of the instrument; she was awed by the way it filled the building and echoed through her entire body.

All of Emma's family was there, even Grandma Thursfield, along with dozens of people Gertrude had never seen before.

Then they were all on their feet and staring towards the back of the chapel as Sarah, on her Uncle James' arm, began the long walk down the centre aisle. What a vision she was. Gertrude thought she looked like an angel! All dressed in white, with a veil covering her face. Through the veil Gertrude could see Sarah's pretty mouth smiling as she saw Felix waiting for her at the front of the chapel.

The ceremony was serious and formal. The minister droned on and on, but Gertrude loved the music and the singing. She was amazed that Emma sang the songs along with everyone else, but not Tom.

The part when Felix lifted Sarah's veil and kissed her was Gertrude's favourite part, and she thought she would cry. She glanced at her mother, but Emma's face was set in stone as she stared at nothing. The vows the couple had taken a few minutes before were ringing in Emma's ears. She wanted to scream "It's all a lie!" and warn Sarah what was ahead for her, but she kept her silence as all the women had done when she had married Tom. *What a cruel joke a wedding was!*

When Sarah and Felix walked out of the chapel, everybody followed, gathering on the steps outside to throw rice at the young couple.

Led by the bride and groom, they all walked from the chapel to the Thursfield home, where a grand feast had been prepared. Gertrude's grandma and aunts had been busy for days preparing the wedding feast and it did them all credit: cold ham, boiled tongue, pig pudding, two different kinds of cheese, thick slices of crusty bread, real butter, pickled onions, ripe red tomatoes, cucumber and onion soaked in vinegar, and pickled red cabbage.

There was a two tier wedding cake, white and glossy, with tiny roses around the edge. Gertrude stuffed food into her mouth and prayed she wouldn't be sick. She thought the ginger pop probably helped keep everything down. The house was jammed with people, all laughing and having a good time. The beer flowed freely, and Tom drank more than his fair share. By the end of the day, Emma told Gertrude and Dolly to take the little boys home, while she went with Tom to continue drinking at the Brown Duck. The four siblings would be home and well hidden in their beds before they came rolling home. Gertrude always remembered Sarah's wedding as the most beautiful day she had ever known.

Another great thing happened as a result of the wedding - Sarah and Felix moved into a house just across the street from Emma and Tom in Edward Street. It was the very same house as theirs, a two up, two down tenement, but in every other way it was the complete opposite.

Felix had a good job in management at a pottery factory. He was manager of the "clay end" at Paragon China, with twenty people under him. He always wore a stiff collar, and black tie and tall black hat. He had a handlebar moustache and didn't smile often, but Gertrude knew just by being with him that he was a kind man.

Sarah's house had lace curtains, a carpet runner from the front door right through the parlour, a tablecloth with tiny blue flowers embroidered in the corners on her table in the kitchen. The whole house smelled clean and was clean. The horsehair sofa in the parlour had red velvet cushions at each end and an antimacassar draped over the back.

There was a framed painting of a lake and mountains over the fireplace in the parlour and a polished sideboard with a glass vase standing on it. The black grate in the kitchen was so shiny it showed a reflection of the room and there was always a pot hanging on the hook over the fire with lobby stew simmering away.

When Gertrude went to Aunt Sarah's she would always be given a bowl of the hot lobby and a crust of bread to dip into it.

Sarah's house became Gertrude's retreat and she spent much of her time there, along with Dolly. They were always treated kindly and it was a wonderful haven away from number twenty seven.

EDDIE

*E*mma gave birth to another son, Edwin, in 1917, probably as a result of the drinking party at Sarah's wedding. He was named after Emma's brother, Edwin, killed in action just a month before the baby's birth. For Gertie and her sister Dolly, the last thing they wanted was another baby in the house. They were both working and shared the second bedroom, and as long as they kept out of Tom's way, and kept some of their wages back from Emma, they managed to find a few joys in life.

Both sisters were striking to look at. Gertie was tall and slender, with jet black hair and beautiful dark brown eyes. Her skin was creamy and flawless and she carried herself gracefully. Dolly was smaller and rounder, with brown curly hair and dimples. Gertrude had a stream of admirers at work and soon was enjoying the flattering company of the young men in the town, but Gertie didn't want to "walk out" with anybody, and preferred to flirt, attracting the attention of young men who were willing to take her out for fish and chips, or to the Empire Theatre to watch the vaudeville.

Things were looking up at the potbank; no more mould running for Gertie. At sixteen she was now a gilder, putting gold bands around the "posh" china. The days were still ten hours, but now she could earn more money, especially because she had a keen eye and a steady hand, and the work went quickly, making her one of the highest paid decorators in the company. She never told Emma what she made, just gave her a shilling to shut her up and keep her in black stout. Gertrude spent the rest on a few good clothes, lipstick and cigarettes. Her hair, which was a rich glossy black, was cut in the newest short bob style, softly curled around her face, when other girls had their hair tied up in a tight bun.

She had a reputation in the neighbourhood. Old women would point their fingers and roll their eyes and say behind their hands, "She'll end up on her arse." Gertie hated them all. Hated the home she lived in and the street it was in. Most of all she hated the poverty and dirt. The smell was always there and it turned her stomach. She paid to go to the public baths twice a week—once a week was considered "very clean." She bathed in perfumed oil and washed her hair in the latest product, called shampoo. People said she was "above herself" and would come to no good. Let them say what they liked, Gertie wasn't going to stay around for long enough to care what they thought.

For Emma, baby Edwin was one more mouth to feed, one more nuisance to deal with and find room for. She made a small bed for William and Thomas in the second bedroom with the girls, so that she only had the new baby with her. The girls complained and complained, but Emma just told them to "shut the bloody hell up." She had enough to put up with in her miserable life. A drunk for a husband, who never acknowledged her except to swear at her, hit her, or bang her. Two teenage girls, who she rarely saw, both of them leaving early in the morning to go to work, and coming home only to change and go out again. Even on a Sunday, the two of them would be up and away to Central Hall Methodist, where they helped cook and eat a breakfast of sausage and oatcakes before the service. Emma didn't know why they bothered. *Probably some bloody boys there who they were making eyes at.*

Emma hated the dirt and smell of the house, now made worse by the baby puke and poop. No point cleaning it. Why bother. They lived in Longton, with black smoke belching from the kilns, covering the buildings, the people, the houses and their contents with the same black film of soot. Emma's whole world was black, it seemed. She, like all the women of Neck End, wore black, because it hid the dirt. The kids were all dressed in various shades of grey (maybe once white), and black. Tom was dressed in black from his cap to his boots. Even his skin was black, except for hands and face, from picking up shifts underground at the pit for extra money. Inside the house all the furniture was black, the only relief being the oilcloth table covering, which was a dull yellow. The bricks in the backyard were black and the lav door was black. *But,* the inside of the lav was whitewashed regularly. An irony, if you like.

Eddie was a sickly, pale-faced baby, whose hair never grew. Emma stopped begging Gert and Dolly to stay with him so she could get out.

"Not on your bloody life!" Gert would say, as she and Dolly ran through the front door.

How Eddie grew was a mystery. He seemed to throw back every bottle of discoloured milk fed to him through the rubber nipple of the crusted glass bottle. Emma's old, tired breasts had refused to provide milk, so she'd borrowed the bottle from the barmaid at the Brown Duck, whose sister had used it for her baby. As was the practice, Emma chewed up food, then fed the mush to Eddie once he was a few months old. He seemed to like the food better than the milk - probably because the flavour of black stout laced everything in Emma's mouth. Without the stout Emma would have gone mad. As the black liquid slid down her throat, she accepted her lot in life. Things would never change, but there would always be more stout.

CHANGE

"*W*ill there be change now?" was the cry from the workers of England, when the war ended in 1918.

"No change," should have been the answer.

The end of the war brought the soldiers who had survived the ordeal home. Emma's brother, William, had been killed a month before the war ended. He was just twenty one, and Grandma Thursfield never recovered from the news of his death. So much grief. Such a sacrifice. Her two sons, and a son-in-law all killed, for what? Would there be change?

The young men of Longton returned to the same streets of poverty and dirt. The jobs they had left were no longer theirs and men begged for work. Working for less and less money and longer and longer hours. The pottery owners and mine owners, already rich from the slave labour force before the war, became richer as production increased and the wage bill was reduced. Men worked in the clay dust or in the pit dust for a pittance, thankful at least for money to buy some food, pay the rent and always to buy beer, which often took priority over the food and rent, leaving families on the verge of eviction and starvation.

The lack of good food and adequate warmth took its toll on the working class. The streets making up Neck End, the worst of the worst in housing, saw death and sickness every day, the very young and elderly being the most vulnerable. Babies died on a regular basis, many not making it through the first days or weeks of life.

Mrs. Walters from Brook Street, next to Edward Street, birthed twenty three babies in twenty years and raised only five. The rest were either stillborn or died shortly after birth.

The kids living in Neck End would do the rounds of the houses where babies had died. Knocking on the door and asking, "can we see ya dead baby, missus?" They would troop into the parlour, saved for laying out the dead, as well as birthing babies, and walk solemnly past the tiny, shrouded figure in the pine box.

"Thanks missus!" they would yell as they left, running to the next dead-baby house.

Death was a part of everybody's life. Not many tears were shed. It was more of a worry where the cash was going to come from to pay for the burial. Most families made their own "boxes," but there was a fee for putting them into the ground at the cemetery. Collections were made between the neighbours; the poor giving to the poor what they couldn't spare. There was always enough somehow. The women scrounged together enough scraps of flour, sugar and fat to make sugar and butter cakes or jam tarts for the bereaved households. Emma always took around the dinged fruit and veggies to help out. Sarah always made an extra bowl of lobby.

Catholic families had a service at St. Gregory's Catholic Church and were buried in the Catholic cemetery.

Protestant families had a service at The Central Hall Methodist and were buried at the city cemetery. No working class folk attended the Church of England; it was the "posh" church for the "posh" people.

The walk to Longton Cemetery was made by most of the neighbours, as they followed behind the family in a bedraggled trail, each one thinking "who would be next?"

Diphtheria killed hundreds of the poor. So did tuberculosis. Whole families lost their lives to that particular horror, wasting away until nothing was left. The graves for those families were left open for the next corpse, which followed quickly, until the entire family was stacked one on top of the other. Jenny Birks, who lived three doors from Emma, watched her husband, Norman, and their six children succumb to consumption, before joining them at the top of the pile. No sugar and butter cake or jam tarts or fruit or lobby needed; there was nobody left!

No change. The miserable lives of the very poor were the same as they always were. The decadent lives of the mine and pottery owners were the same as they always were.

The rich lived in Trentham and Barlaston, in mansions surrounded by walls, with iron gates securing the entrance to their domain. They employed servants, who lived in: Butler, housekeeper, cook, scullery maids, ladies' maids, valets, chauffeur, gardener. Daily help was also hired to help with the gardening, in season, and extra scullery maids for large parties. It was a plum job to be hired in one of the big houses, and much desired by the working people of Longton. Not much money and long hours, but enough to eat and a bed to sleep in high up in the garrets of the house; one day off every week, when the servants would walk the five miles to visit family, often sharing their meagre wages to buy much needed food. Of course, the prestigious positions of butler, housekeeper, valet, and lady's maid were filled by highly trained individuals, who had spent their lives in service.

Mary Ann Thursfield, Emma's sister, was one such lucky woman. She had left her husband, after sixteen miscarriages, and was living with her sister, Sarah, and desperately looking for a job. Mary Ann's friend, Sheila Bradbury from Marsh Street, was a "casual" scullery maid at the Johnson Mansion in Trentham and kept her ear to the ground, when she was there, for the chance of a permanent position. When the housekeeper sent for Sheila to work in the kitchen, to replace the scullery maid, who had "gone astray," which meant "was pregnant," until a replacement could be found, Sheila mentioned the chance of a job to Mary Ann. The following day Mary Ann went with Sheila to the big house and met with the housekeeper, Mrs. Broadmoor. Mary Ann was a quiet, hard-working young woman and the house-keeper thought her well suited for the scullery maid's job. Mary Ann moved into the Johnson mansion the following week.

"Mary Ann's got a job with Johnson's," was the chorus around the streets.

"She's made for life!" said the old women.

"She'll never be hungry!" thought Gertrude. "Or wake up in this hole. She'll be in a beautiful house every day, with clean sheets to sleep in and good food to eat. I wish it was me."

Gertrude trudged to the pot bank at seven o'clock on Monday morning, through the slush and dirt, wishing she was Aunt Mary Ann in the big house in Trentham, helping cook the breakfast.

Gertrude vowed she would get out of this place. *I will not spend my life working in the pots, turning into an unhappy, down-trodden, cruel woman like my mother. Change? Yes, there would be change for me - I'm sure of it.*

OUT ON THE TOWN

*E*ngland was slowly recovering from four years of war. The Potteries would remain depressed. Life, for the working people, would remain harsh. A year after the war, workers worked for small wages, considering themselves lucky to have a job. Never-ending poverty clung to the streets of Longton. Nothing changed for the people living there.

Emma cleaned her step every day and left everything else filthy. The boys were seven, six and two—no more babies, thank God! Tommy and Billy went to school, leaving Eddie playing on the dirty rug in front of the grate. At least Eddie had all six blocks of wood and the one small wooden car to himself while the big boys were out of the house.

Thoughts of Gertrude crowded Emma's head. She'd always been a thorn in her side.

Full of cheek. Stubborn as a mule. Thinks she's something. Little snot.

Emma's thoughts rambled on, as she flicked crumbs from the morning toast onto the floor to join the crumbs from all the other pieces of toast.

She knew why she was particularly bitter this morning. Four days waiting for a "show." She was never "late," unless……. perish the thought! Had that one night, when he'd come home not drunk enough to pass out, done it? It was hardly a memorable night— hardly a successful coupling between two tired, half-drunk strangers, who were married but not connected to each other— barely speaking to each other these days. He'd gone through the motions, but Emma hadn't given it a second thought, certainly never imagining that such a pathetic attempt would result in another unwanted child.

As the days turned to weeks, Emma knew the truth of it. Tom ignored her growing girth, refusing to believe his ill luck. Another mouth to feed. He'd got his sons, now here was that fool woman getting herself knocked up again. He wasn't even sure it was his. He didn't remember doing anything to produce another baby. Maybe his mess of a wife had been letting somebody else dip his wick.

"You bloody cow!" Tom yelled at Emma. "Whose kid is that ya've got in there?"

"Shut your gob," Emma yelled back. Eddie started to cry and crawled under the table with his blocks.

"It's not mine," Tom persisted, packing his pipe with tobacco.

"I wish!" retorted Emma, flinging toast and dripping onto his plate. "How would ya know. Ya can't remember nothing. Ya drink ya face off and come home with a skin full. Ya don't know if ya did it or not do ya?"

Tom lit his pipe. Puffing furiously and sending clouds of smoke into the already stifling air. He didn't say anything else to Emma, just to Eddie under the table, still crying.

"Shut bloody up, you," he shouted at the two-year-old, only making him cry more.

Tom got up and, still puffing on his pipe, headed out the back door and up the yard to sit in the lav. How he hated his life, his wife, his kids.

Over the next months, Emma picked up the baby stuff from Sarah and went through the motions, once again, of preparing for the new life. The parlour was cleaned and the bottom drawer from Dolly's chest was made ready. Newspapers were collected and the midwife from the next street given notice of the approximate date.

In the cold, early hours of a Thursday morning in November, a baby girl was born too soon. No time to send for the midwife. The baby, born in the bed upstairs with hardly a pain to herald her arrival, was weak and underweight. Emma wrapped it in an old towel, with the afterbirth still attached, and waited for the midwife. Tom came clattering into the house with the same woman who had delivered all their children, grumbling about being awakened in the middle of the night and how cold it was outside to be traipsing about fetching midwives.

"Upstairs," he indicated with his thumb towards the stairs off the kitchen. "Didn't even make it into the parlour."

"Here we go then," said Mrs. Hodges, huffing and puffing her way up the narrow winding staircase.

The baby was waving its arms around slowly and sucking in air in tiny gasps. Mrs. Hodges cut the cord and wrapped the placenta in newspaper, putting it into the empty chamber pot under the bed. Then she turned all her attention to the baby girl, rubbing her in the towel gently, breathing into her mouth, holding her close to her buxom chest, keeping her warm. Mrs. Hodges had delivered many babies over her twenty five years as a midwife. She had no medical training and had learned from her own mother the skills of childbirth. She rarely lost a baby that was born alive, although there had been numerous stillbirths in those years. Emma's baby began to breathe easier and lost her palour, her finger tips and toes turning pink. She let out a weak cry before settling into a deep sleep on Mrs. Hodges' breast.

"There you go, little one," cooed the midwife, still rubbing the baby's legs and arms gently under the towel. Gertrude and Dolly had both been awake for hours, listening to the sounds in the next room. Now, they both peeked in the door and, seeing Tom wasn't there, crept in to look at their latest sibling.

"She's a bit small," said Mrs. Hodges. "But I've seen smaller. She'll do all right once she gets some milk into her."

"Mam didn't have any milk for Eddie," said Dolly. "But I know where the bottle is and Mam already bought some Nestles baby mix to put in the milk." Dolly was a mine of information regarding babies, and Mrs. Hodges was relieved that Dolly appeared to know what she was doing. This baby would need all the help she could get.

"Off you go then, Dolly," said Mrs. Hodges. "You go make up a bottle and warm it nicely. We'll see if we can't get some milk into her right away. Gertrude, you can go and fetch a bowl of warm water and a cloth of some kind. I need to clean up the baby and the mother."

Gertrude scurried down the stairs, passing Tom snoring in his chair and joining Dolly in the back kitchen. Dolly already had a kettle of water on the hob over the fire, and had added extra coal to get a good flame. She was now carefully mixing the Nestles mix with milk in the glass baby bottle and giving it a shake. Gertrude looked around for something to hold the water and found a tin bowl under the sink, which she scrubbed with cold water. There was a fairly decent looking rag in the rag bag hanging on the nail in the corner and Gertrude ripped off enough to make a cloth. She put some of the hot water from the kettle into the bowl and hurried back up the stairs, with Dolly behind her carrying the bottle, rubber tit securely fastened to the end.

Mrs. Hodges set to work, washing the baby and dressing it in the prepared clothes from the parlour. She swaddled her tightly in the piece of bed sheet she found folded under the baby clothes and handed the clean, dressed baby to Dolly, who attempted to get the milk into her. Mrs. Holdges turned her attention to Emma, washing her gently and finding some clean drawers. She took the sodden bedsheet off the bed and placed a piece of towel for Emma to lie on. When she left the house, the baby was sucking the milk slowly and Emma was sleeping. Gertrude had gone back to bed.

They named the baby Marjorie, although she was always called Madge. She was born sad and stayed sad. Without Dolly's care, the tiny baby probably wouldn't have survived. Dolly left a note for the milkman to leave an extra bottle of milk every day. Tom grumbled about paying for more milk, but didn't put a stop to it. Dolly made sure Madge had a bottle before she went to work every morning, and another one when she came home after work. She bathed her and cuddled her and fed her again before she went to bed, often getting up in the night, when she heard Madge crying to warm another bottle of milk. What happened during the day while Dolly was at work, she didn't think about—Emma was disinterested in the baby to say the least. Madge survived despite her mother, due to her sister's persistent and tender care.

Gertrude saw the new baby only as another nuisance. *Let Dolly care for her if she wants to. I'm not going to feed her and look after her while Emma sits there drinking stout. Dolly's too soft. Our mam just takes advantage of her. Well, that's not for me. It's not my baby.*

~

"Want to go up town tonight, Gert?" asked Gladys as they walked home from work on a warmer than usual Friday in May of 1920. The friends were eighteen now and always looking for a night out away from the slums they lived in.

"Why not!" said Gertrude, brushing a black smut off her nose. "Better than being stuck in our house with kids screaming half the night."

After a tea of chips and bread and butter, soaked in malt vinegar, Gertie tripped up the stairs to get ready to call on Gladys, who lived one sorry street over.

"Don't think you're goin' out," Emma screamed up the stairs. "It's my bloody turn to get out o' this dump. You can stay 'ere with these little sods. Dolly's working at the Empire."

"No bloody way," Gertie shouted back, glossing her lips with red lipstick and brushing at her hair furiously. "Find some other mug."

She clattered down the stairs in her new shoes, pushed Emma out of the way and headed for the door.

"Get back 'ere, you," her mother started after her.

Gertie was too young and too quick for the older woman, who was, by now, folded in layers of extra fat and slow on her feet. The door slammed in her face as she reached it. Now she was stuck in here again for the night. The children started screaming; not enough food, not enough sleep, nothing to play with, nobody who loved them – screaming was all they knew. Emma slopped past them to the corner cupboard and reached for the black stout and opener, snapped off the bottle top and swigged at the dark, thick liquid. What else was there in her life anyway? The screaming continued.

"Shut bloody up," Emma yelled at the tear-streaked babies.

Gertie ran up the street, passing the grimy smoke-caked row houses with the red steps. Funny that! The women always cleaned their steps. Every morning, every woman would be out there polishing and reddening their front steps until they shone. The only touch of colour in an otherwise colourless world of grey and black.

Gladys was waiting by her house. She didn't want Gertie to knock or call, or she'd be in real trouble. Gladys' dad would have had her hide if he knew who she was going out with.

"She's a right little tart is that one," her dad would say, when he saw Gertie in the street. "You keep well away from the likes of her, do ya hear me?"

"Iya, Glad." Gertie tucked her arm through her friend's and they walked towards the bus stop giggling, enjoying the fact they were away from Edward Street and on their way up town. They hurried along the narrow pavement to Market Street to catch the tram.

Hanley was the only one of the five towns with any life in the City of Stoke-on-Trent. That's where the best shops were, the banks, the hotels—well two hotels anyway. That's where the best pubs were and the biggest picture house. And that's where Gert and Gladys were headed on that Friday night of 1920.

The tram was overcrowded, standing room only, with men coming home from the pits and pots. Half of them covered in coal dust, the other half covered in clay dust. Funny really to see them, half black, half white, with just the circles around their eyes showing their real colour and their lips looking like a fleshy pink gash. They all wore flat caps and they were all silent, worn out by the sheer hard work of a ten or twelve hour day of digging out the coal or making and stacking the pots. The "working class" they were called. A defeated class. A miserable, depressed, hungry, drunken class. All they knew was work and beer and fags—tobacco was on everybody's lips these days, women included.

The rich pointed fingers.

"Why do they complain they don't have enough money. They have enough for beer and cigarettes don't they?"

"Walk a mile in my shoes," should have been the answer. "Work as hard as I do. Feel as hopeless and helpless. Watch your babies die before they have a chance to take their first breath. Live on chips and bread and lard. Never feel warm, or fed, or loved."

Gertrude looked around the bus at the worn faces and stooped bodies, and her eyes filled with disgust. She shouldn't be part of this "class." She couldn't stand their acceptance of all that was bad. Couldn't stand that they didn't want to change things, or didn't care what happened to them. They lived and they died. Life expectancy in the Potteries was forty two years of age, by which time they were old and exhausted and ready to die. Not for her. She would get out.

It was a fine dry night for a change. Nice enough to wear her new cream-coloured dress with the little black bolero jacket. It had cost her eight weeks' pay, but was worth every penny. It was stylish and too short, coming to mid-calf, showing off her wonderful shapely ankles, as she clipped along in her dainty shoes. Gladys was plain by comparison. Her mam still bought her clothes and she, like all other Pottery girls, was dressed cheaply. A navy blue ankle-length dress made of cheap material, with no style and long enough to conceal any hint of legs. Gladys didn't mind much, as long as she was with Gert and out on the town, she was having fun.

"Lend me ya lipstick, duck," Gladys said, as they left the tram, stopping to smear it onto her lips outside a hat shop, where she could see her reflection in the window pane.

The girls paused outside the North Staffordshire Hotel to look through the steamy windows. It wasn't the usual run of the mill pub, like the pubs on every street corner throughout the five towns, where the men went to drink. Serious drinking, and maybe a game of dominoes, darts or crib. Women were never seen in the corner pubs. But the North Staffs Hotel was different. Meals were served and gents took their ladies out for the night. It was a "safe" pub for girls. Although to even go into a pub unescorted was frowned upon, and gave such girls an instant bad reputation. They weren't actually on the street, trying to turn a trick, but they were advertising that they were available as single girls, which was considered very forward—not done by "nice" girls.

It was crowded. Full of people laughing and talking. This was a step up from the working class, and that's why Gert loved going there. They pushed open the big wooden doors, with the brass handles running from top to bottom, and squinted through the smoke-filled room, looking for a table.

"Over there, Gert." Gladys had spotted a small round table with two stools way over by the lavs. They weaved their way through the crowd and managed to snatch the stools, just as a young man and his lady almost beat them to it. The young man glared at them in disgust and stood with his hands on his hips, but his lady friend just pulled him away and stuck her nose in the air at the girls. Gert and Gladys giggled at them for being so ridiculous.

"What ya havin,' Glad?"

"Gin, like always,"

"Two gin and oranges." Gert ordered the drinks from the barmaid, who looked down her nose at them as if they were something crawling up cabbage.

Whenever they were at the North Staffs Hotel, Gert would always attract attention within minutes of walking in. The usual parade of young men would stop by to flirt with her and beg to see her home. She loved the flirting, but took none of them seriously. They would buy her drinks and often a meal, which was a bonus for her hungry, gin-sodden stomach, but she would make no promises of walks home, or no encouragement of an encounter if that's what the young men were seeking. Although she looked the part of a good-time girl, she had never had a steady boyfriend and didn't intend to. All the young men she saw were far beneath her expectations, and she would never have lowered herself to such a level.

She leaned forward as the current young man lit her cigarette. Through the swirling smoke, her half-closed eyes looked across the room and into the eyes of an older gentleman, who was gazing at her with an expression of amusement.

PART III
TOGETHER

EDWARD

*G*ertrude held his eyes. Steel grey they were. He was an old gent, but something about the smile on his lips and the way he looked at her, froze her gaze. He finally looked away, answering a question posed by his male companion, whose back was facing Gertrude.

"What are ya starin' at, Gert?" asked Gladys, turning around to see what had attracted her friend's attention.

"Nothin'. Just thought I'd seen somebody I know, but I didn't."

"Are we havin' somethin' to eat? I've got an extra sixpence in my pay this week." Gladys went on. "I feel like a meat pie. How 'bout you?"

"All right. I could manage a meat pie. Go order two."

As Gladys went to order the pies, Gertrude's eyes wandered back to the steel grey eyes. He met her eyes boldly and there was that smile again. Gertrude looked away quickly. He was old enough to be her father. Why did she keep looking at him? She felt herself getting red and realized she was blushing, something she never did, until now.

The girls ate their pies and drank their gin. Gertrude could think of nothing but the grey eyes and the gentleman on the other side of the room. Why did she feel this way? She didn't like old men. She'd lived with Tom long enough to know what old men were like. But this was a gentleman. She could tell just by looking at him. Lovely clothes. Clean and shaven. And those eyes.

Edward made his way across the room, Gertrude noticing how tall and slender he was. He bowed his head slightly as he reached her table and captured her eyes once more.

"Please excuse the interruption," Edward began. "My name is Edward Wrightson. You must think me very rude, but I wanted to meet you and, as we have no mutual acquaintance here, I have taken the liberty of making the introduction myself."

His voice was cultured and deep. He spoke like a gentleman. He looked like a gentleman. Gertrude was enraptured.

"Well, pleased to meet you Mr. Wrightson, I'm sure." Gertrude replied. "I'm Gertrude Bryan and this is me friend Gladys." She felt herself blush again, aware that her voice was neither cultured nor genteel.

Edward bowed briefly in Gladys' direction, before engaging Gertrude's eyes again.

The smile never left Edward's lips as he drank in all that was Gertrude. Her deep brown eyes and rich dark hair. Her unblemished, smooth skin. Her slender figure, with the hint of full breasts pushing against the cheap dress. Edward could see that she was very young. Younger than a daughter might be. What was it that made her so irresistible? He hadn't felt like this since he had met Clara all those many years ago.

"This is very forward of me," Edward continued. "Would you do me the honour of meeting me for dinner tomorrow night? I would like to take you to The Grand Hotel. You, of course, could bring along your friend as chaperone."

Gertrude looked at her friend across the table. Gladys was sitting there with her mouth open.

"What do you think?" Gertrude asked her.

"Dunno."

Gertrude realized it was all up to her to make the decision. She wasn't going to get anything coherent out of Gladys. It would be nice to go for dinner at the Grand. She had only walked past it once. It wasn't a place for the likes of her, and where she was from. How she would love a chance to go inside and see it for herself. What would the dinner be like? She bet it wasn't pie and chips!

Gertrude looked up at Edward and gave him the tiniest of smiles—she didn't want to appear too eager.

"Sounds like fun to me," she said. "We could meet you outside this pub if you like and we could walk over to the Grand."

Edward was shocked she had said yes so quickly. He thought pleading would have been in his future somewhere. He beamed with pleasure.

"No, no. I will come and pick you up in my car. Just give me your address."

Not bloody likely, thought Gertrude. *Imagine him driving to Edward Street. The car wouldn't fit down the narrow street anyway. He certainly wouldn't stay around long enough to pick me up if he saw where I was from. It's only because I'm all dressed up so nice that he thinks I'm a "cut above" the regular poor.*

"No," cut in Gertrude quickly. "That won't do. I'll only come if we can meet you here."

"Very well." Edward agreed. "If you insist. Would seven o'clock be suitable?"

"That would be very suitable," answered Gertrude, now in a rush to be gone.

Edward turned and walked away and after a few words with his friend, strode through the double doors and out into the night.

Gertrude and Gladys sat at their table staring at each other. Neither spoke or moved.

Finally Gladys broke the silence.

"What are you thinkin'?"

"What do you mean?"

"Sayin' we'll meet him tomorra?"

"I just want to see the inside of the Grand Hotel, duck. To eat a meal there. Can you imagine—us two from Neck End, in the Grand? Anyroad, he seems like a nice gent, don't ya think?"

"He's an old man, Gert. He's older than me dad. What's he up to anyroad, wanting to take us out? He could be up to no good, duck, that's what I think."

"I think he's on the up and up," declared Gertrude. "He wouldn't have invited you to come as chaperone if he was an old lech. Such a gent though. Did you see his clothes? Did you smell how clean he was? I thought he was lovely!"

With that, the girls paid for their pie and gin and made their way back to the tram and back to Longton and the grim streets of the poor.

THE GRAND

*W*hat would she wear? Dinner at the Grand. With a gent. She only had one really decent outfit and she'd worn that last night. Gertrude looked through the small pile of clothes in the cardboard box by her bed and groaned. She was going to look shabby, and the gent, Edward, was going to be ashamed and sorry he'd ever asked her out. Then she remembered, there was a jumble at the chapel that day from ten until two. If she went over there by opening, she'd get the best picks. Sometimes there was stuff from the big houses—Aunt Sarah once told her she'd heard Mrs. Farthingham the owner's wife from Paragon China, had given several boxes of her clothes to the chapel jumble.

At nine thirty, Gertrude was among the first twenty or so in line outside the chapel side door. She'd have to be quick and on her toes once the doors opened. The other women in line would be elbowing their way in, grabbing at all the best stuff. Gertrude had a shilling in her pocket, which was plenty to buy the nicest things.

At ten o'clock on the dot, they heard the locks turn and the heavy door swung open. They all charged down the entry and into the big hall attached to the chapel. Tables were set up around the outside of the room, with "chapel ladies" behind each one, looking smug and stern. Gertrude quickly eyed the tables and made for one in the far corner, where none of the other women had yet reached, many of them absorbed with kids clothing nearer the door.

Jackpot! There was a whole pile of elegant-looking blouses and a couple of good skirts. Gertrude held them up to eye the size and decided on a pretty blue skirt and a cream blouse. Just the thing. She paid her eight pence and still had four pence left over, what a bargain.

She went straight to bath street and rented a bathroom for thirty minutes. She had scented soap with her and sat in the few inches of hot water allowed, washing her hair first with lavender scented shampoo, so she could rinse it in cleanish water before washing the rest of her body. The towel from the bath house, which was included in the rental, was rough and grey, but Gertrude felt a happy surge of excitement as she dried off. *A new skirt and blouse and dinner at the Grand with a gent.*

"Don't think you're going' out again, miss muck," yelled Emma, as Gertrude ran up the stairs to get ready, bag in hand containing the "new" clothes.

"Get back down here. I'm goin' out, not you," Emma ranted. "These bloody kids are driving me mad. It's your turn, lazy, idle, cat! You were out last night. You're not goin' again. If I spend one more night here on me own, I'll kill the whole lot of ya, I swear. Bloody horrible life, I've got. You can take your turn. They're your brothers."

"Shut your gob, you old bitch," Gertrude yelled back, from

the upstairs room. "They're your bloody kids, not mine. I am goin' out and you can't stop me."

Emma started up the stairs at that point, but Gertrude put an old chair under the door knob of the bedroom, so Emma couldn't open the door, and continued to get ready.

Emma banged on the bedroom door, still threatening what she would do to Gertrude. When she realized the door was not going to open, she gave it a final kick before hurtling herself down the stairs again, back to the kitchen and the screaming kids.

Dolly had a weekend job at the picture house ushering people to their seats in the dark, so missed all the "fun" of Emma's tirade. Gertrude waited until the kids stopped screaming and Emma stopped shouting, guessing that the black stout was easing the mood once more. She opened the door carefully and crept down the stairs, shoes in hand, until she could peek around the door at the bottom. Emma was sitting in "his" chair with the bottle of stout in her hand. The boys were playing with pieces of chipped china from the saffruck, pretending it was English planes, bombing Germany, while Eddie watched them. Madge was asleep in the corner of the sofa. Gertrude made a final dash for the front door, but nobody bothered. Emma had given up for today—she was stuck looking after the kids, as always.

Gladys was waiting at the end of Marsh Street and waved when she saw her friend.

"Look at you, Gert. All dressed up. Where did you get the new outfit?"

"The chapel jumble this morning. Isn't it lovely? I dropped on lucky. I think it must be from an owner's house, it's so

classy." Gertrude twirled around in the street, hands in the air.

The two girls made their usual trip, by tram, to Hanley and walked to the North Staffs Hotel. Edward was waiting in the high street, looking at the books in the window of the book store next to the pub. His face lit up when he saw Gertrude and Gladys walking towards him.

"I'm so happy you could come," he said. "Let's take a walk over to the hotel, where dinner awaits."

The girls walked in front of Edward, giggling and nudging each other as they walked. Gertrude looked over her shoulder, stealing a glimpse of Edward and thinking he was the most handsome man she'd ever seen - even though he was so old.

The Grand Hotel was so *grand*. Gertrude thought she would faint when she stepped inside. The thick carpets, the chandeliers, velvet drapes at all the windows, ornate wallpaper, plush sofas and chairs. Gertrude and Gladys tried not to stare at everything. Edward escorted them both, in his elegant way, to the dining room, where a table was awaiting them, a round table for three, with fresh flowers in the centre. The gas lighting was elegant and soft and shed a warm glow on the table. The two girls from Neck End thought they were in paradise, they had never even imagined a place like this.

Edward went over the menu with them, realizing, after their blank stares at the food lists, that they had no idea what it said or meant. He suggested food they may try and they both settled on the same thing, a leek soup to begin, followed by breaded chicken with a mushroom sauce, served with scalloped potatoes and mixed sautéed vegetables. Edward ordered lobster with wild rice, which caused frowns of concern from the girls.

A white wine was ordered, and tiny mini rolls of bread with paté were brought to the table for them to enjoy whilst waiting for their meal. Gertrude could hardly eat, even though the food was the best she had ever seen or tasted. There was a lump in her throat that refused to move. Every time she looked at Edward, he was looking at her. Her knees and head felt "wobbly" and she wondered if she was coming down with something. Slowly, as Edward talked, telling them about his travels and all the wonderful things he had seen, she began to relax. The wine stopped the "wobbly" feeling, and she just felt warm and fuzzy. She forgot Edward was an old man, as she watched him, seeing his grey eyes dance as he talking about America, and the wonderful years he had spent there both as a boy and as a man.

They ate their way through the delicious meal, taking their time to savour the dishes and finishing with a chocolate mousse served in tall glasses and eaten with long silver spoons. Edward wanted to drive them both home, but they insisted they would make their own way. He asked Gertrude if she would meet him in Hanley Park the next afternoon, at two-o-clock, to hear the brass band play at the band stand. This time she didn't even look at Gladys, or hesitate, but agreed immediately.

SUNDAY IN THE PARK

"See you tomorrow then, Gert," Gladys said when they were at the top of Marsh Street.

"No thanks," Gert replied. "I'm goin' on my own this time."

"You're not," gasped Gladys. "What will people think?"

"People won't think nothin', 'cause they won't know, will they? Nobody's goin' to tell them, are you?"

Gladys looked at her friend and shook her head. She knew she was heading for trouble, but she wouldn't be saying anything to anybody about Edward.

Gertrude headed for home with her head full of Edward. He wanted to see her again—tomorrow. She couldn't wait to be on her own with him. She couldn't wait to hear more of his stories and adventures. She thought him the most wonderful man she had ever met, but then all other men were the men of Longton, not to be compared with a real gentleman.

Emma was snoring in the chair by the fire when Gertrude walked in. Two of the boys were asleep on the floor in front of the dying fire, the babies were nowhere to be seen. Probably upstairs already. Gertrude crept past them through to the back and ran up the yard to the lav. Far cry from The Grand Hotel lav, which was painted pale blue with gold motifs around the ceiling, flush toilets, soft tissue to wipe instead of newsprint, hot water to wash your hands and real little towels to dry. Gertrude ran her hand under the cold water tap in the back kitchen then tiptoed past the sleeping boys and up the stairs, where Dolly was waiting for her.

"Mam is after you. She was ranting all night about you being selfish and going out again. Better watch out tomorrow or she'll have your hide. Where were you anyroad?"

Gertrude undressed quickly and slid into her bed.

"Doll, I was having dinner at The Grand Hotel in Hanley. You should have seen it. It was lovely. Me and Glad went with a real gent, named Edward. I'm meeting him tomorra at Hanley Park."

"You can't go tomorra Gert! Mam will kill ya!"

"Don't worry about Mam. I'm going to ask Aunt Sarah to come over and watch the babies and the boys, so Mam can do what she wants for an hour."

Sunday was going to be wonderful for Gertrude and nobody, especially her mam, was going to ruin it for her.

Aunt Sarah came over at one o'clock and took the kids to her house to play, leaving Emma drinking her stout in peace. Emma had gone berserk when she found out Gertrude was going out, placated by the news that Sarah would take the kids.

Gertrude dressed carefully in an old skirt, but a nice pale blue blouse from last month's chapel jumble. The day was sunny for a change. A great day for sitting in the park listening to a band.

Edward was waiting at the park gates, looking distinguished. He walked towards Gertrude as he saw her coming down the street.

"Where's your friend?" he asked.

"She couldn't come today," lied Gertrude.

"Too bad," lied Edward.

They strolled through the park without talking, but somehow content to be beside each other. Edward couldn't remember the last time he was in a park, certainly not with a young lady. He saw several people glance their way as they walked past. Probably wondering if they were father and daughter, Edward though. He had a lifetime of experience when it came to women and Gertrude had none when it came to men. He had to admit, he was quite bowled over with this beautiful girl. He didn't feel the age gap, but felt like he had when he had first met Clara, a warm, wonderful glow inside, which overwhelmed him.

They sat side by side to listen to the brass band from the local colliery play with gusto. Edward so arranged his chair that he could see Gertrude's face as she listened. Every moment spent with her enchanted him more. Gertrude could feel him watching her, prickles danced up and down her spine and her face glowed with the attention.

As the band stopped, Edward took Gertrude's hand as she rose from the chair.

"I would like to spend more time with you, Gertrude," he said softly. "In fact, would you be able to meet me tomorrow night? I would like to show you where I live. Mrs. Bennet will cook a meal for us. I could pick you up at six o'clock."

"I would love to meet you tomorra," Gertrude said, looking up into the grey eyes. "I'll meet you outside the pub if you like."

Edward knew by now that she wasn't going to let him see where she lived, so agreed to the arrangement as he walked her to the tram stop.

"See you tomorrow then," he called as she stepped onto the tram.

Gertrude waved as the tram pulled away, smiling and enjoying Edward's approving gaze.

TWO WEEKS OF BLISS

*M*rs. Bennet cooked a lovely lamb roast, with new potatoes and sweet peas, dressed with mint sauce. Edward had picked up Gertrude outside the pub and driven her to his house in Alsager. The car ride was enough to send Gertrude into raptures, having never been in a car before. The house was equally surreal, tucked into a garden full of trees and shrubs, the picturesque stone cottage, like a fairy tale to Gertrude. Inside, red tiled floor, with rich deep carpet squares, lush sofa and two armchairs flanked by carved tables. The tiny dining room, with round table and four chairs, was laid for dinner. Mrs. Bennet served the meal and discretely left, leaving a delicious chocolate cake on the sideboard for dessert.

Gertrude was enraptured with everything. Edward had to encourage her to eat the meal, as she was so distracted with all she saw around her. The lovely pictures on the walls, the china—all matching, wine glasses, water glasses, gleaming cutlery, linen napkins. She thought about her usual "tea" at home, with chips in a newspaper from the chippy, thrown into the middle of the table for everybody to help themselves. Tin mugs to drink from, if you were lucky. No such thing as cutlery or napkins or glass.

Edwards' intentions were not honourable. He knew he had found something very precious and was on fire, for the first time since Clara, to make love to Gertrude. He had no idea what her background was, only guessing it was very poor, because of the accent, lack of manners, and poor clothing. He didn't give it a second thought. He wanted to take this chance to be happy again. Maybe his last chance to love and be loved.

Gertrude was in heaven. This was beyond anything she had seen or done before. The food was so delicious and the house so clean and beautiful. Then there was Edward, the icing on the cake. He was so handsome. So attentive to her. She noticed everything about him—his beautiful hands, his graceful movement, his greying temples, his straight nose, his broad shoulders. A different species than the men she knew.

Edward remained a gentleman after dinner, sitting on the armchair with Gertrude on a stool at his feet, reading poetry to her. She couldn't understand any of it, but loved the sound of his voice. They drank more wine and ate thick slices of the chocolate cake, Edward laughing as he brushed away the crumbs around Gertrude's mouth. He drove her to the tram stop as usual. This time lightly kissing her on the cheek, whispering how much he had enjoyed their evening together.

Gertrude's next two weeks were full of Edward. She stopped going home after work, taking a change of clothes with her to the pot bank, then getting the tram to Hanley to meet him. Emma was furious to such a point that Gladys offered the sofa at her house for Gertrude to sleep on. Gertrude was happy to sleep at Gladys' house instead of doing battle with Emma. She only needed the sofa for three nights anyway, then she didn't need somewhere else to sleep.

Edward loved her. He had said so. They had slowly moved from touching each other's hands, to caressing each other's hair, to a gentle kiss on the lips. Too slow for Edward, but he wanted everything to be perfect for Gertrude. All he could think of was making love to her. It consumed his every waking moment and it took all of his self control, when he was with her, not to snatch her up and rip off her clothes - to ravish her! Clara was still a dim memory, but Gertrude chased away all distant thoughts of the woman Edward had loved so long ago. This was real. Gertrude was immediate and ageless. Everything about her fuelled Edward's love and desire for her. Her luscious black hair, her slightly crooked teeth, her flawless complexion, her slender figure, her full breasts, her laugh, her almond shaped long-lashed dark brown eyes. Edward felt twenty-five again.

Gertrude, for her part, was swept away by this tall, handsome, genteel man, who talked in a posh accent. She had never been treated even as a real person before, and to have this wonderful man treat her with such respect and tenderness touched something inside her. Tears were often on the edge of her eyelids, threatening to tip over and spill down her cheeks, as Edward held her close and whispered wonderful things to her. No harsh words, only sweet, loving words. No criticism, only encouragement. No ugly swearing, only tender tones, filled with love.

Moving from kissing and caressing into the bedroom was an easy transition. Saturday was spent at the cottage, walking the lanes and stepping over the styles into farmers' fields, full of buttercups. Sitting under a giant oak tree, where Gertrude made buttercup chains and placed an extra long one around Edward's neck, kissing the tip of his nose in the process. Eating the picnic lunch, prepared by Mrs. Bennet. Sharing a bottle of white wine, poured into two glasses carefully wrapped in white linen napkins. Gertrude thought it was a dream. She lay back in the grass after lunch and squinted up at the sun finding its way through the giant oak leaves. Edward watched her, entranced, as always, by her beauty and the feeling he had that this was the first time she had done this.

The fresh air and long walk made them both sleepy and they cuddled down into the soft cushions when they were back in the cottage. Mrs. Bennet had left them a pork roast for supper, ready to reheat in the stove when they were ready. Not yet, though. Gertrude fell asleep first, breathing rhythmically on Edward's chest. Edward buried his face into her hair, drinking in the soapy smell and eventually succumbing to a contented sleep himself.

It was dark outside when they finally roused. They were both famished. Edward hurried into the kitchen to heat the roast, then lit a fire in the living room, then poured wine for them both.

"Gertrude, thank you for spending the day with me," he said, as he handed her a glass. "I can't remember a happier day. I am completely content."

"I feel like I'm dreaming." Gertrude said, looking up into his eyes as she took the glass from him. "You have no idea how different this day has been for me. You have no idea who I really am, or where I'm from. You'd maybe feel differently if you knew where I lived and who my family is."

"Darling, no." Edward replied, putting a finger on her lips as he sat beside her. "Nothing could make me love you less. Your family and where they live has no bearing on the way I feel about you, and never will. I feel you are a part of me. Your life before we met has no meaning for us. Gertrude, I want you to stay with me. Don't go back."

"Don't go back?" Gertrude muttered, almost to herself. *What if I don't go back? Who would miss me? Gladys would! Dolly would! But that's all!*

Don't go back? A smile came to her lips. *No more dirt, grime, stinks, yelling, swearing, chips, beer, crying kids. No more back-yard lav. No more squares of newspaper—Edward's paper was white and soft and smelled of rose petals. No more stomach cramps from hunger, or fighting for broken biscuits and fish heads at the market on Saturday night. No more of Emma screaming at her day and night. No more keeping her clothes in a cardboard box.*

"Edward," she finally said, "I have no clothes."

Edward threw back his head and laughed. She loved to hear him laugh.

"Silly goose." He said. "You will have all the clothes you want. Shoes, dresses, coats, gloves, handbags, pretty under garments, silk lingerie, perfume and jewelry. Anything you desire."

The tears now escaped her eyelids and ran in tiny rivers down her cheeks. Edward kissed them away, putting her glass on the table, and swept her into his arms.

"Does that mean 'yes'?" he asked, looking deeply into her eyes.

"Yes," Gertrude said.

The kiss was soft and firm as if sealing the promise just made.

The smell of the roast pork permeated the cottage and they both laughed, having forgotten entirely that the roast was even in the oven.

"We had better eat that meat," said Edward, "Or Mrs Bennet will not be happy."

The meal was succulent and tender, with bread stuffing, new potatoes and fresh peas to accompany the meat and a dish of fresh apple sauce to enhance the flavour. Gertrude had never tasted pork like this, and she never ate it again without thinking of that meal with Edward, when she had agreed to stay with him.

After the meal, Edward took Gertrude's hand and led her up the winding staircase to the bedroom. She hadn't been upstairs before and she went with no hesitation. All the talking and rumours she'd heard growing up about "doing it" and how horrible it must be were driven from her memory in the hands of this remarkable man called Edward. He undressed her gently and slowly, stopping to kiss her hands, arms, shoulders. He left her scanty, tattered, undergarment on and gently lay her between the crisp white sheets, before going into his dressing room to remove his clothing, coming back into the room dressed in a blue silk dressing gown. He didn't let her see him naked. He joined her between the sheets, letting the gown slip to the floor as he did so.

The first time making love with Edward was, for Gertrude, beyond any imagined or dreamt fantasy. Every moment was filled with pleasure, which mounted into ecstasy as Edward slowly and gently adored his sweetheart. He had made love to many women in his lifetime. He was an experienced and considerate lover, taking his time to help Gertrude become comfortable with his caresses, which became more and more intimate. When Gertrude finally plucked up courage to look under the sheets, she drew in a sharp breath as she saw Edward naked for the first time. She wasn't afraid, how could she be? Edward knew it would be wonderful. He had been so patient and, unlike a younger man, controlled, but now was the time and there was no turning back.

Gertrude lay with her head on Edward's bare chest and one leg draped across his thigh, feeling so light and warm. This had been nothing like the bump and grind stories told to her by other girls in the street. Nothing like the grunts and moans from the room next to hers in Edward Street after a night of drinking. Nothing like the horror stories of young married women, who didn't think she was listening, as they told in whispers of their ordeals at the hands of their rough husbands. This, with Edward, was beautiful. She had lost track of time and space, sinking into a world of sensuous warmth, being filled with Edward as he moved inside her. She wanted to freeze time right here. Stay in this warm, clean, soft bed with Edward's arms around her forever.

Sunday morning, as the sun peeked through the window, Edward turned over to look at Gertrude as she slept beside him. Last night had been everything he had imagined. But he had to tell this lovely young woman about Amy. Just how to put it into words was his problem. There was no easy way to tell the girl he had just made love to and invited to stay, that he was married.

Gertrude's eyes opened cautiously. Where was she? *Please, don't let me be in Neck End.* Then, as she realized where she was, she let the smile grow—she was in bed with Edward in his cottage.

Sunday was spent in a haze of wonder as Edward drew her a bath, then gently washed her body with soft soap smelling of roses. He didn't use a wash cloth, but used his hands, until Gertrude was writhing with pleasure. She didn't wait to dry off, but went from the bath, soaking wet back to the bed, this time urging Edward not to take his time. Sweet Sunday, full of love-making. How many years it had been since Edward had spent such a day? Surely not in these past twenty years or more.

Mrs. Bennet came in on Monday morning as usual. Edward explained to her immediately that Gertrude would be staying, and Mrs. Bennet just raised an eyebrow, but didn't make comment. She just adjusted her housekeeping and cooking accordingly, happy to have a good job and a good boss.

A MARRIED MAN

*T*he conversation had to happen. Edward had put it off too long.

Gertrude had been staying with him for two weeks now. He had taken her into town after their first weekend together, to buy clothes. They went to Huntbach's ladies outfitters in Hanley. Gertrude had never set foot in such a ladies shop before. She looked over the designs of many beautiful outfits, Edward giving his opinion on which ones she should choose. Her measurements were taken and fabrics selected and the gowns ordered. It delighted him to see her dressed as she should be, in the very best fabrics and styles of 1920. The sales assistants were very attentive, making suggestions and finding shoes and accessories for each outfit. The undergarments were discreetly purchased without Edward's help, but he insisted on seeing the negligees, choosing a silky cream-coloured gown trimmed with lace, a pale blue Parisian lace gown and a white chiffon and satin gown trimmed with tiny embroidered pink flowers around the lower-than-decent neckline.

Gertrude unpacked all the parcels, folding everything carefully before placing them into her bedroom chest, bought especially for her by Edward. When the gowns arrived, she hung them in the wardrobe and placed the shoes carefully in the shoe holder under the wardrobe. The bathroom shelves now had a full complement of necessary soaps, shampoos, sweet smelling lavender and rose waters, along with brush, comb, nail brush, nail scissors—things Gertrude didn't know existed. She remembered how she had begged Aunt Sarah for an old comb when she had started going to school. Never again.

On Tuesday night, after eating another of Mrs. Bennet's delicious dinners, Edward sat beside Gertrude in front of the fire, looking serious and concerned. Gertrude's first thought was that he had tired of her already and was sending her packing.

"Gertrude, I need to tell you something important," he began. "I should have told you as soon as we met and have kept putting it off, not knowing how to say it or what you will think about me."

He swallowed hard and rose to get himself another whisky.

Gertrude had grown up in a hard, tough world and had dealt with all kinds of heartaches and disappointments in her short life. She braced herself for whatever Edward was about to tell her.

"There is no easy way to tell you this," he continued. "I am married. My wife is named Amy and she lives near Birmingham. We have been married for many years. We have never lived as man and wife. From the beginning, Amy was cold and frigid and I moved into my own bedroom early in our marriage, realizing that she would never welcome me as a lover."

Edward paused to give Gertrude time to take in what he had said. She just looked at him with her big eyes, not blinking–just gazing as though in a trance.

"Say something, darling," begged Edward.

"Why are you still married to her?" asked Gertrude.

"Ah, well," Edward said. "It's a marriage of convenience, as they say. She was wealthy, and I was not. She likes to have me around occasionally to act as her escort, and in return she provides me with a generous allowance, which enables me to live very well. It is a lifestyle I enjoy, this cottage, an expensive car, the best clothing. I work, of course, but my income is really just a little extra pocket money compared with Amy's wealth."

He paused, choosing his next words carefully.

"Gertrude," he now said, "I have no intention of changing my relationship with Amy. I will remain married to her."

"Where does that leave me?" asked Gertrude.

"Where you are now, darling," answered Edward. "Living here with me, wanting for nothing. You are the centre of my life, not Amy. I will have to travel to her home on occasion to keep up appearances, but other than that, I am totally yours. Please say this will not come between us."

"Edward, I have to think about this," whispered Gertrude. "I didn't think you would marry me or nothing—it's not like I'm a girl a toff like you would marry. But I didn't consider you as a married man somehow."

Gertrude didn't yell or scream or make a fuss. She just moved away and stood by the window, looking out on nothing.

What do I want? I know the answer—not to go back to Neck End. Does this news make such a difference? A toff wouldn't marry a girl like me. Why do I feel disappointed somehow? Maybe the thought of Edward having another life somewhere else that I knew nothing about. A wife. Another home. It seems neither of us know much about each other.

"Edward," she said moving away from the window and looking up at his anxious face. "I will stay with ya, but I want to know everything about ya—who ya are, where ya've lived, who ya've loved. Everythin'—no secrets."

"Darling Gertrude, you shall know all," he said smiling at her, even as the tears stung his eyes. "I will spend the next days, or weeks, or months telling you about my life—just let me know if you get too bored."

"I also want ya to know about me," continued Gertrude. "Where I come from. Who me family is. What me life has been like 'til now. It's not a pretty story."

Their life together really began after that Tuesday night. Edward telling instalments of his life each day, from the beginning. Gertrude telling Edward about Neck End and her life with Tom and Emma in Edward Street. His face grew dark with concern for her, as she told stories of poverty and abuse he could hardly believe.

Gertrude asked Edward to drive her to Neck End one Saturday morning. She needed to see Dolly and Gladys. She had disappeared without a word to them and felt badly for it. As the car approached Longton and the misery of the streets in that part of the city, Edward shuddered with the knowledge that his love had lived here until a few weeks ago. No blade of grass grew here. No tree or flower. Just black buildings on black streets. Gertrude gazed out of the car window and shuddered for a different reason. Coming back here wasn't easy, as all the memories from the past unhappy eighteen years flooded in.

She asked Edward to park the car on Brook Street and to wait for her there. She hoped she would find Gladys at home, remembering that Saturday morning was "bath" morning for Gladys, but she usually went down for her bath before nine, while the baths were somewhat clean. Gertrude knocked on the front door, noting the red step, newly polished that morning. Gladys answered the door and stared with disbelief at the vision before her, her mouth dropping open.

Here was Gert dressed to the nines in an olive green dress and long jacket made of some fancy material, matching shoes and bag. Hair done like a lady. Here was Gert, smiling at her.

"Hiya Glad," Gert said. "Don't tell me you've forgotten me already?"

"My God, Gert," Gladys finally got out, "what's happened to ya? Me mam said you were probably dead. Your mam thinks the same. They was going to have a memorial at the chapel for ya."

Gertrude laughed loudly at this. A memorial—for her? They had to be kidding!

"Well, sorry to spoil the party," she said still laughing. "Aren't you going to ask me in?"

Gladys opened the door for Gertrude then looked up and down the street to see if anybody had seen her go in. Lucky for Gladys that her dad was fishing at Longton Park with his mates.

"Glad," said Gertrude, "Would ya go over to Edward Street and see if our Dolly's in? Ask 'er to come over 'ere if she is. I don't want to see Tom or Emma."

Gladys set out on her errand and returned very quickly with Dolly in tow.

"Our Gert," sobbed Dolly, "where've ya been?"

Gertrude held her sister close.

"I'm sorry, Dolly," she said. "I've left it too long to let ya know I'm alright. I've met the most wonderful man and I'm staying with 'im. I'm not coming back to Neck End. I'm done with this life. We live in a lovely 'ouse in Alsager and I have everything I need. He's a kind man. Not like the men around here. E'd do anything for me. I'm just 'ere to let ya know I'm doing well. Tell Mam for me. I don't want to see 'er."

"Oh Gert," sniffled Dolly, "I miss ya, duck. Life's still shit, but worse without you. Are you livin' in sin Gert?"

"It doesn't feel like sin, Doll," said Gertrude. "It feels like heaven."

"One more thing," continued Gertrude, "Will you go see Aunt Sarah and tell her you've seen me and that I'm fine? She was always good and kind to me since I was a little girl. I wouldn't want her to worry about me."

Dolly nodded her head. She hugged Gertrude one more time and ran out of the house, still sniffling.

Dolly understood why her sister was staying with the toff in Alsager. She had heard Gertrude swear so many times that she would get out of Neck End somehow, and this was how.

She didn't blame her, she was better off where she was—nice clothes, good food, a good man.

"Good luck to 'er," thought Dolly. She went straight to Sarah's house to give her aunt the news.

Gladys told her friend she'd been walking out with a young man named Sidney. He helped out with the breakfast on Sunday mornings at the chapel. Gladys had started going to the worship service with him after breakfast. He was a decent chap, according to Gladys. He was a carpenter and worked for Sheltons Wood Company in Fenton, which was the next town to Longton.

Gertrude was happy for her friend and hoped the relationship with Sidney would work out. She took her leave of Gladys, promising to keep in touch when she could, then hurrying back to Brook Street, where Edward was waiting for her.

She breathed a sigh as she sunk into the seat beside Edward.

"That was hard to do." She said. "But I had to come, and I'm glad I did."

Edward patted her hand and drove the car out of Neck End and back to the green fields and trees outside the dirty city. He wanted to erase those years spent in the grime of Longton from Gertrude's mind, and make sure she was surrounded only with lovely things from now on.

SECRET LONGING

*T*he roses bloomed in a profusion of colour and perfume around the cottage. Edward clipped the best of the blooms for the house, bringing them in and presenting them to his beloved Gertrude. They filled vases and bowls all over the house, the most perfumed beside the bed, filling the air as they slept and made love.

The weekends when Edward was away were never without tears. Gertrude resented the visits to Birmingham and sulked, begging Edward to stay with her. But he was bound to Amy and to his duty as her husband and he had agreed to escort her and be seen in society as her husband. Any indication of Amy's loving relationship with Alice would have been completely unacceptable by any society, especially the circles in which they moved.

Amy wrote down the dates she expected Edward in Kings Norton and he complied with no complaints. His manner had changed lately and he seemed happier. He looked younger somehow. Amy suspected he was in love, but never entered into a conversation about his private life in North Staffordshire.

Edward drove south for the various social events he was expected to attend, staying overnight and returning north the following morning. Gertrude would be waiting, feigning sadness at his leaving, then pressing her pouty lips against his lips, making him feel joy throughout his entire being. He loved her more and more, his desire for her increasing each time he was away.

Mrs. Bennet was teaching Gertrude to cook real food. How to bake bread and her own cakes and cookies. Gertrude was anything but domesticated, but she gave Mrs. Bennet her full attention and surprised Edward with the dishes she had made.

She preferred to go into town with Edward and browse around Huntbach's ladies outfitters, attending the fashion shows and choosing a new outfit from the latest styles. She had her hair done every week. Her nails manicured. Heads turned as she walked down the street and she revelled in the attention, knowing she was nothing like the women around her, who were mostly drab and poor.

Edward had only one regret in life. He envied his old friend Mac. He remembered the days, playing with Mac's children. How he had enjoyed them. He had always pictured himself a future father, surrounded by small children, but it had never happened. Not with Clara. Certainly not with Amy. Now, he lived with a young girl with her whole life before her. He was older than her parents. Surely too old to now father a child. The dream, however, kept pushing itself into his mind. A dream he never shared with Gertrude. How could he? It would have been selfish.

He made sure there was no pregnancy. He was careful that he always had protection beside the bed. Gertrude knew no different than the life she had with Edward, and never questioned the use of a condom. She learned, early on, that putting it on for Edward was exciting for him. She adored giving him pleasure in every way she knew. She never questioned why he wore it. It never occurred to her that it was preventing pregnancy. Only that maybe it was less messy, more genteel, something the toffs did.

When they had been together for six months, Edward decided he would risk telling Gertrude his dream. What could he lose? It was so crazy that he still wanted a child, she would probably laugh, but he needed to tell her.

The evenings were spent walking, reading, cuddling, talking. Sometimes taking a bath, each soaping the other's body, laughing as they slid against each other in the bubbles. After such an evening, they were both in dressing gowns, sitting before the fire, drinking tea and eating crumpets with butter dripping through the holes onto their fingers.

"Gertrude," Edward began. "I have a secret longing that I want to share with you and I don't want you to laugh."

"What?" she laughed.

"You're already laughing!"

"No, no, I will be serious."

"I'm just going to jump in and say it," declared Edward. "I have always wanted to be a father."

He waited for her to say something. She looked at him for a long time. Not laughing, but wondering if he was really serious.

A baby? Her experience with babies had been miserable. Screaming, hungry, dirty babies. Spoiling her sleep, making the house stink, taking so long to grow up.

Edward sat looking at her, giving her time to ponder.

A baby? He would never leave me if I had his baby. He would leave his wife and marry me. A baby would seal our future for sure. I would live with Edward forever, in this beautiful cottage. Mrs. Bennet would help me. Edward would be truly mine. This would be my insurance that he would never leave.

"Edward," she finally responded. "If this is your dream, I will be a mother for your baby."

She watched his eyes fill with tears. She loved him so dearly. He would be a wonderful father to her baby. She had no experience of a "good" father, except possibly Sarah's husband, who was always kind and never yelled.

They didn't say anything else. The secret had been told and there was no discussion. How would it happen? Easily. The package from the bedside was put away and Edward joined with her with a joy he had never experienced, knowing that this could be the beginning of his own child.

A COLD WINTER

*I*t was a cold January in 1921. After a snowy Christmas, spent eating the food Mrs. Bennet had been preparing for weeks ahead, and enjoying the small gifts they had wrapped for each other, the couple settled down to survive the January storms with frigid temperatures and dark nights. Early nights, with the fire in the bedroom burning brightly and Edward reading Great Expectations to Gertrude, often ended with loving each other, hoping to create a baby.

January came and went, and by the middle of February Gertrude was counting each day that she didn't bleed. Edward knew immediately and anxiously monitored each day, hoping the cold January nights had eventually led to a pregnancy. The first of March, they tentatively celebrated. Edward kissing her belly and whispering to the tiny being inside of his love and devotion. Gertrude laughed and laughed and called him "sloppy."

Edward took her to a gynecologist in April to confirm the

pregnancy. Yes, it was confirmed and the baby would be born in September.

Gertrude didn't like how her body changed. Even though she was outfitted with the loveliest maternity clothes, she was mortified at the loss of her figure and the ugly little marks appearing on her growing belly and at the sides of her breasts.

Mrs. Bennet was thrilled beyond words at the prospect of a baby in the house. She had six grown children and was full of advice on what should be bought and how Gertrude should look after herself. Of course, it was a baby born out of sin, which would be frowned on by everybody in the neighbourhood, but Mrs. Bennet wasn't one to judge. She liked Edward and tolerated Gertrude because he loved her so much. She would stick by the two of them, and help all she could. She went to Hanley to help Gertrude shop for all the baby clothing, crib, nappies, bits and bobs. The small room upstairs was cleared of Edward's files and painted a pale yellow, with new drapes at the windows and soft carpet on the floor. Edward bought a white rocking chair for Gertrude and set it beside the cradle. Even Gertrude, who had some misgivings about motherhood, was getting excited and enjoying all the lovely new things for the baby.

Edward had arranged for her to go to Blackpool in Lancashire to have the baby at a private hotel, with a good reputation for taking care of the confinement, and nurturing of the new mother and baby for two weeks after the birth.

Blackpool was a popular seaside resort and the sea air was said to be very healthy. Edward drove out there himself in August to take a look at the hotel and set his mind at rest that all would be well. Nothing could go wrong with this pregnancy now they had come this far. He was to be a father at last.

Gertrude's bump was big now. To his delight, Edward could see the baby moving inside her. He lay with his head on the baby, cooing and singing to his unseen offspring, waiting for any sign of movement. Gertrude thought he was crazy. She'd never seen a man so excited about a baby he couldn't even see. She'd never seen a man so enamoured with the mother of his baby as Edward was with her, despite her distorted shape and swollen ankles. He lay next to her in bed stroking her hair, her shoulders, her swollen breasts. Still desiring her. Still wanting to make love to her. Gertrude didn't think it was safe to make love when the baby was getting so big, but Edward was so gentle, assuring her the baby was fine.

BLACKPOOL

*T*he final check-up with the gynecologist was at the end of August, and he advised Edward to drive Gertrude to Blackpool within the next few days.

Gertrude packed her bag and a bag for the baby. Edward loaded everything into the car and they set off for Blackpool. Gertrude had never been to Blackpool, but had heard about the seaside town from Mrs. Jones at the corner grocery store, whose sister had been there on her honeymoon.

"It was luvly," Mrs. Jones told the shop full of women. "Sand and sea. A lovely prom to walk up and down. Flowers in pots. Even a merry-go-round. Of course they stayed in a bed and breakfast boarding house and couldn't sleep in the same room; men in one room, women in the other. But nice to get away!"

What kind of honeymoon was that? Gertrude had thought. *Not even sleeping in the same room.*

The hotel Edward drove her to was on a quiet side street in

the north end of the city. A lovely white double-fronted building, with shrubs and flowers in the front yard. Mrs. Phillips greeted them at the front door with a smile.

"Please come in," she said. "Mr. and Mrs. Wrightson, I presume."

"Thank you," said Edward.

Mrs. Phillips took them into a sitting room, inviting them to make themselves comfortable while she sent for tea.

Gertrude's bags were taken upstairs by a young porter and tea was served by a young lady, along with scones and jam.

"We'll have tea, then get you settled in," said Mrs. Phillips. "We are just a few minutes from the promenade, where you will be able to walk and enjoy the fresh sea air, Mrs. Wrightson."

Gertrude almost laughed at being addressed as Mrs. Wrightson. It sounded so funny. Edward frowned at her as he saw the corners of her mouth crinkling and she swallowed hard to suppress the urge to giggle.

After tea, Mrs. Phillips took them upstairs to room number eight, which was large and cozy. Decorated in shades of pale green, with cream-coloured drapes at the bay window overlooking the back garden. The double bed had cream-coloured bedcovers and cushions to match the drapes and there was a sofa and chair in the bay window forming a small sitting area. The two chests of drawers were dark wood, as was the lady's wardrobe in the alcove opposite the bed. This was where their baby would soon be born.

"What provisions are there for the baby?" asked Edward.

"A cradle and baby storage chest will be brought into the room after the birth," explained Mrs. Phillips. "Everything will be provided for the baby's needs, as soon as is needed."

Gertrude thought about the parlour in Edward Street where she and the other babies had been born to Emma. The stack of newspapers ready to soak up the mess, the horse hair sofa, the drawer from the chest for the baby's crib, the woman from the next street who came to bring the baby into the world, the swaddling clothes passed down through many families to wrap the newborn. How different it would be for her baby.

"Thank you," said Edward. "Everything seems to be in order."

"Then I'll leave you to get settled," Mrs. Phillips added, as she left them alone.

"Do you like it, darling?" Edward asked.

"I do, Edward," Gertrude replied. "How could I not? It's so comfortable."

Edward watched as she filled the chest with her clothes. He wanted everything to be easy for her. She knew nothing of birthing a baby. He knew very little. Only that it could last a long time and be very painful. He wished he could somehow protect her from the labour of childbirth, but knew it was something she had to go through herself. He wasn't sure how brave she was.

Edward had to leave to drive back to Staffordshire. He had a project that needed his attention. Mrs. Phillips promised to telegraph him when labour began to give him time to drive to Blackpool. As it turned out, the telegraph wasn't needed. Edward planned to make the journey back to the seaside the following Saturday, after his week of work. Amy had sent word that he was needed in Kings Norton that weekend, but he made his apologies.

Gertrude was rosy and bright eyed when Edward saw her at the hotel. She had spent the week walking on the promenade, as advised by Mrs. Phillips. She had eaten wonderful food and slept soundly in the big double bed, but was bored with her own company and longed to see Edward. She greeted him with a smile of joy and a long sweet kiss. She was so happy to see him, wanting to show him the sea and the flowers and walk with him in the sun.

No sign of the impending birth.

It was already September thirteenth and Edward was impatient for the baby's arrival.

"Edward," Gertrude said, smiling up at him. "The baby will come when it is ready. I don't feel it will be soon."

They walked together in the afternoon, returning for a quiet supper at the hotel. They retired early, Edward longing to share the bed with his lovely "wife." Gertrude lay on her side and Edward lay behind her, cradling her on his lap and encompassing her swollen belly in his arms. The baby was still. He rubbed his hand over the baby, but there was no movement. It wasn't usually this still for this long. He wondered if all was well. Gertrude slept peacefully beside him, while he continued to monitor the unborn baby.

He must have dozed off eventually, because he woke with a start while it was still dark and realized he was very wet. Warm liquid flowed over the front of his thighs. It was coming from Gertrude.

She stirred and moaned quietly, not aware yet what was happening.

"Darling," whispered Edward. "Wake up. Something is happening. Do you need the bathroom?"

She rolled onto her back, eyes wide in the darkness, as Edward lit the gas lamp. Feeling the fluid seeping from her, she was suddenly aware of the flood in the bed beneath her. Edward ran to the door, calling for Mrs. Phillips. Then he remembered the bell pull he was supposed to pull if they needed her. He grabbed the pull and yanked it.

Mrs. Phillips came hurrying into the room, assessing the situation with a glance.

"Your water has broken, Mrs. Wrightson," she explained. "Not to worry. You will go into labour soon. Now let us get you up and change your nightwear and the bedsheets so that you are comfortable."

"We will also give you an enema, so that your bowel is empty."

Mrs. Phillips calmly took care of everything. Rose escorted Gertrude to the bathroom for the bowel evacuation, while Edward quickly dressed, ready to be of any assistance. He sat beside Gertrude on the sofa, holding her hands in his and reassuring her, as two young women came into the room with fresh bedsheets, towels, bowls and jugs and two baskets of other necessities. Soon Gertrude was back in the dry bed with soft towels under her and between her legs to absorb any more liquid. Mrs. Phillips said it could be a few hours before the onset of labour and that Gertrude should try and get some sleep. Edward knew he wouldn't sleep again, but sat beside his love, stroking her hand. Gertrude couldn't sleep either, but was calm and serene with Edward beside her.

"Edward," she asked. "Will you stay with me through it all? I would be brave if you held my hand. I would be scared if you left."

"I will stay with you," Edward assured her.

Daylight came with still no sign of labour beginning. The young woman called Rose brought them a tray with toast and tea. Edward couldn't stand the tension and paced up and down the room.

"How much longer?" he thought.

The labour began shortly after their toast and tea. Gertrude bending over in pain, her face going white, her eyes wide with fear. It had begun!

The painful contractions lasted only a few seconds at first, with twenty minutes before the next one. Edward read another Dickens novel, David Copperfield, to Gertrude as she waited for the next pain.

Mrs. Phillips checked in on them regularly, monitoring Gertrude's progress. Drinks and snacks were served through the day. Edward ordered a whiskey and soda half way through the afternoon. This was taking much longer than he had imagined, but he had no experience to draw on. This was one of life's mysteries for him.

The labour became more and more intense, and Edward felt more and more inadequate as he watched Gertrude suffer. Mrs. Phillips insisted this was a normal labour for a first baby. She suggested Edward go for a walk and stay down-stairs on his return. No fathers were ever present for this long into the labour—it was most unusual.
"Mrs. Phillips," Edward said. "I not only will not go for a walk, but I will not be leaving this room until the baby is

born. I will stay here beside my wife and support her throughout this process."

"Mr. Wrightson," Mrs. Phillips replied. "I urge you to reconsider your decision. No father has ever been present at the birth. You would be in the way. You may faint. Men are not equipped to witness childbirth. It's something women have to endure with the aid of other women."

She sniffed at the end of her speech, sure Edward would now see sense and go for a walk and remain downstairs.

Edward sat on the bed beside Gertrude and changed the cold cloth on her forehead.

"Don't worry, darling," he murmured. "I am right here. I am not going anywhere."

He looked at Mrs. Phillips as he said these last words, emphasizing his commitment to staying where he was.

Mrs. Phillips sighed and looked at Rose. She couldn't insist. After all, Edward was paying the bill.

It was agony for Edward to watch the labour.

Gertrude screamed and cried. She pleaded and begged for it to stop.

Edward was distraught. He rubbed her back. He held her hand. He wiped the sweat from her head and neck and arms with cool cloths. He watched her belly form a tight ball with each contraction, until the hard belly stayed hard as the contractions followed each other without a break. Gertrude gasped for breath, thinking she would die. She clutched at Edward's shirt, soaking from his own sweat, asking him to make it stop.

Rose rang the bell and Mrs. Phillips came bustling in to

check again on the birthing progress. She looked under the bed sheet, asking Gertrude to bend her legs and let them fall open at the knees.

"Baby is ready," she announced.

Edward's heart began to beat faster and faster. Hours of waiting. No, years of waiting. Now his baby was about to be born.

"Now Mrs. Wrightson," instructed Mrs. Phillips, "we need you to push the baby out. So with the next contraction, I want you to push like you are going to the bathroom for a bowel movement."

"No," screamed Gertrude. "No, no, no."

Edward held her face in his hands, looking into her eyes.

"You can do it, darling," he encouraged. "You have been so brave. Now it's the very last bit. Our baby will be here very soon. Stay brave."

"Fuck off, Edward," she yelled.

Edward almost laughed. It was so out of character for her. He looked at the shocked look on Mrs. Phillips' face and Rose, redder than a beet, rinsing out cold cloths. He continued to hold her hand though, as she gritted her teeth and pushed for all her worth. He pulled the edge of the bed sheet back from Gertrude's knees, so that he could see what was happening.

"Mr. Wrightson, what are you doing?" snapped Mrs. Phillips in alarm. "That is Mrs. Wrightson's private parts."
Edward looked in wonder at the opening which was Gertrude's vagina, usually so small, stretched now to allow the baby's head to descend. He could see the dark, wet hair of

the baby appear as the opening widened and stretched, tiny tears appearing around the edges.

"I have seen my wife many times, Mrs. Phillips," he said. "But this is the most beautiful I have ever seen her."

As the baby's head emerged from Gertrude, she let out one last scream of agony.

Mrs. Phillips waited for the baby to turn and slowly helped out first one shoulder and then the other, allowing the rest of the baby to slide out with ease. Edward was in tears as he watched the miracle. His baby. His baby girl.

He cradled Gertrude in his arms, both of them crying.

Mrs. Phillips cut the cord and passed the baby to Rose. Rose gently wiped the baby clean, as the newborn cried lustily, kicking her legs in fury at being in the cold room and out of her warm baby bed. The afterbirth was delivered and disposed of and Gertrude was washed and made comfortable.

Edward never took his eyes off Rose as she swaddled the tiny girl and laid her on Gertrude's chest. So soft and sweet smelling; she would never be this clean again. Edward was in awe of her! He touched her tiny hand, each touch provoking more tears from his already wet eyes. Gertrude looked down at her daughter in wonder. Black hair, a red face, funny little ears. She had done it. She had given Edward a child. He was a father. His dream had come true. She picked up the infant and handed her to her father.

Edward held the tiny baby in his arms. She was so small. So light. So precious. He was overwhelmed by her. He was fifty-two and a father at last.

"What will we call her?" asked Gertrude.

"Let's call her Dorothy," said Edward at once.

"Dorothy's nice," agreed Gertrude.

Edward's daughter.

PART IV
FULL CIRCLE

AMY ALONE

en days after Dorothy was born, Edward packed up the car and took his family home to Alsager. Mrs. Bennet had been busy preparing the house for its new inhabitant. The nursery was ready, with cradle covered in white frills, nappies washed and in a fluffy pile beside the baby cart where the creams, talcum powder and wash cloths were stored. Edward had ordered a dozen pink roses for Gertrude, delivered before they arrived home and arranged by Mrs. Bennet in a glass bowl on the dining room table.

The first weeks with Dorothy were a challenge. Gertrude was grateful to the housekeeper for the instructions and help she gave, staying well past her usual time to make sure Dorothy was feeding well, helping Gertrude latch the baby to her breast and showing her how to move any air trapped in Dorothy's stomach.

Gertrude had no idea how to look after a baby. Emma certainly had not been an example of motherhood. The new mother struggled with changing nappies, feeding and bathing the tiny child. She was so small. So fragile. She cried for no reason. She didn't sleep during the night. Feeding her never went well without Mrs. Bennet there to help. Gertrude was so tired.

Edward, however, delighted in his daughter. He couldn't wait to come home after a day in the city to pick her up and cuddle her close. He didn't seem to mind changing her nappy, or waking in the night to comfort her. He even bathed her, his shirt sleeves rolled up to the elbows and his big hands supporting Dorothy's tiny head and body. She never cried when Edward bathed her, laying in the warm water and letting him wash her gently with the special baby soap.

He often took Dorothy into bed with him, laying her on his chest, which was her favourite place to sleep.

"She'll never sleep in her cradle, Edward," criticized Gertrude. "You're just making it harder for me to look after her when you're at work, you know."

Edward smiled contentedly.

"She won't be small for long, darling. I'm going to enjoy every minute."

Gertrude thought he was being a bit daft about the baby. Men didn't pay attention to babies. Babies were women's work. They certainly never changed them or bathed them. Gertrude even felt a little jealous of the attention lavished on this small person, when she had become used to Edward's undivided attention.

As Dorothy grew, she looked more and more like her mother. Her hair was thick and dark and naturally curly. She had the same dark almond-shaped eyes and full lips. She had sturdy dimpled arms and legs and was soon crawling around the cottage investigating everything.

She was adored by her father, who thought her to be the most beautiful baby he had ever seen. He wanted everybody to see her and took her for long walks in her pram, so that she could be admired by the village folk. He frequented Huntbach's infant department in the big Hanley store, buying his daughter more outfits than she could ever wear.

"You're spoiling her, Edward," grumbled Gertrude.

But Edward couldn't be stopped. He had waited far too long to become a father, and now he was making up for all those years without a child to spoil.

Amy still gave her dates when Edward was expected in Kings Norton and he still complied, reluctantly leaving his family while he attended a County Ball or some other important social event.

One particular weekend, as he arrived at the big house near Birmingham to change, before escorting Amy to a dinner party at Lord Bellingham's house, he was greeted by his wife at the door. She looked distraught and had obviously been crying a great deal.

"Edward, thank God you're here. Alice has had a fall. She missed her footing coming down the main staircase. She has been taken to the infirmary in Birmingham."

"Do you want me to drive you there?" asked Edward.

"Not now," Amy replied. "How would it look if we didn't go to this dinner party? How would I explain?"

Edward followed her into the sitting room, pouring her a glass of brandy and sitting her down. She was obviously very upset and he didn't see why they couldn't cancel the dinner.

"You're not thinking straight," he said. "I will go to the dinner alone and make your apologies. Say you're unwell. They will understand."

Amy smiled up at him, sipping the strong drink, the colour coming back into her face. She nodded her agreement, and Edward, without asking Amy's permission, rang for Hodges, the butler, and made arrangements for the Daimler to be brought around to the front of the house.

"Mrs. Wrightson is going into Birmingham, to the infirmary to visit Miss Bridgewood. Please make arrangements for Clifford to drive her and wait for her," instructed Edward.

"Very good, sir."

Amy changed her clothes and washed her face. She was on her way to Birmingham within ten minutes and Edward on his way to Lord Bellingham's.

Alice didn't survive the accident. When Amy arrived at the hospital, her friend was already gone. Not realizing the significance of the loss, Amy was treated as a friend of the deceased, the nurse showing her into the cold, dark room smelling of disinfectant and leaving her there.

Amy grabbed the rail of the narrow bed where Alice lay in an effort to stay on her feet. She slowly pulled the white sheet away from Alice's face to look at her beloved friend. She stood for a long time, staring at the white face with the forehead blackened from the fall, then felt under the sheet for a hand and held onto it as the tears finally spilled down her cheeks. She pressed her lips to Alice's lips, willing her to be alive. Amy's life without her would be nothing.

Amy had nobody to comfort her—nor would she.

MOVING SOUTH

*E*dward stayed with Amy for a week, sending a telegram to Gertrude saying he had been delayed and would be home the following Monday. Alice was buried quietly, with only Edward and Amy in attendance. Edward knew how tragic it was for Amy to lose her friend. She begged Edward to stay with her now, wanting the comfort of a familiar person in the house, who knew what she had lost.

"Amy, I can't stay with you," he said. "I have no life here. My life is in North Staffordshire now. We both made a choice long ago to go our separate ways."

Amy looked long and hard at Edward.

"Never forget, my dear," she began, "you still have an obligation to me—your wife. It's my money that rescued you from debt and humiliation. It's my money that has provided you with a generous allowance, giving you a quality of life you could never have had without me. It's my money that has made your life in North Staffordshire, with your whore, even possible. Never forget who you are beholden to, and how I could use your dependence on me against you, if you should ever think of leaving this marriage."

Amy stormed out of the room, giving Edward no chance to recover from her harsh words. He stood in the middle of the room, shaken from the confrontation. *Allowances must be made for Amy, in her grief, although I know everything Amy has said is the truth. I also know that any hint of scandal in our marriage would cause widespread exclusion in the fickle, social circle we are part of. I must think of my family, who are part of that same circle. They would suffer the same shunning, suddenly not being included in invitations—people they considered friends, becoming estranged and distant. No, I am trapped in this marriage and must continue to be at Amy's side when needed. Gertrude never understood the implications of cutting the tie with Amy, because in her world there is no such thing as social circles, or inclusion into society. I wonder sometimes, who is the better off?*

The house in Hawthorn Road, Kings Norton, was put up for sale the following month. Amy couldn't stand to live there alone! She bought a large comfortable house in Maidenhead, near Windsor, a short journey from the capital city. She told Edward that she expected him to move close to her, so that he could spend the weekends with her as usual. The pretence was to be kept up.

"I will not move!" shouted Gertrude when Edward told her of the new arrangements. "That woman has you wrapped around her finger, Edward. Why don't you tell her you have a new family? Why don't you tell her you want a divorce? Why don't you tell her you have a daughter?"

"Gertrude, you don't understand," he answered. "I cannot leave my wife. Such a scandal would ruin both of us."

"Sod you, Edward." Gertrude yelled. "You could leave if you wanted. Blokes leave their wives every day. They disappear and leave their wives with a house full of kids. They think nothing of it—they just bloody well walk out."

"That's the working class, Gertrude. My situation is far different. The code of honour is never broken. Marriage is forever. I am the one at fault for finding you, God help me, and loving you, and living with you. Please try to live with this dearest. Aren't you happy?"

Gertrude choked back tears. She didn't answer, but turned away with her fists clenched and her cheeks blazing.

Questions poured through Gertrude's mind. She was shocked Edward was still visiting his wife on the weekends and keeping up the pretence of being married. She thought he would leave his wife once the baby was born, but he hadn't.

Gertrude liked living in the cottage in Alsager. Edward would give her a ride into Newcastle sometimes and she'd meet Dolly at the market cafe and catch up on all the news from Neck End. Gladys, her best friend, was married. Dolly was promised to Norman, who was a bit of a dope. It was nice to hear all the gossip.

Edward promised they would not move soon. He would delay it as long as it was possible. He never answered any direct questions regarding Amy though. He never said he would leave her, or divorce her. He never promised to marry Gertrude.

When Dorothy was three years old and Amy had been in Maidenhead for two years, Edward, tired of the travelling at the weekend, found a small cottage just outside London in

Cobham. It was perfectly located. Near to London, where Edward had the promise of a good job and closer to Maidenhead for the weekend journeys to visit Amy.

After many tears and tantrums from Gertrude, she finally agreed to move, still believing that she could persuade Edward to stay with her and leave his wife. She planned to get pregnant again—surely with two children, he would have to choose her.

Edward drove Gertude and Dorothy to the new cottage on a calm, cool day at the beginning of May. It was like a foreign land to Gertrude, who had never been south of Staffordshire in her life. How green everything was. How big the trees were. Everybody talked differently than her. People smiled more. There were no black buildings. She saw cows and sheep and horses in fields surrounded by hedges. Brightly coloured flowers by the side of the roads. Washing hanging out on lines, bright and clean—white with no black smuts. People with pink faces, shopping and walking—no clay white or pit black faces.

The furniture from Alsager was already delivered ahead of their arrival and two men were busy carrying it into the cottage. Edward ushered Gertrude and his baby girl into their new home, steering them towards the bright kitchen, where a round, pleasant-faced woman greeted them with tea and scones and a dish of apple sauce and fresh strawberries for Dorothy.

Mrs. Medwin lived nearby and was happy to have a few hours' work helping the new family settle in.

"Come on in, dear," she said to Gertrude. "I've a nice cuppa tea for you."

Edward gave instructions to the furniture men, sending them to the various rooms with the right items. Mrs. Medwin began unpacking the boxes marked 'kitchen' that Mrs. Bennet had packed up in Alsager.

"Do you want to place everything yourself, Mrs. Wrightson?" asked Mrs. Medwin.

"No, you do it," answered Gertrude. "I'm not bothered where you put stuff."

Mrs. Medwin found a spot for all the dishes and pots and pans. She put the food into the small pantry and the table linens into the sideboard. She had arranged for the milk man to deliver two bottles of milk each day and had purchased eggs, butter, cheese, and a fresh loaf.

Gertrude looked around at her new home. It was nice, she had to admit. Dorothy was running around investigating every nook and cranny, stopping frequently in front of Edward to be lifted up and kissed. Anywhere daddy was, was home!

Life in Cobham was very different for Gertrude. She was lonely. She didn't know the village or its surroundings. Edward had been hired in London by an engineering consulting firm and was only home after six. He didn't drive to Maidenhead every weekend, and when he did have to go, he didn't leave until Saturday after lunch and was back by Sunday evening. Nevertheless, Gertrude resented every trip he made. Dorothy asked for him all day when he wasn't there.

"Daddy coming home?" was her constant cry.

"No. Not yet."

Gertrude tried not to show her annoyance, remembering how she was talked to by her mother and vowing she would not speak to her daughter that way. Sometimes, she admitted to herself that she felt like screaming "Shut bloody up!"

DOUBTS

"Have you told her about us?" Gertrude asked Edward one evening after Dorothy's bedtime.

"Yes, I have."

"When?" gasped Gertrude. "You never said."

"I didn't tell her about *us*. I told her I had a daughter."

"What did she say?"

"She said 'never speak of it again.'"

"The cow!" squealed Gertrude.

Edward put his arms around her and cuddled her close. She was so dear to him, yet he hadn't left Amy. Amy was his bread and butter. Gertrude was his caviar. He had been careful there weren't more babies. He had the beautiful daughter he wanted—that was enough. More children would complicate his life even more.

Gertrude resented her daughter more as she grew. Dorothy

was Edward's daughter, and she didn't even feel like the child's mother much of the time.

What am I doing? I'm already twenty-four years old! I'm missing out on life. Stuck here with an old man and a little girl. Where will I be in ten years time? Nothing has worked out for me. Edward hasn't left his wife and married me, like he should have. Dorothy's growing up loving Edward more than me. Dorothy will have the life of a rich kid. She doesn't even talk like me. Everybody in the village talks with a snotty-nosed accent and looks down on the likes of me. I'm not part of their culture, I'm an outsider, and I don't belong. But Edward does and so does Dorothy, with her little posh accent.

As Dorothy grew from baby to little girl, Gertrude became more discontented with her life in the south. Edward couldn't be seen with her in London, so she never went into the capital city. He doted on his daughter and became less tolerant of Gertrude as she whined and complained.

They had lived together for six years. Gertrude was still a young woman. Edward had turned fifty-seven years old. Dorothy was often mistaken for his granddaughter. The age difference between the couple suddenly seemed vast and divisive. What was once an attraction for both Edward and Gertrude became a chasm between them. Edward felt old when he was with Gertrude. She seemed silly and common. He wrestled with his feelings, knowing that Gertrude had left such poverty to become his companion and mother of his baby.

When Edward came home, he was no longer greeted with affection, but with a sour look and miserable countenance. Gertrude had come to the end of her tolerance for the situation she was in.

"Tell her you're leaving her," she snapped at Edward one night after dinner. "Tell her you want a divorce. That you have another family, another home. I will not live here with you one more day, Edward, unless you promise to marry me and leave her."

"Let's not go over this again Gertrude," sighed Edward. "I have explained all the reasons why I will not leave Amy. She is wealthy and I am not. She provides a lifestyle I couldn't possibly live without her. She provides this very cottage and the car I drive. All she asks in return is an escort to the occasional engagement, and in return we live very well, with no money worries. I have no intention of divorcing her, no matter how many tantrums you have."

Gertrude was furious! She had given him six years of her life —given him a daughter!

She slammed out of the dining room, through the kitchen and out the back door into the garden, breathing in the cool night air to calm her racing heart. Where would she go if she left? How would she start another life, especially with a child in tow? Who would want a woman with a bastard child?

Edward had gone to bed when she finally went back into the house. She crept upstairs, undressed quietly and lay on the edge of the bed, as far away from Edward as she could without falling off the edge.

When Edward left for work the next day, Gertrude sat at the kitchen table and began writing—she was no scholar, and the letter took her a long time to write, a letter to Edward saying she was returning to The Potteries to begin life again, and didn't want Dorothy to go with her. She was sick of living in Cobham with all the snobs, looking down their noses at her. She wanted a fun time. She wanted to go dancing and to the pictures. She didn't want to be stuck in a cottage with a child for the next ten years.

Then she packed all her beautiful clothes, left Dorothy with Mrs. Medwin and caught the train north, changing trains in Crewe then on to Stoke.

Edward read the letter several times. Dorothy, sitting on his knee sucking her thumb, looked at his serious face and wondered if she should cry.

Mrs. Medwin said she could stay and help if needed, realizing that Gertrude wasn't coming back.

"Thank you," said Edward quietly. "Could you arrange to take care of Dorothy for the next few days, while I make some alternative arrangements?"

"Of course, sir," agreed his housekeeper. "I'll be here at eight o'clock in the morning. I'm sorry sir—about Mrs. Wrightson."

"I think we both know she was not Mrs. Wrightson," said Edward quietly.

Edward gave Dorothy a bath and dressed her in her favourite pink nighty. He brushed her wet hair carefully and warmed up her milk, serving it with two small sugar cookies. He carried her up to bed and read Peter Rabbit for the tenth time. It was a normal bedtime for her. Except for an occasional Saturday night, Daddy always bathed her and put her to bed. Nothing unusual that night.

The next morning Mrs. Medwin was already in the kitchen when Dorothy crept down the stairs, rubbing her sleepy eyes.

"Where's Mummy?" she asked.

"She's gone to visit her family," explained Edward. "It's very far away, so she will probably be gone for some time. Is that all right with you, darling? Mrs. Medwin and I will take great care of you."

Dorothy looked at her father with trusting eyes. Everything was all right as long as Daddy was there.

Edward picked her up and held her close, planting a kiss on the end of her nose.

"See you this evening, poppet," he smiled. "Be a good girl for Mrs. Medwin."

Edward didn't go into the city, but drove to Kingston-upon-Thames.

BOARDING SCHOOL

$\mathcal{T}$he Kingston School for Girls was an impressive estate, converted from a grand aristocratic manor into the well-renowned girls boarding school. Edward had telephoned earlier that morning and Miss Eleanor Preston was waiting for him in her office.

"Edward, how delightful," she greeted him. "The last time I saw you was about seven years ago at Lord Sutherland's New Year's party. You look very well."

Edward greeted her with a kiss on the cheek. She was lovely as ever. Dressed appropriately for the head-mistress of the prestigious school, in a navy and white outfit, not disguising her slender figure. Her hair was gathered into a soft bun, wisps of the soft brown curls escaping around her oval face. Seven years ago, they had spent several months in each other's company, sharing discreet dinners and intimate evenings and parting as friends.

"Eleanor, thank you for seeing me on such short notice. I'm

here to call on your good nature. I need a huge favour. I'm in a tight corner, or I wouldn't bother you."

Edward sat down in the offered chair, rubbing his hand over his eyes as he thought how to explain his complicated life.

"Eleanor, I have a daughter. Her name is Dorothy," he began.

"A daughter? Surely Amy has past the age of child bearing?"

"She isn't Amy's child. I have lived with a woman for six years and Dorothy is our child. I don't want to go into all the details, except to tell you that Dorothy's mother has decided to leave. She had no intention of taking our daughter with her—she wants to restart her life with no attachments."

Eleanor stared at her old friend, hardly believing what she was hearing.

Edward has a child! Edward, who is almost sixty years old! Edward, who is everybody's favourite dinner guest, every woman's dream lover, every man's sought after companion, a father?

Eleanor only nodded as Edward continued his story.

"We live in a cottage in Cobham, but that cannot continue now that the child's mother has left. I am dependent on a village woman to take care of my daughter during the day, and that is unacceptable. I still have to travel to be with Amy in Maidenhead on occasional weekends, which would be difficult. I have been thinking all night about a plan for the future—for Dorothy's future. If you would agree to take Dorothy for me, I could find a flat in London and visit her frequently. She would be safe with you. She would have the other girls for company. She would have a good education. She would learn social skills. She would grow up with every advantage. Eleanor, please say you will help me."

Edward paused to give his friend time to absorb all he had told her. She poured coffee for them both from the carafe on the sideboard, her hands shaking slightly as she handed a cup to Edward.

"How old is she?"

"She is almost five years old."

"She's a year too young. We don't take boarders until they are turned six."

"Couldn't you make an exception?"

Eleanor sipped her coffee slowly, looking at Edward over the rim of her cup.

"If I take her, it would have to be under my guardianship for a year, until she is eligible to board."

"Will you do it, Eleanor?" asked Edward, his eyes fixed on her.

"When would you want to bring her here?" asked Eleanor.

"Soon."

Eleanor came around her desk to face Edward. How dear he was. She nodded her head in agreement, grasping both his hands. "We'll give it a try. Bring her on Monday."

"I promise you, my dear friend, you will adore Dorothy as much as I do. She is a delightful little girl and she will blossom under your supervision. I can never repay you."

"There will be paperwork to take care of, Edward," explained Eleanor. "I must insist we have a copy of the child's birth certificate and details of how to contact her mother in case of emergency."

Edward realized it was a legal matter. Although Gertrude had abandoned her daughter, the birth certificate was a legal document, stating that Gertrude was Dorothy's mother and that the father was 'unknown.' Edward had no legal claim on the child.

Edward explained everything to Dorothy. She was to go to a beautiful school with many other girls. She was to stay with Miss Eleanor Preston, who was the headmistress and an old friend of Daddy's. All her clothes, books and toys would go with her. Daddy would come to see her often, and he would take her to London with him, and show her all the sights in the capital city. She would grow up to be a lady.

Dorothy took all the changes in her stride. Edward drove her to her new school the following week, where she met Miss Preston. A lady named Miss Spicer took her to a room with four beds, and unpacked her belongings, placing them in a wooden chest beside the bed. Miss Spicer would be her house mother and she would take care of Dorothy. The three other little girls in the room were already six years old and bigger than Dorothy, but they smiled at her, sharing their lemon drops to make her feel at home.

Edward stayed with Dorothy the first day. He sat on her bed beside her, holding her hand and stroking her curly hair.

"You are my precious princess," he whispered to her. "You will love living here with the other girls, and I will see you on Friday. I have a special gift for you, Dorothy. Because you are staying here without me, I'm leaving you my Prussian Captain as your guard." Edward took the well-worn toy from his pocket and placed him beside Dorothy's bed. "He has been my constant companion since I was about your age. Now he will keep you company, help you to be brave, and remind you how much I love you."

Miss Spicer showed them through the school, showing them the dining room, Dorothy's classroom, the music room, the chapel. It seemed like an enormous building to the little girl and by the end of the school tour, her eyes were wide and scared. Edward picked her up, planting the usual kiss on her nose.

"Don't worry, darling," he whispered. "Miss Spicer is your house mother, remember. She will be with you whenever you need her."

"Will she read Peter Rabbit to me?" asked Dorothy.

Miss Spicer smiled up at her, cuddled in her father's arms, and nodded. "Of course I will."

Dorothy was brave when Daddy left. Miss Spicer was kind and took her hand to lead her to the dining room for dinner, where she sat with her bedroom companions to eat.

It will be all right, even without Daddy. I will see him soon. I will make him so proud of me. I will pretend to be six and learn to read and write.

NO ROOM

*G*ertrude was back in Edward Street. It seemed dirtier than she remembered. The smell of beer, pipe tobacco and poverty sticking in the back of her throat. Emma bombarded her with questions.

"What're you doin' back here? Where's the bloody kid ya had? Kicked ya out, did he? Always knew ya'd fall on your arse."

Tom wasn't home when she arrived, thank God.

Gertrude lit a cigarette and ignored the questions, only saying "I'm not staying long. Just need a place for now. Left the girl with her dad."

"Well, there's bloody well nowhere for ya to sleep my girl." Emma said, poking the fire to get a flame under the kettle.

"I'll sleep in the parlour—on the sofa."

"The parlour's not for sleepin'. The boys are upstairs. Madge is in with me and him. How many bloody bedrooms do ye think we have? There's nowhere for you." Emma glared at the younger woman smugly. She couldn't just show up after all these years and think there'd be a place for her.

Gertrude dragged her bags into the parlour and sat on the horse hair sofa, looking around at the dingy room and the rain running down the small window. Regrets poured through her mind, thinking of the life she had left.

What am I doing back in Neck End? Why did I leave Edward and Dorothy? The lovely cottage, so clean with lace curtains and cozy furnishings. Mrs. Medwin to help with the housework and cooking. I must be mad! I'd forgotten how awful it is here. I could have lived with Edward until Dorothy grew up, then started over. But how old would I be then? Too old! Anyway, Edward didn't want me anymore, he only wanted Dorothy. Well, let him have her all to himself. I'm only staying here until I can find another way to get out—this time it'll be with a bloke who'll marry me.

News travelled fast through the Longton streets that Gertrude was back. Aunt Sarah lent her an old mattress, so she could sleep on the parlour floor. She left her clothes and shoes in her bags by the fireplace nook. Dolly wanted to hear all the details. Why had she left Edward? Why had she left Dorothy? The two big questions that Gertrude wouldn't answer. Dolly, along with most of the women in the streets, whispered their versions of what had happened, coming to the conclusion that whatever had happened, nobody, including Gertrude, could ever make the break with Neck End.

Nothing had changed at number 27 Edward Street. The boys were at school. Tom still selling from his barrow, and drinking the money away at the pub. Emma still chugging bottled stout. Chips for tea most nights. No privacy. No hot water. Newspaper squares in the lav. All the horrors of her former life invaded Gertrude's life again, like an old nightmare.

She found a job at Newport China, convincing the decorating supervisor to give her a try as a gilder. Gertude picked up her old skills quickly, securing a permanent position at the prestigious china factory. How easily she slipped into the old way of life, hating every minute of every day. She thought about Edward and Dorothy constantly, imagining them at the cottage, sitting at the kitchen table, enjoying hot buttered toast and honey for breakfast. At night, as she lay on her mattress in the parlour and pictured Edward asleep in the cozy, clean bed, between clean sheets. Was he missing her?

So many times she almost packed her bags to make her way back to Cobham, but she stopped herself, thinking about why she had left and looking to a future when she would leave Longton for good and have a better life. Edward had probably thrown himself on his wife's mercy and begged her to let him take Dorothy to Maidenhead. Dorothy would forget who her real mother was. Edward would grow old with Amy and forget the six years he spent with her.

LEGAL RIGHT

When Gertrude had been 'home' for two months, a letter arrived from Kingston on Thames. It was from Miss Eleanor Preston, Headmistress of The Kingston School for Girls, informing her that Dorothy was a student. It was a very formal letter, stating that as legal next of kin to the girl, it was the duty of the Headmistress to send the information of Dorothy's enrolment to her mother.

A bloody boarding school! Well, he's managed that very nicely hasn't he? No worries for Edward! Amy not involved or inconvenienced in any way. The stream of money not jeopardized. Edward coming out of it all smelling roses, as usual. And Dorothy! In a boarding school was she? What a life she was going to have. Best of everything. I'm stuck here in this hole and there she is living in a snotty boarding school in Kingston. She'll have everything I never had. Well, I don't much like that, I don't. If Longton was good enough for me, it should be good enough for her.

Gertrude's jealousy of her daughter returned with a vengeance. She didn't want her girl to have all the privileges she never had. Doesn't every mother want what's best for her offspring? Gertrude didn't.

She thought of nothing else for days after the letter came. Dorothy living in a boarding school with all the toffy-nosed snob kids. Dorothy growing up never knowing her own mother. Dorothy never even imagining a place like Neck End.

I'll fetch her and bring her to Longton, that's what I'll do. She'll live like I had to live. She's not growing up in that place surrounded by rich kids. She belongs here, in the dirt, with me. Just think how Edward will hate his beloved daughter being here in the slums. How he will hate that she's here with me and not with him. The last laugh will be on Edward!

The more Gertrude thought about it, the more she liked the idea of bringing Dorothy to Longton to live with the family. Everybody knew about her anyway.

Gertrude told Dolly about her plan. Dolly wanted to tell her sister to leave the little girl where she was. Why did she want to bring her back to such a place? But she was always a little afraid of Gertrude, and she kept quiet, promising herself she would do everything she could to help make her niece's life bearable.

On the last Saturday in April 1926, Gertrude made the train trip to Kingston on Thames. It was a long journey, first to London, where Gertrude spent an uncomfortable night at a traveller's hostel near the station. Early the next morning she travelled from London to Kingston by train. She had brought all her savings with her; not amounting to much, but she hoped it would be enough to pay for a car hire to the school, and the return trip to Staffordshire for her and Dorothy.

Gertrude stepped into the car outside the station and gave him the destination.

"Wait for me here," she said when they reached the white gates of the impressive building. "If I'm not out in thirty minutes, go on your way." She handed him the fare for the one-way trip and the driver promised he would wait thirty minutes.

Gertrude didn't have time to waste. She hurried to the entrance and banged on the door, pushing her way inside when it was opened by an alarmed young lady. She was asked to wait in the foyer, but instead followed the young lady to a door at the far side of the large entrance hall. She didn't wait to be announced.

Eleanor Preston stood up behind her desk, she didn't appreciate being disturbed in such an impolite manner. She had no idea who this wild woman was with her hair sticking out from under her hat, but she soon found out.

"Where's my girl?" said the woman loudly. "Dorothy Bryan, that's who I've come for. Go get her now. I have identification and I have her birth certificate. I know my rights. She's mine and I want her fetching this minute."

"Please, Miss Bryan," began Eleanor, "sit down. Let's discuss this sensibly. Dorothy has only been here a short time and is settling in nicely. Her father has taken great care to make sure she has the best care. He visits very regularly, often taking her to London with him. They are very close."

Nothing could have annoyed Gertrude more than the words this hoity-toity, snobby woman, talking in her posh accent, said about Edward's relationship with Dorothy.

"Get her now," she demanded. "I'm taking her with me and you can't bloody stop me."

Eleanor nodded to the younger woman who had been standing at the door with her mouth open watching the scene unfold. She quickly ran across the entrance hall and into the classroom corridor. Gertrude stood in the centre of the room never taking her eyes off Miss Eleanor Preston. They couldn't keep her child, of that she was sure. She had the legal right to her—a legal right Edward didn't have. Eleanor knew it too. It would be against the law to keep a child against the will of its legal parent. She had done everything Edward had asked, but she would not risk the reputation of the school for this one child.

Dorothy came into the room holding Miss Spicer's hand. She ran to her mother as soon as she saw her.

"Mummy, you came back for me," she smiled, hugging Gertrude's legs.

"You're coming with me, Dorothy. We're going to live with my family now. Where you belong."

"Please reconsider," pleaded Eleanor. "Think of all the advantages for your daughter."

"Shut your trap," snarled Gertrude. "She'll have plenty of advantages living with her own kind, growing up without you filling her head with stuff she doesn't need to know. She'll not grow up toffy-nosed, looking down her nose at everybody from north of Coventry. She'll grow up knowing how to work hard for a living and that's more than I can say for any of you lot."

She grabbed Dorothy's hand and pulled her out of the room. Miss Spicer said she would pack up Dorothy's things and mail them to the address they had for Miss Bryan. The little girl's feet hardly touched the ground as her mother hurried her towards the gates at the end of the drive. A taxi waited to take them to catch the ten o'clock to London.

Dorothy started to cry. Why was her mummy taking her away from school? Daddy hadn't said she would come and take her. Why did Mummy look so mad? Why didn't she talk to her? Where was she going? She felt sad and worried—that's why she cried. She wished Daddy was here. He would explain everything to her and make her feel better. Her mother ignored her, not even wiping her nose or eyes. She used the sleeve of her sweater to clean her face, not daring to say anything.

It was dark when the two travellers arrived at Longton Station. Dorothy was tired and hungry. She trudged beside Gertrude up the hill from the station. It seemed a long way to walk for a small girl who had only had a sticky bun and a cup of milky tea all day. By the time they arrived at number twenty seven, the house was in darkness and Gertrude lit a gas light in the parlour.

Dorothy spent the first night in her new home laying beside her mother on a thin mattress, covered with a blanket that smelled of onions.

Dorothy was traumatized by everything she saw.

What is this place? Who are these people? Where is my daddy?

It was the opposite of everything she had ever known. The dirt, the smells, the lack of food, the toilet up the yard, the big black grate, the chipped mugs, the unhappy, unkind children and the miserable foul-mouthed adults. This was where she lived now. These people were her family!

LOST CHILD

hen Edward arrived at the Kingston School for Girls the following Friday evening, Eleanor Preston was waiting for him on the front steps. His face twisted with concern as he approached her, sensing immediately that there was something very wrong.

"Eleanor?" he spoke her name in a question. "What is it?"

"Come into my study, Edward. Dorothy is safe and well, but I need to tell you the whole story." She hurried ahead of him across the hallway and into her study. "Please sit down my dear friend. I was about to write to you, but realized you would be here before the letter would get to you."

"Where is my daughter?" was all Edward could utter.

Eleanor explained as calmly as she could, telling him about Gertrude's visit, and the subsequent departure with Dorothy.

"She was here only a matter of fifteen minutes, Edward. She just grabbed the child and left," Eleanor explained tearfully. "I don't know what to say, other than the mother had every legal right to take her—she had Dorothy's birth certificate, and it said "father unknown."

"Dorothy's clothes and few processions were quickly gathered together and taken with her. The only thing left behind was an old toy which we found under her pillow."

Eleanor opened her desk drawer and took out the Prussian Captain, handing it to Edward across the desk.

"She would never have left this behind," choked Edward. "It was a gift from me and she will be lost without it."

They sat in silence—Eleanor drying her tears and twisting her sodden handkerchief into knots, Edward staring through the window at the driving rain washing the garden. He had not even imagined Gertrude would do such a thing. She hadn't wanted Dorothy. She had left Dorothy. If she wanted to hurt Edward, she had managed it very well, but what about the child? How was she feeling?

She must think I don't love her. She must be scared and lonely. I have to clear my mind and think what to do. I can't give my baby up. I can't let her go. I have no legal right to her, but she is all mine even so. Oh, my Dorothy—my beautiful little girl, where are you? You left the captain behind, my precious. Wherever you are, I will find you and give him back to you. I will not let you be ripped from my life like this. I will find you.

"Do you know where Gertrude was taking her?"

"Only that there was a hired car waiting to take them to the station. No, wait, she did say something about going to live with her family."

"Then I know where to find her. I remember the very street."

Edward put the captain into this pocket and moved around

the desk, taking Eleanor into his arms and hugging her close. He didn't have to say anything, she knew how he was feeling.

"Good luck, old friend. I hope you find Dorothy safe and well. Bring her back to us soon."

Edward's mouth was set in a firm line as he left the school and headed home. He packed a small valise with some of Dorothy's favourite outfits and a few things he would need for the journey and, within the hour, had the Bentley on the road. He would be in Staffordshire in four hours with some luck. It would be too late when he arrived to do anything that day, he decided, but he would be able to get an early start tomorrow and be at number twenty-seven Edward Street before their day began.

He booked into the Grand Hotel and spent a restless night waiting for dawn. He remembered bringing Gertrude to this very hotel for their first meal together. How beautiful she was and how smitten he had been by her. He remembered the lovely young woman he had lived with for six years and how happy they had been. He thought of his beloved Dorothy and where she was now living. Morning came as a relief.

As planned, he was at the top of the street of row houses in Neck End by eight o'clock. The men had left to work at the pot banks or the pit heads an hour or more before. Now there was the hustle and bustle of women cleaning steps and yelling at their children to get ready for school.

Edward left the car parked on the slightly wider road at the top of Edward Street and walked down the steep hill to the Bryan house. The rain soaked street smelled of mould and coal dust. The pavement was slippery under Edward's feet. This was where Gertrude had brought their daughter to live.

He knocked on the door loudly, wanting the first knock to be heard and answered. The door flew open and there stood Gertrude, hair in curling rags, wearing one of her beautiful silk nightdresses, her bare feet sticking to the dirty linoleum on the parlour floor.

She stood, with her mouth gaping open, at Edward—his tall frame almost filling the doorway.

"What the bloody hell are you doing here?" she whispered at him, through clenched teeth, all the time glancing over her shoulder for signs of Dorothy, who was in the kitchen eating lardy toast.

"You know why I'm here," replied Edward calmly. "I came for Dorothy. You can't imagine I would let you take her away from me and keep her here with you. Why would you do such a thing, Gertrude?"

"Shut your mouth," she hissed back. "She's mine—all mine. You're not even on her birth certificate. It's my name on that piece of paper—not yours. Now bugger off, you're not wanted here. You're not seeing her. She doesn't want to see you. She's happy to be here with me. This is where she belongs."

Gertrude tried to shut the door, but Edward put out a hand to stop her. He was very angry, which was rare for him. He grabbed Gertrude's arm and pulled her out into the street. If she wanted a fight, then it would be a street fight, fitting the habitat she had chosen to live in. She tried to turn and get back into the house, but Edward had a firm grip on her and turned her to look directly into his eyes.

"Where did that beautiful girl I met go? What are you doing, Gertrude? Think of our daughter instead of seeking revenge on me. She has a chance to grow up in an elite girl's school and have the very best of education and a life of privilege. You can't give her anything but poverty and hardship. That was the way you grew up and you couldn't wait to get out— why have you come back to this world?" Edward spoke quickly, looking into the lovely eyes he had so adored such a short time ago.

"And what can you give her?" Gertrude threw back in his face, meeting his eyes with a hostile stare. "A visit every bloody weekend, when you can fit it in with Amy's requirements. What kind of family is that? At least here she's surrounded by family. My family. Her family. Growing up a snob isn't for her. She'll learn the value of a day's work and learn to stick up for herself instead of being spoiled by you."

She wrenched her arm away with a quick snap and this time Edward let her go. As she stepped off the street, he once more stopped her from closing the door on him. She had to see sense. He pleaded with her now.

"Please Gertrude, don't do this. Let me take her back with me. She deserves better than this—everything here is ugly and sad. Do you really want her to grow up here, under the influence of Emma and Tom—think what it did to you."

"Go back to where you belong, Edward," she spat. "Back to your snobby friends and your weekend 'wife.' Go back and forget about us. Forget you ever had a daughter. I will never talk about you and she'll soon forget you. She has nothing to remember you by."

Edward fingered the Prussian Captain in his pocket. She would always remember him if she had the captain with her. The thought of Dorothy being a few yards away was more than he could bear, but he didn't want to frighten her by bursting into the house and grabbing her. What could he do?

He searched his mind for an answer. How could he change Gertrude's mind? She was the most stubborn, self-willed woman he knew, yet there was something...

Edward let the door close and walked back to the car. He wasn't giving up, just changing strategy—compromising maybe. As he drove back to the hotel in Stoke, he considered his options.

Why did Gertrude agree to live with me? What attracted her to me in the first place? Why did she agree to leave her home and family so quickly? It wasn't because of my good looks, or my "posh" accent, or my motor vehicle. It was because I had money. Money was the key ingredient to the whole affair. A lifestyle that Gertrude never imagined, with beautiful clothes, jewelry, shoes and hats. A lovely home where no expense was spared on furnishings. Everything she wanted and had never had.

Is money the answer now? If Gertrude is determined to stay in Longton with our daughter, then I can make sure the child is well taken care of, can't I? I can send a monthly allowance to provide the very best of care for my little girl. She will still have the finest clothing and the best school in the area. As soon as she is able to travel by herself, she could come to London on visits. When she is grown, she could still go to finishing school—Gertrude won't be able to hold onto her forever.

Edward spent the next two days formulating his plan. He found a private Church of England school within walking distance of Edward Street. Dorothy would be enrolled there and stay there at least until she was twelve years of age. He would send the fees directly to the school. He needed to find an ally now. Somebody who had the best interests of Dorothy at heart. Dolly! Gertrude's sister Dolly! He had only met her briefly when dropping Gertrude off in town, but the way Gertrude had talked about her, Edward felt she would be the sympathetic ear he needed. How would he know where to find her? Was she married or did she still live in Edward Street?

He drove back to Longton the following day, parking the Bentley farther away from the streets of Neck End this time, behind St. Gregory's Catholic Church. He walked the length of Marsh Street and went into the small corner shop on the corner of Edward Street. Mrs. Shaw, the shop keeper was busy behind the counter, sorting the daily papers. She looked up as the bell announced the arrival of a customer. She sized Edward up in a minute as an upper class 'toff.' Mrs. Shaw was all smiles as Edward removed his hat and greeted her.

"I'm sorry to trouble you, dear lady," Edward began. "I wonder if you are acquainted with a Miss Dolly Bryan."

"Well, yes m'lord," Mrs. Shaw stuttered. "But she's not Miss any more. She married Norman Cooper last year."

"Ah! Did she?" smiled Edward, using every ounce of his charm. "Do you know if she still lives in the area? I wouldn't trouble you, but I have some important information for her."

Mrs. Shaw almost shook with excitement. It wasn't every day a "toff" walked into the shop with a mysterious message.

"She's Mrs. Cooper now and lives just down the next street at number thirty-nine. Her back yard is behind her Aunt Sarah's house, down here on Edward Street. Her mam and dad, the Bryans, live down 'ere as well, on the same side as the shop."

She was a mine of information, as she babbled on, giving Edward all he needed to know in a very short space of time. He beamed at her and bowed slightly in thanks.

So Dolly was married and living close by. What luck.

When he came out of the shop the stream of working girls, heading for the pot banks were leaving their houses and plodding through the rain to earn their day's wage. Edward walked back one street and peered down the steep slope at the women and girls walking towards him.

She was easy to spot. A short, plump girl with dimples and dark curls, dragging her feet along the pavement, through the rain. Edward hurried down the street, intercepting Dolly's path. She looked up at the stranger barring her way.

"Dolly," Edward began. "Do you remember me? I am Dorothy's father, Edward Wrightson. Could I speak to you for a moment?"

"I'll be late for work," Dolly said, trying to push past him. She knew who he was.

"I'll walk with you, if you don't mind. I don't want to make you late."

He stepped aside and walked beside her, turning up the collar of his coat against the steady downpour of fine rain.

"Dolly, I need your help. I know I'm asking a very difficult thing by going behind your sister's back like this, but I have no other option."

"Don't think so," Dolly quietly said, gazing up through the rain at the tall, handsome man beside her. "Gert 'ud kill me if she knew I was even talkin to ya."

"I am only interested in helping Dorothy," Edward went on. "I want to make sure her life is as good as possible. I need you to help me with that. I have enrolled her into the Church of England school in Webberley Lane. I will pay the fees directly to them, but I need your influence to make sure Dorothy attends. As long as she attends the school regularly I will send a generous monthly allowance to the Bryan family, for Dorothy's clothing, food and expenses. It would stop should she be withdrawn from the school."

Edward paused for breath. Even though Dolly's little legs were no match for his very long ones, she clipped along at such a speed, Edward had a hard time keeping up and talking at the same time. They were now at the factory gates where Dolly worked and she stopped to answer him.

"I want what's best for Dorothy. It's not her fault to be born like she was." She shrugged her shoulders and blushed a deep red, embarrassed at having to allude to the sensitive situation of being born out of wedlock.

"I'll have to tell Gert of course, but she'll not turn down the chance of a bit of extra money. Life's hard in this part of the world and there's never enough. I'll be your go-between if you like—for the girl, of course."

She shook the rain from her wet curls as she turned to go into the gates.

"Thank you, Dolly," Edward said softly. "One more thing. Would you please give this to Dorothy? There's a note inside, which I would like you to read to her. Kiss her for me, will you, and tell her to be brave."

Edward handed her a small box tied with a pink bow, and she turned into the factory to punch her time clock and spend the next ten hours stacking plates.

He had done what he intended and was pleased Dolly had agreed to his plan. Maybe Dorothy's life would be easier with his help. Who could tell.

He walked back to his car in the persistent rain. His life would never be the same but he consoled himself with thoughts of his beautiful daughter. Even though she was out of his reach for now, he was still her father and would, one day, have her back. He was sure of it.

He drove slowly back to the cottage in Cobham. He would sell it now and move into the city of London—probably find a nice flat. He loved London, and would busy himself with city life. Maybe he'd look for a different job—even change careers.

*D*olly hurried home after work. The rain had stopped, leaving streaks of soot running down the outside of all the buildings. She had the box from Edward safely in her pocket, and wondered what could be inside. She put the stew pot on the hod over the fire and lit the paper under the coal, waiting for the flames to heat the coal and start the stew simmering for Norman's tea, before she left the house to run over to see Dorothy. She hoped Gert wasn't home, so she could see Dorothy on her own and give her the package. But Gert was home, and getting ready to go to the pictures with a young man she'd met in the market. As usual, she was done up like a dog's dinner. Her hair curled and her skirt too short. Her lips cherry red and her eyes dancing at the thought of a night out.

Before Dolly could speak, Gert rushed in, "Doll, can you watch Dorothy for me tonight? I'm off to the pictures with this real nice man. He doesn't know about her. I'd be ever so grateful."

"Yea, course I will. She can come home with me and have a

317

drop of stew with me and Norman, then we can go for a walk to see the trains or somethin'."

She was happy Gert was going out. It would give her a chance to talk to Dorothy alone and give her the gift from her dad. Dorothy was at the kitchen table eating the last of the chips from the newspaper. She smiled up at Dolly, looking forward to spending time with her aunty.

After Gert had left, Dolly took Dorothy into the parlour, away from the prying eyes of Emma, and sat her down on the sofa.

"Dorothy, I saw your dad today," she began.

"Where?" Dorothy cried out, jumping up from the sofa. "Where is he? Is he coming to take me back to school? Please say yes. Please say he's coming to take me back."

Her big brown eyes filled up with tears at the mention of her father. She hadn't seen him for so long. She thought he had forgotten all about her. Knowing Dolly had seen him that very day filled her with hope and longing.

"No, Dotty, he can't take you back to school. Your mam wants you to stay with her, duck. But your dad loves you and he wants you to have this."

She put the box into Dorothy's hands as though it was the most precious thing in the world. The little girl sucked in her breath and wiped the tears from her cheeks with the back of her hand. The box was from Daddy. Her daddy loved her.

She opened it carefully, untying the pink ribbon and laying it aside—she would save it to tie up her hair because it was from Daddy. Inside was fluffy white tissue paper wrapped around something hard. She gasped as she uncovered the Prussian Captain, letting out a squeal of delight.

"It's Daddy's Prussian Captain, Aunty Doll. He gave it to me when I went to school to keep me brave. It's my captain now and I'll think of Daddy every time I look at it."

She held the worn toy close to her cheek and closed her eyes, imagining she could see Daddy. She would never forget him. Not ever.

"There's a note as well, Dotty," said Dolly.

"I promised your dad I'd read it to ya, duck."

My darling Dorothy,

Here is your Prussian Captain. I know how much you must have missed him. I love you very much and will always love you. Keep being brave, sweetheart. I will come to see you every time it's your birthday. I will write you a letter every week and Aunt Dolly will read it to you.

— DADDY

"So, I have to stay here?" asked Dorothy.

"Yes duck, ya do. But it's not all that bad is it now? A letter from dad every week and he's paying for you to go to a posh church school an' all. He's sendin' your mam money to buy your clothes, duck. He must really luv ya a lot. He said once you're bigger and can go on the train, you'll be able to go up to London an' visit him. How's that then? Off to London to stay with your dad. Things aren't that bad, duck."

Dorothy folded the note and wrapped the captain with tissue paper, placing them both back into the box.

"Don't tell Mummy about all this, Aunty Dolly."

She looked serious and older than her years, as she looked at her aunt.

"Oh Dotty, I'll have to tell ya mam. She has to know about the money part of it. But maybe not about the little toy and the note hey." That much Dolly could promise.

They found a space for Dorothy's box behind a piece of loose wood at the side of the hearth. She would be able to take it out whenever she wanted to. Whenever her mother wasn't around. She clung onto the message in the note: her daddy loved her and always would. That made her feel wonderful. No matter what happened, her daddy loved her.

Gertrude laughed when Dolly told her about the monthly allowance.

"Conscience money that is, Doll," she said. "For leading me on, and putting me in the family way, and never intending to marry me. Well, he can pay now. That suits me."

The letters arrived weekly as promised, addressed to Dolly and secretly read to Dorothy. Letters full of stories about London, full of love and kindness. Dorothy always held the captain while the letters were read to her, feeling the closeness of her daddy.

The monthly allowance arrived regularly on the first day of the month. None of it was spent on Dorothy. Most of it on new clothes for Gert, some of it on stout to keep the old woman happy.

Dolly made it clear that the allowance would stop if Dorothy wasn't attending school. Gert walked with her the first day to show her where to go, but after that she walked to the Webberley Lane school on her own. She was a robust little girl, benefitting from the first five years of her life of nourishing food and healthy living. She managed the walk very well, through good and bad weather, and enjoyed the Church school. She learned to read quickly, spurred on by the thought of reading her father's letters by herself.

Gert was always in the background. She worked and went out at night, leaving Dorothy with anybody who would watch her—mostly with Emma, who couldn't stand the sight of her bastard granddaughter. Good that she spent so much time in the parlour on her own, while Emma drank her stout.

Gert had been seeing one particular man for a few months. Mr. Owens was his name and he had good prospects. He was from Sheffield and was working in the Potteries for a few months. He had plenty of money and a house back in Sheffield and Gert set her cap at him, thinking this was her chance to get out of Staffordshire once and for all. Mr. Owens would marry her for sure. She'd be set for life then. Out of Longton for good, married, living in a house. The only problem was, he didn't know about Dorothy.

"What do ya mean, you can't watch her?" Gert yelled at her mother, Emma. "Where are ya going? Ya never go out. Just 'cause I'm bloody goin' out isn't it?"

"Ya'll have to take her with ya," Emma retorted. "Won't kill ya. She's your bloody girl, not mine. I can't watch her. I'm off to the pictures with our Sarah."

Gert wasn't happy! *What would she say to Mr. Owens? Oh, by the way, this is me daughter Dorothy. I don't think so!*

Gert washed Dorothy's hands and face in the cold water in the back kitchen, and told her to go up the yard to the lav before they left. Dorothy walked beside her mother along the high street towards the cafe where she was meeting Mr. Owens.

"Don't call me Mam. Call me Gert. He doesn't know about you and I don't want him knowin,'" Gert instructed her little girl as they neared the cafe.

Dorothy's eyes stung with tears. Even at her young age she knew her mother didn't want her. Daddy would never disown her. He wanted everybody to know she belonged to him.

Two weeks later Gert left for Sheffield with Mr. Owens to begin a new life. She didn't tell him she had a daughter. It was her ticket out of Neck End—for good this time and she grabbed it with both hands, leaving Dorothy behind with Emma and Tom. She would send for Dorothy, once she was married and had told Mr. Owens about her past life, but it never happened.

Emma gave up all hope that the parlour would be used for births, deaths and posh visits and moved Madge's mattress in with Dorothy.

The two girls were complete opposites in every way, and had little to do with each other despite sharing a room to sleep in. Madge was spiteful and mean. Her demeanour showed in her appearance—small, skinny, sour-faced and sharp-tongued. She never said a kind word to her roommate, seeing her as an intruder who nobody wanted, not even her own mother.

Emma resented the very presence of her granddaughter, who lived under her roof without invitation, and reminded her daily that Gertrude had abandoned her own child, leaving Emma to raise her. Now the parlour was a bedroom. A fact which made Emma cringe with embarrassment every time she thought of it. No special room for birth and death in the house now, it was socially unacceptable, and Emma knew everybody in Neck End was talking about it and looking down on her. As a result, Dorothy was constantly reminded what a nuisance she was, and what disgrace she brought on the family. People in the neighbourhood pointed and whispered when she walked by, and boys yelled, "There goes the bastard." Aunt Sarah and Aunt Dolly were her life-line and she spent most of her time at one or other of their houses. Anything to avoid Emma.

Dorothy had her father's spirit of gentleness. Although she was very sad most of the time, she would pretend she was living with Edward and escape into an imaginary world, where Madge and Emma didn't exist.

With her mother gone, Dorothy took her Prussian Captain from its hiding place and sat him on the wooden crate, which held her clothes, beside her mattress. She gazed at the worn little figure, and remembered all the stories Edward had told her about his adventures with the captain beside him. Stories about New York, the biggest city in the world according to her dad, the tall buildings, the theatres, the bustling streets, buying the soldier in a brand new store that had a whole floor devoted to toys. The train ride across America, from one side to the other, taking days and days, seeing mountains and great rivers and hundreds of miles of wilderness. The wonders of life in California, riding horses, not wearing shoes, living in a castle, loving the Chinese servants who took such care of the family. Edward's devastation when they had to move back to England, and the years of school and college, when he gazed at the captain and relived his years in America. Dorothy remembered so clearly how her father's face would light up when he talked about that land, how he wished he could have stayed there forever.

Dorothy's eyes misted with tears as she reached for the captain and held him close to her chest. She clung on to him, willing herself to be brave, even though she missed her daddy so much it hurt her somewhere inside. She often fell asleep holding him and had wild dreams of riding horses without her shoes, her hair flying in the wind. She would look at the rider on the horse beside her and see Edward smiling at her. They rode together across the wild countryside, gulping the clean, crisp air into their lungs. When she awoke to the stark, dark world around her, she kissed the captain on top of his head, and placed him back on the crate, feeling braver and stronger each day.

To Dorothy, the Prussian Captain meant there was somebody in the world who loved her—her daddy.

THE STORY BEHIND THE STORY

It was 2005. My mother, Dorothy, and I sat on the beach, in our deck chairs, watching my grandchildren, her great grandchildren, Rebecca and Sarah, playing in the water. Nana, as my mother was known, loved being with babies and having toddlers around her. She had moved to Canada in 1981 at sixty years of age, and lived in a small apartment in Winnipeg, but she spent most of the weekends and summers with us, loving our cottage on Lake Winnipeg.

"I used to live in a boarding school," she suddenly said.

"What?" I said. She'd never told me anything about a boarding school before. Where was this coming from? For the lower class in England in the 1920s a boarding school was unheard of. A place where only the very rich sent their children to be educated.

"Yes," she continued, "I was really young. My father took me there. I think I was about four or five years old. He knew the head teacher there. I was really too young to board, but she said she'd make an exception for his daughter."

"Mum," I began. "Why haven't you told me about this before?"

"Because I've only just remembered it," she sniffed. "I can see it as clear as a bell. I even remember the red velvet coat I wore, with matching muff and hat trimmed with fur."

I wondered what else she remembered from the past. I had heard that some elderly people remember their early childhood very clearly.

"Do you remember anything else?" I asked her.

It was like a flood gate had opened. She remembered all kinds of things from her early life that neither me nor my sister were aware of.

She loved the boarding school and the kind head teacher. She missed her father, but he came every week to see her and when there were holidays, she would go to the cottage in Cobham with him, and stay overnight. She couldn't remember how long she was at the boarding school. A short time she thought. Maybe less than a year.

Her mother came and picked her up one day and took her away. Away to North Staffordshire, to live with her mother's parents in a terraced house in Neck End.

I knew all about Neck End–the poorest part of The Potteries. I remember the very house she was taken to. My great grandparents lived there until I was nine years old, and I remember that house and the street it was in. The smell of poverty and dirt. The dark rooms, back kitchen with cold water tap, the out house in the yard. I remember my great grandad's chair up the corner by the black fire grate, the parlour where nobody was allowed to sit. I was born in 1944 in that parlour, while my dad, a tank gunner, was in France with the Welsh Guards.

As my mother continued to remember, she told me my grandfather, Edgar (called Edward in the book), moved to London in 1927, but kept in touch with her, sending money to her grandparents, Emma and Tom Bryan, so that she could be sent to private school, be properly fed and clothed. She did go to a private church school until she was eleven, but the rest of the money was spent drinking at the pub, not on Mum. She was treated like an outcast–barely fed, barely clothed, never loved.

I need to write this all down, I thought, *before it gets lost in my memory too.*

When I told my sister, Christine, about Mum's memories, she shared some of the stories she had heard over the years about our family. Between us we had snippets of information, dropped as comments from time to time by Mum. Much of what we knew was disconnected and confusing. It wasn't until we were both well into our adult years that we realized Mum was born out of wedlock. A big scandal in 1921! We also realized that we knew very little about our grandparents, Edgar and Gertrude.

Christine began to dig around in online ancestry sites and uncovered details of their lives from census documents. As these details came to light, I was more convinced than ever that this was a fascinating story that I needed to tell.

My sister found out that our grandfather's family were indeed wealthy and well education, and lived at Nine Elms, in Kings Norton, on the outskirts of Birmingham. But according to the census, they were no longer living there in

1878. Discovering they had made their way to Wild Horse Valley, California, was a huge surprise.

Ship's documents, and Castle Garden (before Ellis Island) listings confirmed that the family had journeyed from Liverpool to New York in 1878.

The family must have returned to England in the late 1880s, as Francis Wrightson's death certificate shows he died at Nine Elms in 1890. Annie Wrightson and the children are listed as residing at Nine Elms in the 1891 census.

As I wrote the chapters of The Prussian Captain, more and more details were uncovered, and I often had to go back and exchange the story I had written for the facts, which were far more interesting than anything I had dreamed up. My sister would call me or email me, beginning with, "Guess what I've just found?" I knew it would mean a rewrite of part of my story.

One moment sticks out in my mind above all others. The genealogical society in Napa Valley forwarded two newspaper articles, describing the house the Wrightson's lived in as a chateaux, which the local people called "the castle." The articles described the fused window facing west, along with other details of the house and contents. I was dumbfounded! I had written the description of their home in Wild Horse Valley as a farmhouse made of logs.

The book is based on a true story of two very different people, divided by social class, background and age. A young girl from the poverty of the working class industrial midlands, who had never done anything or been anywhere. A middle aged man from an aristocratic family, who was well educated, cultured, and had travelled extensively, living in America on two separate occasions for a number of years.

Writing this story was such a labour of love. My mum was so unique. I have a much better understanding of who she was now I know more about her parents, and her early life.

I hope you enjoyed reading about Gertrude and Edgar, who were the unlikely parents of my mother, Dorothy.

WRIGHTSON FAMILY

Francis Wrightson (Feb. 27, 1817 - Aug. 6, 1893)
married to
Ann Prosser (1837 - Oct. 29, 1907)

Their children:

- Richard Albert (1860 - 1863)
- Frances Louise (1861 - ??)
- Arthur (1862 - ??)
- Percy Herbert (1864 - 1865)
- Margueritte Laura (Aug. 1, 1866 - 1940)
- Alberta Violet (1868 - 1954)
- **Richard Edgar** (May 2 1869 - Nov. 24, 1952)
- Harold (Sept. 22 1870 - ??)
- Lucy Marianne (1872 - ??)
- Robert A. Baldwin (1876 - ??)
- male child born Oct. 12 1877 in Napa - died
- Fanny Charlotte (1880 - ??)

BRYAN FAMILY

Thomas Crossley Bryan (July 22 1877 - Aug. 13 1961)
married to
Emma Thursfield (1879 - Oct. 4 1963)

Their children:

- **<u>Gertrude</u>** (Feb. 6 1902 - 1948)
- Sarah Ellen (Dolly) (1903 - ??)
- 2 children born who did not survive
- William (1912 - Aug. 1933)
- Thomas (1914 - Aug. 1933)
- Edwin (1917 - 1984)
- Margorie (1918 - 2004)

ACKNOWLEDGMENTS

I owe a huge debt of gratitude to my sister, Christine Podmore, who was my research assistant extraordinaire! She spent countless hours on genealogy research, finding births, deaths and marriages on census forms. Dates, times, journeys to and from America—searching through ship's manifests and Ellis Island records. Christine's trip to the Napa Valley in 2015 revealed more fascinating information about our grandfather's time there. Thank you so much Christine for helping untangle the details of this story.

To Matthew Brough, my son and publisher, who has spent many hours helping me discover the world of computers. Your support has been invaluable. I have learned so much from you. Who knew computers could do so much of the work!

To Tracey, my eldest daughter, for reading and rereading the book, and for her editing skills. To Cheryl, my daughter-in-law, one of the first readers, for her insight and suggestions. To the rest of my family, who have encouraged and supported me throughout.

To my husband, David, who patiently sat through me reading chapters to him, in no particular order. Thank you for reading the final product with such enthusiasm. Thank you for telling me "Go write something" when there seemed to be so many other things I should have been busy with. Thank you for believing I could actually finish this book.

To my editor Lauren Craft, for her encouragement, great suggestions and "fixings".

Lastly, a posthumous thank you to my mother, Dorothy, for the vivid memories that came with old age, inspiring me to write this fascinating story. Mum was feisty, hard-working, belligerent and fiercely protective of her family—no wonder, when you consider her start in life.

ABOUT THE AUTHOR

My name is Ann Brough, daughter of Dorothy Podmore (nee Bryan or Wrightson?)

I live in Manitoba, Canada, in a wonderful lake community, called Lester Beach on Lake Winnipeg, with my husband David.

I was born in 1944 and immigrated to Canada in 1967 and again in 1978, with a seven year residence in England during that time.

My husband and I have three wonderful children and five incredibly wonderful grand children, between the ages of seven and twenty. Our lakeside home is filled with family, love and lots of sand every summer. It's everybody's favourite place to be!

This is the first book I've written and I have enjoyed every minute.

For more about Ann:
annbrough.com

JUN 25 2018

GIFT